THE
GARDEN
SPOT

SCOTT HENDRIX

The Garden Spot
By Scott Hendrix

Paperback ISBN: 978-0-57838961-5

Cover design by BespokeBookCovers.com

Find out more about the author
Instagram: @scottdavishendrix
Facebook: scottdavishendrix
Email: scottdavishendrix@gmail.com

"Some must die so that others may live"
-Winston Churchill

Garden Spot: Golf Term
The ideal location for placing a tee shot, usually thought of in
terms of an ideal angle and lie from which to approach the
green.

CHAPTER ONE

The buzzing phone jolted Jaimey Crawford awake. Exhaustion tempting her eyes to remain closed while she picked up the receiver and placed it next to her ear. She answered the call with a forced hello.

The male voice on the other end was raspy and rough, obvious to Jaimey that her potential client was a smoker. As he spoke, she heard a short silence and then a light sucking sound as if he were drawing from a cigarette, immediately followed by a cough. The cough was loud, and he made no attempt to pull away from the phone, and he blasted Jaimey's ear. As she listened to the caller, experience told her there wouldn't be much money involved. The caller promised a tip, if things went well.

The address was strange: 134 ½ Waterway Road.

As she followed the directions, she meandered loosely through neighborhoods that had no real boundaries and looked as though they were scarce of good incomes. There was, however, no scarcity of large pickup trucks nor Jon boats. Confederate flags adorned each yard and flew at equal height to the black POW/MIA flags, each looking as if it had been flying there since the war in Vietnam had ended.

The neighborhood consisted mainly of men. They moved around their yards like ants- hosing out boats, mending and folding nets, rigging lines and filling tanks. Men seemingly happy with their monthly retirement checks, aging trucks, and a boat to fish from.

She continued making her way between rows of long and narrow shotgun houses, the kind seen around most southern coastal towns. The houses so close you could easily stand between two, extend your arms, and touch each one on either side.

She glanced frequently at her notes as she began noticing the landmarks that her client mentioned. She had taken the notes carefully, sure to add every small detail.

She passed a row of old shrimp boats that appeared as race horses put out to pasture, never to be used again. She passed Big Sal's Seafood and Bait Shop with the neon silhouette of a shark overhead. It suddenly turned on as she approached and then blinked on and off as if it couldn't make up its mind. She drove another one-eighth of a mile and turned right at Mike's Girls strip joint. She knew Mike, and her skin crawled.

She noticed three of Mike's "girls" leaving through the door looking like death warmed over. The phrase "rode hard and put up wet" filtered through Jaimey's mind, and she wondered if people thought that about her.

She began to slow as the even house numbers on the left side of the road started nearing 134. The slight crunch of oyster shells filled the quiet of the day, almost lulling her to sleep as she crept, looking. The muffled echo of men talking in the distance woke her, and she sat up straighter.

Her eyes growing more alert, darting from house number to house number.

She finally arrived at 134 Waterway Road and slowed to a crawl. She eased forward and saw 136 on the next mailbox. Glancing behind her she noticed a worn, sandy trail that led to a travel trailer. An unpainted plywood addition attached to its side. She turned in and parked beside an orange 4x4 truck that sat on large, mud-grip tires, a winch bolted to its homemade front bumper. The truck next to it looked to be blue at one time but now, severely rusted. Bondo filled various dents, hand painted racing stripes chipped from age, peeled along each side.

On the rear right side of the bumper, a sticker informed the world that the owner's best friends were people called Smith and Wesson. On the back glass directly behind the driver, a cartoon of a little boy urinating on a Ford symbol caught her eye.

As she sat in her car morosely contemplating, Jaimey noticed a white metal mailbox with an address handwritten in what looked like permanent marker. Her racing heart slowly moved into her throat as she spied how far back the trailer sat in a thick clump of pine trees. She stared at the trailer. Forty dollars was on the other side of the door that sat crooked on its hinges.

She opened her purse to be sure her gun and mace were inside and easily within reach. She cut up and snorted a line of coke on her dashboard before opening the chamber once again to be sure the thirty-eight was fully loaded. She replaced the handgun and checked her makeup in the rear view before heading down the trail.

The yard was littered with various parts of engines from old cars and boats. Old fishing nets were draped over a molded boat filled with empty beer cartons. The mildewed shell of an old Snapper riding mower, its engine long stripped, sat littered with pine needles, and was held in place by honeysuckle vines.

As she approached the door, a pit bull reached the end of its chain, barking at the same time, and she jumped back almost losing her balance. She could hear her heart thumping as she started back toward her station wagon. As she turned, the creak of a screen door sounded, and her appointment quietly asked her where she was going.

"The dog scared me," Jaimey said as she turned, finally seeing the man that lived at 134 ½ Waterway Road.

Danny "Crabs" Williams looked as though he had not owned a razor in several years. With sunglasses, he could have passed for a member of ZZ Top. He stood with two twenty-dollar bills in his hand, and he rubbed them together between his index finger and thumb, waving them at Jaimey. She barely noticed the cash as she stared at him. His once white t-shirt was stained and crusted with food, dried, as if it had been there for days.

Ironically, the song *Sharp Dressed Man* began playing in her mind. She smelled him from the ten feet they stood from each other and was quickly repulsed. She had been with a lot of men before, but none had ever disgusted her the way Danny Crabs did.

He raised a beer to his lips and took a long, slow drink, finishing it and added the can to the many more already littering the yard. Jaimey noticed his dirty fingernails were in need of a cleaning and a manicure. His hands bore witness to the life of a hard-lived commercial fisherman that suffered from blisters and an aversion to bathing. They were yellowed from years of smoking cigarettes and pot.

"Come on in," he said, as if inviting a family member into his home.

"I've just remembered another appointment, I'll have to reschedule," Jaimey said, her voice shaking.

"You're here, you might as well come on in, won't take long," Danny said, his grin showing what was left of his yellowed teeth.

"I really think I just need to re..."

As Jaimey turned-and before she could get another syllable out, Danny Crabs bound down from the top step of his travel trailer, his patience finished and grabbed Jaimey by her hair. He began pulling her backwards up the stairs and into his trailer.

"I said, come in, Whore!" Danny shouted as he turned and used his other hand so he could get a better grip on her.

Jaimey, screaming, begged him to stop. She grabbed his wrists to take the pressure off her roots and kicked her way into the trailer. He threw her toward a small loveseat and immediately reached into a nearby cooler for another beer.

Danny's "home" looked as if it had never been cleaned. There were empty beer and whiskey bottles littering the floor and kitchen counter. The half-eaten contents of fast-food bags and pizza boxes lay scattered on the floor and furniture. A now yellowing poster of a nude centerfold that had been ripped from a magazine and unfolded was taped to the wall. It smelled of rotted food and the stench of beer and urine... it smelled like Danny Crabs.

Jaimey's stomach began to churn. Danny threw himself on top of her and began groping and kissing her just because he could. His breath was a stale combination of cigarettes, beer and the absence of toothpaste.

Jaimey vomited in his mouth and pushed him away at the same time. He quickly threw her to the ground, spitting and gagging. He spat on her and slapped her repeatedly in the face. He stood and kicked her in her stomach, and she vomited again; and as quickly as he started, he stopped. Danny grabbed a bottle of whiskey, took a drink, rinsed his mouth out and spit out the door.

His body odor permeated the small space. She brushed off the dried crumbs that were hidden in his beard, and stuck to his shirt. She lay on her back, staring up at the dust-filled ceiling. Cobwebs connected the two sides of the room. She brought her hand to her face and wiped blood from a cut under her right eye.

Danny wiped his mouth with his forearm and sat back on the arm of the couch littered with old Hustler magazines and stained sheets that covered the holes in the cushions.

Her breathing labored, Jaimey, now on all fours, rocked with unsteadiness. She was still dazed by the sudden violence that was a part of daily life for Danny, and becoming more so for her as her clientele began to wither in wealth. The carpet under her hands was matted and sticky.

"I just want you to watch," Danny Crabs said, struggling for air as he stood and dropped his pants.

"I don't even want to touch you again."

Jaimey was immediately relieved. She had done this before, just watched, although she never understood what this did for her clients. As long as she was paid, she usually didn't care. At this moment, however, the money wasn't important anymore. As badly as she needed it, she just wanted to leave and never come back to 134 ½ Waterway Road.

Both their breathing finally eased, and Jaimey moved from the floor back to the loveseat, which wasn't much cleaner. She picked up her purse, her hand touching the thirty-eight inside. She considered using it and getting the hell out of there, but since she wouldn't have to touch or be touched by Danny Crabs again, she would take the money, and become a voyeur for thirty minutes.

"I need to be paid before we get started, and we need to get going because I've got other dates today," Jaimey said with authority, attempting to appear as if she wasn't frightened.

Danny threw two wadded twenties at her feet.

"You're going to like this," Danny said as he called out to the mystery date in the back room. Soon the slow creak of a door opening caught Jaimey's ear, and a small girl dressed in a green and blue plaid school uniform stood before her.

Jaimey's mottled brain slowly started putting the scene before her together. The sickness she had experienced earlier came back tenfold. She looked at this sweet little girl standing with her head down staring at the floor. Her unwashed hair was pulled back in a ponytail, and the once white shirt of her school uniform was now almost black with dirt and grime. The girl slowly looked up at her, her eyes speaking volumes about her current life.

"Come here, baby, what's your name," Jaimey asked, extending her hand to the girl.

"Madison," she said as she reluctantly walked toward Jaimey uncertain of what was coming next. Danny smiled as Jaimey squeezed her hand and pulled her closer.

"She's a doll," Jaimey said.

She adjusted her purse strap on her right shoulder. Her right hand slowly eased down inside and shook around the grip of her pistol. Her heart began beating wildly. She eased the safety off and stood at the same time.

Danny hovered over a makeshift coffee table snorting a line of coke. As he raised his head, he was staring directly into the barrel of Jaimey's thirty-eight. She guided the girl behind her and started backing toward the door.

"You, bitch!" Danny said as he started to stand.

"Sit down!" Jaimey shouted.

He didn't, but instead lunged toward the gun. Jaimey closed her eyes and pulled the trigger, then heard a thud. When she opened them, she saw Danny lying on the floor on top of a widening puddle of blood.

Jaimey quickly picked up Madison and ran out of the door. She stumbled down the step and fell, Madison tumbling as they hit the ground. The pit bull rushed toward them and was stopped by the chain just inches from their heads. Jaimey stared into the dog's mouth as saliva dripped from his furled lip. She grabbed up Madison and made her way to her car.

"My doll." Madison said, "I need Sara."

Jaimey looked into Madison's tear filled eyes, unwilling to turn her down after what she'd been through.

"Oh God, where is it?"

"In the bedroom," Madison said through deep sobs.

"Ok, but if I don't come back out you run, you hear?"

"Yes, Ma'am."

Jaimey placed Madison on the back seat and told her to lie down before cautiously going back inside to grab the doll. The screen door closed behind her with a thud, as she stepped back in the travel trailer. She gripped her pistol with both hands trying to steady them. Shaking uncontrollably. Danny Crabs lay on the floor motionless, bleeding from a gash over his eye.

She sprinted inside and went directly to the room, staring at Danny, still on the floor the entire time. Inside the room, she saw the doll on the bed, grabbed it, and turned to leave. Her eye spotted an army green duffle bag with dollar bills poking through the opened zipper. Beside that was a baggie of coke. She grabbed them both and ran out the door. Danny still lay motionless, and she picked her feet up higher as she ran past him.

The pit bull barked and stretched the chain again as Jaimey ran by. She pointed her pistol in its direction in case it should break free.

Finally in the car, she threw the bag in the back and handed the doll to Madison then turned the ignition key. The car chugged. Three more tries, and she smelled gas.

"Dammit! I'm flooding it!" She screamed.

She turned the key again, and after a couple of seconds, the engine roared. She immediately threw it reverse and left. Tires spinning. Dust and rocks and shells kicking into the air. She began driving with no direction in mind. Her hands still shaking; her heart beating wildly, not knowing whether she'd just killed a man. She still smelled him.

As she drove away from 134 ½ Waterway Drive, Jaimey couldn't still her hands, couldn't slow her heart, and couldn't imagine what Madison was going through. The years she had spent as a call girl had toughened her. She'd had held her gun on her clients before, but never pulled the trigger.

Pictures of her childhood shot through her mind like the fast-closing credits after a movie. Her own abuse at the hands of her uncle was contained in the first half of the credits, and her imagination of the utter hell that Madison had endured at the hands of Danny "Crabs" Williams repulsed her for the second half.

Thirty years of hating her uncle and never having the courage to tell anyone her secret steamrolled through the flesh of Danny Williams from a thirty-eight bullet. It all happened so fast, and now she was forced to make a decision.

Jaimey's mind buzzed. She watched Madison in the rear-view mirror. She realized they shared a common bond, a bond that too many young girls and women have. For the last twenty-seven years, she imagined how it would have felt to have killed the man who stole her innocence. She despised him.

As the station wagon made a right turn on I-10, Jaimey's heart rate began to slow; her hands began to steady.

"You ok, baby?" Jaimey asked Madison as Madison caught Jaimey's eye in the rear view mirror.

"Yes Ma'am, are you taking me to my momma and daddy?" Madison asked, now crying again. She held the wild look of uncertainty in her eyes, unsure if she could trust this woman or not.

"Where do you live, baby?" Jaimey asked.

"1423 Moss Creek Drive in Ocean Springs, Mississippi," Madison said quickly, almost forcing it out as if she would forget it, relieved that she got it all out.

"I rehearsed it," Madison said.

"Rehearsed what, baby?" Jaimey asked, looking at her in the rear view as they spoke.

"My address. Just in case I was found, so someone would know where I lived."

"That was smart," Jaimey said.

"I made up a little song called the address song. I sang it quietly to myself everyday just so I wouldn't forget. Are we going there now?"

Jaimey drove. She was unsure where, she just had the car in drive, and she was driving. The adrenaline started again, pumping hard and fast through her body. As soon as it started to slow, she would think of what she had just done and her heart would start racing all over again.

She looked down at her dress, specks of blood splattered upon it. She looked at her face in the mirror; there was a red handprint on her right side and a cut below her right eye. Blood ran from her nose down her neck. Yellows and light purples were already starting to form on her skin.

She read a highway sign up the road, highway ninety, north or south or east... her head spun, filtering the signs telling her where she should go. Filtering the voice in her head that had confused the direction of her entire life up to this point.

She drove blindly, yet seeing everything before her. She saw a sign for Gulfport, and as soon as she reached the exit for Highway forty-nine, she took it.

"Where are we going? Are you taking me home?" Madison asked, her voice cracking with fear.

It took a long time for Jaimey to answer her. She opened her mouth, but found it difficult to form words.

"I'm thinking baby... got to let me think. Just a minute."

Her mind was racing, unsure what she would do if she was pulled over. Unsure of how to explain the blood, the cuts, the bruises. Unsure she could explain who Madison was. Unsure she could explain a duffle bag full of cash with the man's name she just killed written in large block letters.

Her imagination jumped around her current predicament like a paranoid junkie. The police were already searching for her, bulletins put out over police scanners. Her gun was stolen, there was coke in her purse and bloodstream. The car tag and inspection sticker were both out of date. The passenger-side tail light was broken. The money, the blood, the girl... her profession.

She stared at her still shaking hands. She came to a

roadside park and rest area. She pulled in. Families with children on vacation littered the area like ants after their bed had been kicked. She kept driving. Her eyes darting around her, searching for something to tell her what to do next. Searching for something to tell her where to go. As she veered into to the left lane and onto Highway forty-nine, a Mississippi Highway Patrol car came in to full view, lights flashing, closing in on her quickly. Fear crept into her psyche and grabbed a foothold.

"Oh, God, they've found me. Oh shit, oh shit, oh shit," Jaimey muttered, as she beat the steering wheel. She quietly wept.

She veered back into the right lane ready to pull over, the patrol car sped past her. She pulled onto the shoulder of the highway, put the car in park and sat with her head in her hands frantic, crying, exhausted.

More sirens blared, her eyes searching all around her. A patrol car fast approaching in her rearview mirror and then another soon passing her at a high rate of speed. She looked around the inside of her car and grabbed a pair of jeans. Jeans she had stared at for the last two weeks. She turned to Madison and asked her to reach in the back and give her the milk jug filled with water. Kept handy when the radiator started steaming. The full jug was heavy and hard for Madison to pick up, but she finally pulled it over the back-seat and handed it to Jaimey. She slid over to the passenger side, opened the door and held the jeans out of the car and doused them good with the water and began wiping her face off. The water felt good on her skin and it calmed her. She stepped outside the car and began wiping the blood specks off of her dress, remembering other clothes she had in the car.

Jaimey searched in the backseat, grabbing a t-shirt,

shorts and a pair of Rod Laver Adidas. Sitting back on the driver's side, she slipped her dress off and stuffed it under the front seat. She dressed in the shorts and t-shirt unzipped the knee length slut boots and replaced them with the tennis shoes. She wiped her face off again and brushed her hair. She touched up the cuts and bruises as best she could with makeup and rinsed the blood from her mouth with water. She now looked more like a mom than a prostitute. She stuffed the bag under the spare tire.

She took a deep breath and slowly exhaled. Another highway patrol car sped by, and she imagined there must be a wreck on up the highway. She scanned the front seat of the car to make sure nothing was showing from her quick change and cleanup, and started the car down the highway. She noticed the traffic slowing and starting to gather, the vehicles in front of her now at a standstill.

As she slowed, she craned her neck, peering around the cars in front of her. She saw the exit ramp ten car lengths ahead. She started slowly along the shoulder of the highway following other cars that had the same idea.

"Where are we going, miss?" Madison asked with a fearful tear trickling down her cheek.

Jaimey could not remember telling Madison her name.

"Baby, my name is Jaimey, and I'm a mommy too," Jaimey said. "I'm going to get you home, I just need a minute."

Jaimey reached the overpass and glanced down at the line of patrol cars with their lights flashing. An overturned semi lying on its side rested a quarter mile down the high-way. She turned back on forty-nine heading south. As she reached the next exit, she turned into a McDonald's and ordered Madison a Happy Meal. She looked in her purse, and grabbed a twenty-dollar bill. As she handed the twenty to the cashier, she noticed a spot of blood on it. She pulled it back and grabbed the other one. She unfolded the bill, smoothed it out on her lap and flipped it over. It was clean.

After she paid and collected the change, Jaimey pulled into a parking space and sat in the backseat with Madison and helped her with her food. Madison ate quickly.

"When was the last time you ate sweetie?" Jaimey asked.

"I had a bag of chips yesterday, early."

Jaimey gave Madison the rest of her fries and watched the little girl. She brushed the hair from her face and gave her a tight hug.

CHAPTER TWO

The blood stopped flowing. Danny had lain on the floor for so long that the blood pooled and dried under his cheek. The bullet grazed his right cheek and went through his shoulder, and for the last several hours his face had been stuck to the matted carpet. He woke along with the pain and slowly sat up and leaned against the love seat. He had no use of his right arm. Pain moved from his head down through his arm. His back burned from falling along the edge of the coffee table. He sat in the middle of the floor, naked from the waist down, trying to wrap his brain around what had happened. It all had happened so fast. He slowly looked around his trailer.

"Madison... Madison!"

The only sound he heard was his heart beating wildly in his ear.

"Oh shit, no, no, no, the girl!" He got up and stumbled backwards. He fell onto the love seat. He returned to his feet and continued calling to her, stumbling into the bedroom. He looked behind the bed hoping to find her cowering in the corner. Nothing.

"She took her. That bitch took her."

The memory of Madison peering at him from behind the prostitute, holding onto Jaimey as if she were scared. The prostitute pointing a gun at him, the coke, the shot- it all came flooding back.

His mind quickly raced through all of the planning that had gone into her abduction, the money that he spent on the videos, the money from renting her out. That money... was all gone now.

He felt blood drip down his face from where he had just separated it from the floor, ripping the scab away. He put his hand up to the wound and felt the remnants of carpet stuck to his cheek. He snapped his fingers near his right ear. He could hear nothing but the ringing that began the moment he was shot.

He immediately went to his bathroom finding nothing for first aid. He went back to his bottle of Jack Daniels and poured it on the wound gritting his teeth as he did. Watching in the mirror he began plucking the carpet fibers out of the wound, cleaning it the best he could. The longer he stared at himself the angrier he got.

He fumbled around the couch for his cigarettes, cocking his head to see out of the one eye that wasn't swollen and bloody. He felt his right arm, it was still numb. He found a cigarette and lit it. A sharp bolt of pain ran along his wound as he took a long hard pull and swallowed the smoke.

Danny Crabs' travel trailer was a 1975 pull behind and basically consisted of a bedroom that was added on to the side, a small sitting area and bathroom. Through his pain, he continued looking, walking to the door and watching toward the street, hoping to see Madison. Back inside, he fell to his knees and looked under the bed one more time. He looked in the closet finally satisfied she really was gone.

He sat on the bed and grabbed the bottle of Jack Daniels from the floor and took a drink.

He lit another cigarette, and rubbed the back of his neck. He looked again out of the door, toward the street, and then around his trailer again. Searching the same places for the fourth time. Finally, his eye stopped at his old army chest where his duffle bag of money had been kept, it was gone. He sprang to his feet, light headed, ignoring the pain and unsteadiness and bound over to the chest, opening it, knowing full well the bag wouldn't be there.

Spinning around, his eyes danced like flames from a fire. He surveyed the rest of the room, looking for the color green. Nothing. For the next thirty minutes, he trashed the trailer knowing all the while exactly where it should have been.

"Biiiitch!" Danny screamed.

CHAPTER THREE

Randy Crawford was drunk and close to being passed out for the rest of the afternoon when Jaimey hurried through the door dragging Madison by the hand. Madison stayed stuck to her, not letting Jaimey out of her sight.

"I can give you directions to my house." Madison said.

Jaimey immediately went to the refrigerator and grabbed a beer, opened it, drank most of it. She grabbed another one for Randy and dissolved two sleeping pills before handing it to him

She disappeared into her bedroom and started throwing clothes and framed photos along with the baby's photo album detailing every day of Russ's first year into a plastic garbage bag. She dropped in shoes and boxes of knick knacks, loose change and more clothes that needed to be cleaned.

She tore through the apartment with Madison right on her heel. Madison trotted to keep up with her, holding her doll, looking back at Randy, watching him. Jaimey stopped when she came back into the room where Randy was, she stared at him. He was sitting in a chair slowly drifting off to sleep. The thought of leaving him raced through her mind. *Would Russ even care?*

She moved back into the kitchen and stared at the full bottle of sleeping pills on the counter. A whole bottle would do it. It would kill him, she thought.

At the same time, she felt Madison pull on her belt loop and heard Randy behind her.

"You got any money? I need some beer and smokes."

Money was the first and only thing he ever wanted from her. He existed on cigarettes and beer.

"Sure, Honey, we'll get it on the way out of town." Jaimey said as she continued around the apartment grabbing clothes, packing bags and taking them out to the car.

"Where the hell are we going?" Randy mumbled, confused.

"Lewiston, I need to go check on mom and dad's house," Jaimey said hoping his hazy brain would just go along and not question anything further.

"Okay, well, let's stop at the liquor store before we get on the road," Randy said.

He opened the refrigerator and pulled out the last six pack inside. Randy pulled a beer from the plastic ring and popped the top open, and drank until it was empty.

"Who's she?" Randy asked.

Madison continued staring at the floor and slid behind Jaimey as Randy noticed her.

"Just a friend's kid, we're dropping her off at home on the way out of town. She lives over in Ocean Springs."

Hearing this, Russ, Jaimey's son, came into the room, and noticed the cuts and bruises on her face.

"Where are we going?" Russ asked.

"Going to Lewiston for a while, but first we need to

drop Madison off at home. Go ahead and get packed, we need to get on the road." Jaimey said as she followed Russ into his room.

Jaimey shut the door behind her with Madison glued to her.

"Russ how would you feel if we just moved to Lewiston?"

Russ's eyes lit up. He smiled.

"For good, and live in Papa and Grandmother's house?"

Jaimey simply nodded.

"Yes!"

As they hugged, Russ pulled away from Jaimey and looked at Madison and then his mother.

"Is dad coming?"

A long silence filled the room as they stared at each other trying to read the other's mind.

"I can't just leave him here Russ."

Russ let out a big breath and nodded and started packing.

"You're taking me home to 1423 Moss Creek Drive?" Madison asked crying.

"Yes, baby, back to your mom and dad."

Jaimey and Madison went to the car with two garbage sacks full of their belongings. She adjusted the duffle more flatly under the spare and placed the garbage bags on top.

With the car finally packed, Randy fell into the passenger side on the front seat, his twelve-pack cooler on the floorboard between his feet. Jaimey drove toward Ocean Springs. Madison stood behind her with her arms wrapped around her headrest. As they drove closer, Madison gave Jaimey directions to her house.

"Turn that way," Madison said as they arrived at the gated community where 1423 Moss Creek Drive was located. The gate was opened. Repairmen were removing a portion that was bent looking as if it had been plowed into by an impatient driver.

"Russ, this sort of looks like our old neighborhood, doesn't it?" Jaimey asked.

"Yeah, it sort of does," Russ said slowly as if he missed his old house.

The French Acadian style homes framed by moss-draped oak trees lined the quaint street. Residents walking their dogs and pushing strollers fighting the 98 degree day. The humidity clinging to them like cockleburs on a sock.

As they rounded a curve, Madison quietly said, "That's it," as a tear quietly ran down her cheek and her lip quivered. She pointed toward a beautiful two-story home.

Jaimey stopped one house down, and put the car in park. She got out and opened the back door for Madison.

"Sweetie, I'm so sorry this happened to you; I'm so sorry you had to see what you did today. I can't walk you to the door because I might be in trouble for what happened today, but I'm going to watch you and make sure you get inside to your momma, OK?" Jaimey said, wiping tears from both of their eyes.

"Thank you… for what you did," Madison said between sobs.

"Oh, you are so welcome; now you go see your momma Baby."

Madison started slowly walking toward her house. She held her doll, Sara, tightly to her chest. She turned to wave one last time to Jaimey and then ran the rest of the way. Jaimey waved back and returned to the driver's seat, watching Madison. She wiped at her face, Madison looked back at Jaimey again. When she reached the door, Jaimey watched Madison stand to her tiptoes and ring the doorbell and knock as if she were a guest. The door opened and a lady stood erect looking down at Madison, unbelieving, her hand over her mouth. She took Madison in her arms, knees buckling. They both crumbled in the doorway, tears flowing. Madison was finally home.

"They act like they've never seen each other before," Russ said.

Jaimey saw Madison turn and point in their direction, and she quickly drove off. As they drove back through the gate, she realized that of all the terrible things she had been through in her life, maybe this day is why she had to endure them, to return Madison home.

CHAPTER FOUR

As Jaimey turned the station wagon north, she was glad for once that they lived a transient lifestyle. They had nothing to leave behind except rent. No real jobs to leave, no friends to give explanations to. Their apartment was a monthly rent that included the furniture. There was one week left before rent was due, and before this morning she didn't have the two-hundred and fifty dollars anyway. A beautiful house, vacant since her mother's death, sat waiting for them.

The road stretched on for miles ahead of her. She watched the mirage of water disappear from the pavement as the miles clicked by. She spotted three patrol cars parked beside each other in the median. One had a speed gun leveled right at her, and her eyes dropped to the speedometer. She was five miles over the limit, so she slowed. She kept her head straight only moving her eyes watching to see if they pulled out behind her. Sweat beaded on her face and forehead. She let out a long, slow breath, and moved her hand to her chest, and wiped her face.

"Man, the cops are all over the place today; there must be an escaped criminal on the run," Russ said looking back toward the line of patrol cars.

Jaimey stared at Russ in her rear-view mirror.

"You really think so?" Jaimey asked. "You never know who could be out here on these roads."

"So, what's the first thing you're going to do when we get to Lewiston?" Jaimey asked.

"Go to the golf course! Can I play right when we get there?" Russ asked, his face bright with excitement.

"Sure, won't be much daylight left though," Jaimey said as she watched the excitement build in Russ.

They finally reached the city limits of Lewiston after the four-hour drive from Biloxi. As she turned off of Hwy 15 onto Columbus Avenue, Russ sat up in his seat when he spotted the Beau Chene Country Club sign. The sun sinking in the sky barely peeked over the horizon. Memories of playing with his grandfather shot through his mind. His heart raced with excitement. He turned and got to his knees and watched as the golf course disappeared when they made the turn toward home.

As Jaimey pulled into her old neighborhood, golf carts of every make and color were finding their way back home. Russ quickly jumped out of the car and opened the back hatch. He heard his father mumble something and ignored it. He grabbed his pull cart and strapped on his bag and started running. Russ slipped through three neighbors' backyards, and stood on the number eight tee box. He stared ahead of him and looked down the fairway for the green. It was empty save for a family of mallard ducks making their way to the pond that lie in front of the green. He bent down and pushed his tee in the ground and placed his ball on top and heard the distance voices of his father and mother as they argued. He struck the ball and watched it before the dusk covered it. He walked toward his ball and away from the voices and wandered the course most of the night, staying away.

CHAPTER FIVE

The hazy summer morning air wreaked with a mixture of heat and freshly mowed grass. A light fog held tight and low between William Capstick and the number one green. He reminded himself his approach shot would stick hard as it landed. The early morning dew still held tight to the edge of the greens.

Capstick extracted his lob wedge from his bag and lined up. His concentration was easy, he was the only one on the course at 6:30 in the morning on the first day of the week. Retirement allowed this love affair to happen frequently.

He flipped through the menu in his mind, *ball back in stance, swing through, don't break the wrist.* His concentration, his mind, his body were all perfectly in sync as he exchanged glances with the flag and white ball in front of him.

His wedge flowed back like honey being poured without gravity, and he committed to the strike. Just as he struck the ball, all of his preparation fell into place. He watched as his ball fell near the flag. He was dancing.

He stood posed as if someone were taking his picture,

trying to hold on to the memory of how it felt so hopefully he could reinvent it later. He stood this way many times after a shot, wrangling his body into the pretzel-like form, thinking every time he struck the ball, his body would flow into the same movement, making his game more consistent.

As he pulled his body back into its normal stance, he heard a rusty car door slam. It squeaked as it shut, rusted metal rubbing against rusted metal.

"Who in the hell?" he said in disbelief as he wheeled around toward the row of cart houses to see who was intruding into his life of tranquility.

"Damn, kid, what in the hell is he doing out here this time of morning?" Capstick asked himself through gritted teeth. He watched the kid lean into a rusted station wagon through the window and kiss the driver.

She lowered the back glass as the kid walked to the rear, raised to his tiptoes and reached inside and extracted a golf bag and pull cart. He waved bye to her as she pulled away.

His appearance caught Capstick's attention. He was a skinny kid, long waisted with no calves and little ankles. His shirt was not tucked in, and he was wearing flip flops. The bill of his cap advertising Gatorade was frayed, looking as though he had rubbed it hard on a brick wall. It resting on a thick tuft of long blonde hair that curled hard around his ears. He looked more like a surfer than a golfer.

His shirt hung long and looked as though he were wearing a dress when he adjusted his shorts, pulling them up on his frail torso.

The boy ambled over to the number three tee box and pushed his hand into the old bag and pulled out a golf glove that had too many holes in it to be effective. He then extracted a persimmon wood driver.

He threw a florescent orange ball down near the markers, played around with it, and set it up on a thick mound of grass. He looked toward the green one time and struck the ball. It sailed down the middle of the fairway low with a slow rise and fell just beyond the one-hundred-yard marker.

He slid the driver back into the bag and began the slow, arduous walk toward the number three green, pulling his cart uphill behind him. As he made his way toward the green, Capstick noticed the kid looking around the course. The boy stopped and shoved his hand inside his bag and retrieved one lone cigarette. He tapped it on the handle of his pull cart, and lit it with a lighter from the baggy cargo shorts that kept sliding from his waist.

Capstick laughed to himself. He followed along watching. He was caught off guard by the boy. The maturity with which he approached his shots, the keen confidence he portrayed while playing, the creativeness of each shot, the quick decisions he made about his game. All of this combined with his physical presence impressed him. The kid's body was simply suited for golf.

Capstick was mesmerized by the boy and stayed in the dense clump of pine trees slowly stalking him, watching to see if the lanky boy would ever evolve from a PGA pro into a normal teenager. And then it happened- the boy hooked one, and it slowly rolled to the left about one hundred yards from the tee box and rested near the root of a pine tree.

Capstick eased his cart along the row of trees still watching the boy. He watched as the kid arrived at his ball, took a drag from his smoke, pulled it from his mouth threw it down using the ground as an ashtray. The kid pulled out what looked like a wedge again, lined up his shot and placed the ball right on the edge of the green. He bent down, picked up his cigarette and walked toward his shot.

With the advent of many recent deaths, William Capstick was quickly becoming the "old man" at Beau Chene Country Club. He was a sweet man full of time and attention for any young boy that wanted to learn what he had to teach about the game of golf.

He had just turned sixty. A youthful sixty. He had snow white hair and a thick, fluffy moustache that he kept curled on the ends. On his head, he wore a booney hat that kept additional sun off of his already perfectly tanned face. His eyes were small and happy, always looking as if he was glad to be wherever he was. His crow's feet turned upward from a constant smile. His legs and arms were dark from the sun. He stood close to 6'4" tall and walked with a smooth, dignified gait.

On the course, Capstick was typically surrounded by teenaged boys. All begged his attention, eager for the lessons they all placed so much value on.

All of his white hair seemed to fade away when he was surrounded by the sea of dark-headed boys, who could hit three-hundred-yard drives effortlessly. Some drove that long because Capstick had taught them, while the others just had natural ability.

Beau Chene became a babysitter of sorts for the boys in the summer. Their mommas would drop them off at the rows of cart houses, and then go to the pool or beauty parlor or shopping with the girls. The boys would play, and Capstick would coach, and the boys were good.

In Lewiston, golf was one of the few things there was to do in the summer besides work. Sacking groceries and mowing yards somehow escaped these boys, possibly in hopes by their parents that they would someday get scholarships and endorsements and become famous.

Capstick rounded the second hole and saw the boy again pulling his cart toward the spot where he had been dropped off earlier that morning. As he watched the kid, he saw the rusted station wagon again as it turned slowly into parking lot. He watched as it stopped and saw a blonde woman get out to help the kid with his clubs. She was small and wore large sunglasses and little makeup. She looked anxious, and in a hurry, rushing the boy. A lawnmower handle extended from the back of the station wagon and slid to the opposite side as they turned out of the parking lot.

Capstick finished his last hole and sat under the sprawling oak that the course was named after, Beau Chene, French, meant beautiful oak. The tree was over 100 years old and had survived tornadoes and several attempts from chainsaws. Every man on the course had cussed the tree at one time or another because it sat smack dab in the middle of the fairway.

An errant tee shot sparked their creativeness to get around the massive tree. At the end of the day, however, it provided a shaded meeting place where the men would have a drink and tally up their scores. Stories about "that shot" and holes-in-one almost made often told there. Inches always dictated success and lower scores.

Capstick was counting his strokes for the morning when he heard a truck pull into the parking lot. He looked up in time to see the muffler dragging the ground, sending sparks flying, as it hit potholes and scraped against rocks.

He didn't recognize the driver but was sure he was driving Noel Mitchell's old truck. The driver drove slowly in a large circle as if he were looking for someone and finally came to a stop. A man, tall and slight, exited, hitching his pants keeping them on his bony hips. He kept his finger through a belt loop and looked around. When the man walked, he stumbled and had to rest, keeping one hand on the truck to steady himself.

The man pushed off of his truck and walked between a row of cart houses. He made his way to the end and started up the next, bracing himself along the wall as he did. He stumbled a few times and eventually made his way back to the truck. He drove toward the clubhouse and Capstick followed him, cutting across the course. The truck weaved as he drove down the road, the driver scanning the course the entire time. When he reached the clubhouse, the man walked inside, but no one was there; it was still too early. He made his way back outside and around the side of the clubhouse toward the pool, where a group of screaming children were taking swimming lessons.

Capstick pulled up to the front of the clubhouse and timed his exit from the cart just as the man rounded the corner.

"Good morning!" Capstick said, his booming voice forcing the man to acknowledge him. The man only nodded.

Capstick continued speaking, hoping his presence would at least inspire the man to ask if he had seen whomever he was obviously looking for.

With careful thought to pronunciation, the man asked Capstick if he had seen a young boy.

"He's a skinny little shit with long bony ass legs and thick blonde hair, around fifteen years old, goes by the nick name 'Country Club' the man said, slurring his speech.

Capstick was certain he was describing the kid.

"Uh, no, I've been here all morning and haven't seen anyone that fits that description. What's his real name?"

"Russ," the man said with a sneer.

"I'm William Capstick, everyone calls me Cappy." Cappy said as he stuck out his hand. His hand hung in midair ignored.

"If you see him out here, tell the little bastard to get home."

CHAPTER SIX

The sound of falling rain and thunder woke Jaimey. Her senses stirred at the same time the weather man reported rain for the rest of the day and the remainder of the week.

The summer day was unusually dark and gloomy. She sat on the edge of her bed and stared at the developing day before her. A smoky grey sky replaced the clear blue one from the day before and she inhaled and exhaled heavily. The breathing exercises calmed her, eased her mind. It helped chase the fear and loathing away.

The day's weather added to the anxiety that coexisted with her daily. Russ wouldn't be able to play golf or cut grass, and the weather meant that Randy would be home all day as well. She lay in bed and tried to stop the traffic speeding through her head. The events of the last week kept playing on repeat like a bad song that gets stuck in the mind. A thought was sprinkled among her memories, and it kept repeating: *my mind will only take me to imaginations that I dare not repeat out loud.* She wondered where had she heard that. Were they her own words, or was she repeating something she'd heard before?

Still shots of her naked client lying on the floor in a widening puddle of blood kept popping in and out of her mind like someone flicking a light switch on and off. Sometimes she saw him as Danny; other times she imagined her uncle. She secretly hoped it was Randy. She shot Danny because her life was in immediate danger, because she imagined what he had done to Madison. She now wished Randy was dead. She couldn't imagine living with him much longer. She could see no future in it. She couldn't see that he was ever going to change or be the man she married.

"Self-defense," she thought. Russ would be a witness. There was history. There had been past reports of abuse made. Police had pictures of both her and Russ bruised, cut, and bloody. She only wished she could take a picture of the words that had come out of Randy's mouth. Words said to his son, his only child. Words that hurt more than any punch or slap or near-death choking. Words that last a lifetime. Hurtful words.

"Do you fear for your life?" the police would always ask as they sent her back to her husband.

What if I had just said 'yes' once; what if I just shot and killed him? She asked herself the same questions over and over again, a million times over the last five years.

Russ. He was always the answer. She could never allow Russ to witness his mother kill his father. He had already been witness to too much. He lived in a world that she partly created. A world that wasn't good, that wasn't wholesome. A life of anxiety and drug use, alcohol abuse, and prostitution.

She and Randy threw that in Russ's face every day for

most of his young life. "Which would be more detrimental," she asked herself, "the death of a father or a lifetime of abuse?"

Now that it was all behind her, Jaimey replayed in her mind how easy it had been to shoot and kill Danny. She relived the shot. She remembered what it felt like- the surge of adrenaline, the shaking hands, the fear of getting caught. How fast it all went down. How much easier it would have been if Madison hadn't been there and she didn't have anyone but herself to consider. *With a little planning, she thought...that's premeditated murder.* Her mind bounced like a tennis ball back and forth. First one thought, then the polar opposite.

She lie in her childhood bed, in her childhood room, in her childhood home listening to the thunder, smelling the steam rise from the pavement outside. It was almost relaxing in some odd reminiscent way. A feeling of familiarity. The thought of Randy no longer being around soothed her. She allowed her mind to imagine things *she dared not repeat in public*; and it became more and more real to her.

Russ sat on the edge of his bed staring out the window at the rain, thinking of a way to leave the house. The only thing he grabbed before the quick exit from Biloxi were the only two possessions he had in this world- his golf clubs and his record collection. The clubs were some old ones he purchased at a yard sale after Randy sold his good ones for beer money. The record collection spanned a good mix of seventies and Southern rock, Led Zeppelin, Aerosmith, to the most current Van Halen and Cheap Trick.

His favorite song was Van Halen's "Jaimie's Cryin'." He placed the record on the turntable and moved the needle to the beginning of the song. The familiar static scratch soon erupted into Eddie Van Halen's guitar rift and David Lee's voice belting out over and over again. He sat with his ear close to the speaker so he could hear. He had the volume turned down low.

He studied the self-titled debut album cover. The four members of the band clad in spandex and long hair. Russ stared at David Lee Roth the lead singer. He had long blonde hair like Roth did, and he decided let his start growing. He looked in the mirror at his mullet, imagining being the lead singer in a band.

He turned the volume up when the chorus began,

"Oh, oh, oh Jamie's cryin'..."

As he tilted his head slightly to better hear, a hand grabbed the back of his shirt and pulled him across the floor, throwing him into the wall.

"I told you to never play that shit again." Randy said, wiping spit from the corner of his mouth and holding his pants up with his free hand.

Randy grabbed Russ by the front of his t-shirt and stood him up.

"Quit looking so pitiful, you little wimp. You're such a piece of shit! How many times have I told you not to play that song? How many?"

"A lot," Russ said, staring down at the floor.

"Look at me, dammit!"

Russ slowly raised his head, his eyes red, now swimming in tears, that rolled in fat drops down his cheeks.

"I had it turned dow..." Russ's explanation was interrupted by the back of Randy's hand across his mouth. Russ could immediately feel the blood start to trickle and soon felt the familiar sting of flesh swelling.

Wobbling, Randy reached down and ripped the record

from the player and broke it over his knee shattering it. He then picked up the larger of the pieces and tried breaking them as well but wasn't able. He reached for the rest of Russ's record collection.

"Stop, Dad, please!" Russ begged, grabbing Randy's shoulder to stop him from picking up another record. Randy pushed Russ on the bed, and shoved a knee in his gut. He pinned Russ down and started slapping him, trading licks with each side of his face.

Jaimey heard the broken record playing in the next room. The same shouting, yelling, slapping, and punching. She shot up from the bed and moved toward her purse. Russ's cries and begging were piercing her ears with every moment that passed. She took her revolver in her hand and opened the chamber. She saw the pierced center of the shell that she shot Danny with and she closed it shut.

She moved toward her door but couldn't do it. She couldn't let Russ be witness to his mother killing his father. She threw the gun on her bed and ran in Russ's room forcing her way between them to block the blows and started kicking Randy off of the both of them.

"I told him not to play that damn song in this house!"

"So, you're going to beat the hell out of him for playing a song on a record player?! I own this house Randy, and he can play any song he wants to! If you want to go back to Biloxi, you can sit in silence there all by yourself. I wish we had left you there to rot! If we make you so unhappy, why don't you leave?" screamed Jaimey.

Randy was sober enough this early in the day that Jaimey's words stung. It was the first time she ever said that she wanted him to leave. It was hard for him to realize that she does own the house, lock, stock, and barrel. He had very little control over her anymore. She really didn't need him for anything. If anything, *he* needed *her* now.

He had no claim to the house. Her parents were smart enough to place the property solely in her name. Randy had already investigated that option when he needed money and thought he could sell the house. He had planned on leveraging the house for money to invest in a condo on the beach. His mind still worked in real estate, although he could no longer had the capacity to put deals together. He didn't have the money needed. There was no way he could stand in front of investors, looking the way he did, and expect any success. He only dreamed of what was and what could still be... if he had just made different business decisions when he could have.

It was the first time he realized neither of them really needed him for anything. He stood before them suddenly frightened, remorseful for how he had just treated his son. He looked at Russ, Randy's eyes floating in tears.

"I'm sorry; please forgive me," he said.

He walked out of the room, and, at 9:00 A.M., he walked to the refrigerator for a beer.

Russ and Jaimey stared at each other.

"He apologized. He was crying. Did you see that?" Russ said. They both stood in shock; he had never apologized before for anything.

"Did you see him crying?" Russ said uncertain of what just unfolded in front of him.

"Yeah, that almost looked real," Jaimey said, a glimmer of hope filling her mind.

CHAPTER SEVEN

onday night was men's poker night at the Country Club. Men arrived in hoards with coolers, cigars, and card playing on their minds. The Beau Chene clubhouse looked much like every other small-town clubhouse, nothing extravagant but nothing terrible either. The membership over the years ebbed and flowed, seeming to follow the current economic conditions. Beau Chene's membership was healthy mainly due to a large number of local boys who decided to stay home and raise their families in Lewiston instead of moving to the larger cities of Atlanta or Birmingham.

With a recent increase in membership, they had completed a much-needed renovation of the property. The exterior of the clubhouse got a fresh coat of paint. The bathrooms were completely gutted, re-plumbed and re-tiled. The greens and fairways fitted with an irrigation system were now lush and green. New grasses that had exotic sounding names were planted.

The poker room was set up and ready for the weekly game. Several large, round card tables were sprinkled all over the room. Each table dictated its own antes. There were the usual one- five- and ten-dollar antes. But the big table, as the usual group called it, saw much larger antes.

One legendary card game back in 1975 involved the title to a '56 Porsche Roadster. Dr. Greene won the title from Bill Perkins, a local pharmacist. It was Bill Perkins's first ever car, handed down from his father. Dr. Greene knowing how much Bill loved and cherished the car- and how much bourbon he had that night- never signed the title and simply enjoyed driving it for a month. He finally returned it, full of gas, to a tearful Bill Perkins, who rewarded the doctor with a big bear hug.

There had been many other legendary games; many that included a few, cocky, redneck types who came into some money and could finally play with "the big boys"- only to go home empty-handed with their tails between their legs.

There was a lot of old money in Lewiston, so you didn't see the usual strain of doctors and lawyers like you would at most country clubs in the bigger cities. It wasn't unusual to see old oil and lumber money sitting next to no money at all at these social events. These men not only played golf together, but many were in hunting clubs together as well. In the spring, they made their way to the Delta bream fishing. The first of August usually found them in a dove field together, and then a small wing of the group attended races in Bristol and Talladega. They knew each other well.

The room became much louder as the poker tables filled. The talk on this April night centered around fishing reports from the Delta and what the water levels and rain were looking like for the next week, which for some was a segue to talk about investments, crop reports and futures speculation.

There were also the usual stories regaling crazy shots, holes-in-one and seeing one of the wives peeing in the woods off of the ninth green.

"Fours, whores, and mustache growers' wild boys," Bubba Stewart sang around the fat cigar stub protruding from his mouth. He deftly dealt the cards.

"Everybody, ante up!" Wads of green dollar bills pulled from pockets and lay in mounds on the table. A roar of laughter erupted from one of the tables as a player had already lost a hand.

"You cheatin' sumbitch!" a player laughingly shouted as his hand plunged into his pocket to retrieve more cash.

Cappy threw a five into the center of the table and leaned over to Bubba Stewart who was sitting on his left.

"Hey, Bubba, you ever see a kid out here early in the morning playing by himself, real skinny, can hit the ball pretty good?"

A thoughtful frown came over Bubba's face. "Real curly blonde hair?"

"Yeah, that's him."

"I think I saw him yesterday actually; why?"

"Well, you ever stopped long enough to watch the boy play?"

"Naw, I don't guess I've ever really paid that much attention to him."

"The boy can hit the ball; I mean next level" Cappy said. Bubba wished he had paid more attention to the boy.

"I would love to know what he shot on this course today," Cappy said, as he picked a moist piece of tobacco from his tongue.

"You know, I bet that's Noel Mitchell's grandson, Jaimey's boy. Charlotte told me that they recently moved back here from the coast; I think Biloxi."

"You know the last name?" Cappy said hoping Bubba had actually been listening to his girlfriend as she gossiped about the new family in town.

"Yeah. Crawford," Bubba said, proud that he had remembered.

Cappy made a mental note, "Russ Crawford."

"You know, the father is a real piece of work; he's a drunk. He had a real successful real estate business until the casinos came in, and he gambled everything away. I mean, this kid was pulling in some serious money, and he lost it all. After that, what little was left, he lost because he drank it away. I also hea…"

"He isn't paying a visitors fee every time he plays, is he?" Cappy asked.

"I don't think so. We let the kid play on Mr. Noel's membership. Ms. Ruth paid three years in advance before she died. She kept it for the grandbabies. You know, Mr. Noel still has a cart and cart shed out here too; was the kid walking when you saw him?"

"Yeah, pull cart," Cappy said.

"Hey, Cuss!" Bubba yelled across the room to Cuss Stringer, the recently elected secretary at Beau Chene. "Could you get me a cart house folder?"

"Sure, which one?"

"Should be under Noel Mitchell, or maybe Ms. Ruth now?"

"Be right back," Cuss said as he jumped up to retrieve the file.

Cuss was young, fresh out of college, and had moved back home just so he could do what he's doing right now- hang out with these men, many of whom he grew up with, all of whom he loved. His nickname derived from church when, as a young boy, he stood, leaning against the back of the pew, elbows propped on either side of him, tired of a long-winded preacher praying for far too long, asked out loud, "When is this son-of-a-bitch going to be finished?" His father quickly removed him from the congregation and nicknamed him Cuss that day.

"Here ya' go," Cuss said as he tossed the large envelope toward Bubba.

"Cart shed 25," Bubba said.

As he opened the envelope, a key with a piece of paper attached to it fell out. On it, in shaky handwriting was a note:

For Russ from Papa and Grandmother Ruth

"Hey, you mind if I go take a look inside and see what shape the carts in? I'll give the boy the keys when I'm done."

"Sure," Bubba said, handing Cappy the key.

Early the next morning, Cappy made it out to the country club and drove to the row of old cart houses. Noel Mitchell's cart shed was two sheds down from his own. He parked his powder blue '66 Ford Bronco in front of number 23 and scrounged around in the tool box in the back for a can of WD-40.

Before inserting the key, he doused the key hole and watched as rust colored lubricant flowed from the lock. After waiting several seconds, he inserted the key, and, after a couple of tries, the locked popped open.

The hinges slowly wept as he pulled the door, and he sprayed them as he walked inside. The interior was dusty and full of cobwebs. A large spider crawled out of his sight. Five golf caps were neatly lined up on the wall directly above four pairs of golf shoes that were once spit-shined daily. There was an old refrigerator that looked as if it might still work so Cappy plugged it in. He opened the door, and the light was on. He noticed two large plastic stadium cups full of quarters won from playing for a quarter a hole. On top of the refrigerator were trophies from past tournaments. The largest one he remembered watching Noel win in 1980. Propped in the corner was another pair of golf shoes.

With the exception of the dust, everything was straight and had been well cared for. The cart shed itself was still in good shape. As Cappy turned to open the other door, the entire wall before him was filled with framed photos of Noel Mitchell with various members, photos that spanned over forty years. Some yellowed with age. Cappy studied them, wiping the dust, smiling at faces as they became clearer. Most of the men in the photos had passed. There were photos of Noel with the grandkids, and he searched for a kid that might be Russ. In one, he saw the drunk with his father-in-law standing on what must have been the number ten green.

Cappy found the light switch and turned it on so he could get a better look at the cart itself. He opened the second door flooding the room with more natural light.

The cart was British green with whitewall tires and chrome hubcaps. Cappy pulled up the seat to check out the batteries, and the tops were green showing little corrosion but looking good overall. He checked for water in the batteries, and, as expected, they were bone dry. He knocked off a few dirt daubers' nests and wiped the driver's side seat down. His eye caught a score card on the steering wheel. He brushed the dust off of the card and recognized Noel's handwriting. The scores for he and "Ms. Ruth," as he called her. Cappy smiled as he said out loud, "He played his last game with Ms. Ruth."

He walked back up to his own cart shed and retrieved

his cart and drove it down to twenty-five. Tying a pull rope between the two, he pulled it over to the cleaning pad where he was able to fill the batteries and brush off the connectors. He washed it, having to scrub in some places where the dirt was thickest. He filled the tires with air and returned to twenty-five. He plugged the cart to the charger pumping life into the batteries.

"To have been sitting unused for two years, the cart's not in bad shape," he said out loud to himself.

Before pulling the cart back in, Cappy grabbed a broom and began knocking down spider webs and dirt dauber nests, then swept the floor. A plume of dust bellowed from the doors. He wiped down all of the photos on the walls and cleaned Noel Mitchell's shoes. He opened the refrigerator, stuck his hand inside, and was surprised to find it was beginning to cool.

After a quick trip to the store, he loaded the ball holder with a fresh sleeve of new balls, placed a full bag of tees on the seat and attached a new medium right-handed glove to the steering wheel. He stuck a new scorecard and pencil in the holder and wrote Russ's name on the card. He removed a thumbtack from a two-by-four holding a yellowed newspaper article about his club win in 1980 and added Noel's and Ms. Ruth's score card over it replacing the thumbtack.

CHAPTER EIGHT

Two weeks had passed since Danny "Crabs" Williams was shot. He arrived late to his doctor's appointment. As he walked through the front door, the smell of fried wontons and egg drop soup filled his nose. He walked through the restaurant into the kitchen and out the back door. Once outside, he walked through a small courtyard and to a metal door with a horizontal slot head high. He knocked three times and a man opened the slot then stared at him. Short, the man stood on his tip toes. He opened the door and let Danny in.

It had been only weeks since Danny's doctor had been released from jail. With his license stripped, he was no longer able to practice medicine legally. He now resorted to working under the radar from the back of a Chinese restaurant in Chinatown on the outskirts of Biloxi. His stint in federal prison for Medicaid fraud shut his practice down completely. He was desperately trying to rebuild, and relied on relationships from his other life to help.

Danny knew the doctor from being a part of the network of men that made and peddled kiddie porn, and today he brought with him his payment for medical services rendered. Ten never before seen tapes that Danny personally made. Some of them were of Madison, the others were several different girls he had molested while the good doctor was in prison.

The doctor's professionalism that was once a part of his daily life had left him the longer he spent behind bars. He walked into his examination room looking as if had arrived from a beach vacation rather than just being released from prison. He wore long board shorts and a Hawaiian shirt. Bamboo thongs adorned his feet. A silver toe ring hung loosely around his second toe. His white beard had not been trimmed, and the straw hat sat back on a thick head of white hair.

He stood in front of Danny and lit a cigar. Taking his time to hold the flame on the end, twisting it back and forth to get an even burn.

He took the tapes from Danny and looked at them individually, then thanked him. He walked over to the cabinet behind his makeshift desk and pulled a tape from underneath a large brown box and handed it to Danny.

"Here, take this with you, I got it while I was in prison. So, what the hell happened to your face?" He asked, finally looking at Danny.

"I got shot."

"By whom?" The doctor questioned, as he examined the wound more closely.

"I hired a hooker to watch me and the girl; she shot me and took the girl."

"Damn, is the girl in any of these?" the doctor asked as he motioned toward the stack Danny brought to him.

"The one marked Madison, school girl outfit, fourth one from the top."

The doctor cleaned the wound, bandaged it and gave Danny an antibiotic shot.

"Oh, by the way, you need to call our friend in Southaven; he has something for you."

"Good, thank you."

CHAPTER NINE

R andy woke early the next morning and sat in the backyard in his boxer shorts. It was still dark. An orange skyline edged with a blue tint sat just above the trees. He held his head as it pounded; then lit a cigarette. The sting of Jaimey's words still rang in his ears. The sick feeling that he was virtually alone turned his stomach. He lay awake most of the night with the image of his son's face burned in his memory. A face that wore fear. A face that shook from wincing, bracing against another barrage of violent outburst.

Randy was smart. He knew he had gone too far. He knew that his existence, grotesque as it was, served to only save face. He had to protect the little pride he had left, hold on to the little pieces of power that he could eek out of each day. Days filled with memories of defeat and loss. Days filled with memories of walking around like the cock-of-the-walk with his chest poked out, proud of the busi-nessman he had become. Figures floating in his head. Amounts in this account and that account. Figures of what had been paid for cars and jewelry and toys and houses.

Multi-million-dollar figures of business deals closed over drinks. Figures of women he lusted after. Dark figures of them lying in the bed as he left the next morning.

It all added up to failure; he took his eye off the ball, and now his family feared him. His wife now wanted him to leave and his own son couldn't look him in the eye.

He fought the urge to drink. He looked down at his hands as they shook. He clasped them together, one hand trading places with the other, holding each one still trying to calm his mind.

He sat waiting for an hour until the sun rose well above the pines and the day began to warm. A neighbor walking his garbage can to the street glanced toward him. Randy still sat in his boxers rubbing his hands together tighter and tighter until they started to become hot.

He knew what he had to do, but he couldn't bring himself to do it. Time would eventually heal the wounds. Apologies would go a long way toward righting the ship.

He stood, but quickly fell back into the chair. The force of the fall tipped the lawn chair, and he fell to the ground. He slowly got to his hands and knees and, eventually, to his feet. He was still unsteady and wobbly. He made his way back into the house. He dressed in the cleanest clothes he could find and brushed his teeth and combed his hair and put on a cap. He sat down and tried to tie the laces on his shoes, then opted for a pair of loafers and slipped his feet into them.

He walked down the hallway and stood at Russ's door trying to muster the courage to simply speak to his own son. He had a plan in mind, a day for them to spend some time together. The demons were at bay for the moment, and he felt oddly at peace. He felt hope.

He opened the door and walked to the edge of Russ's

bed and placed his hand on the boy's shoulder. Russ turned and saw him, and immediately retreated against the wall, recoiling as if Randy were a snake prepared to strike, Russ appearing like a fearful little boy.

"It's okay son, I just want to tell you I'm so sorry for all of it," Randy started. A long quiet filled the room as Randy struggled to find the words. He wanted them to be right, they had to work. "I don't expect you to forgive me immediately. I know it will take time, but I've got to try. I'd like for us to go fishing today...if you will."

Russ kept pushing his feet against the bed trying to create space between himself and Randy. He wasn't sure of what he was hearing. He wasn't sure who the man was in front of him. At the same time, a strange relief washed over Russ. He wanted peace for himself and Jaimey so badly that he accepted the words.

Russ couldn't bring himself to speak; he simply nodded. As he did, Randy's eyes filled with tears and relief flowed from his mouth in a rush of air.

"Thank you," he said as he started to pat Russ's knee but thought better of it.

Russ dressed and met Randy outside by the truck. Randy held the keys in front of Russ, allowing him to drive.

"I can drive?" Russ asked, astonished, wondering when the man before him would snap back into the father he had known most of his life.

They grabbed some cricket buckets and two bream poles from the storage room and threw them in the back of the truck. Russ drove them to the ice house and bait shop for crickets. Russ gave the two buckets to the man to fill with bait as Randy walked through the store. He stood at a rack filled with donuts and got two packs, then walked to the coolers for two milks to wash them down. As he neared the coolers, beer signs for every flavor stared at him and begged him to grab a six pack. His hand shook as he opened the cooler holding the milk and took two. He finally turned and walked away, his hands continuing to shake.

He took out a twenty-dollar bill, holding it in his hand as the cashier totaled their items. Russ noticed Randy's hand shaking. He quietly took the money from Randy and completed their purchase. He eased Randy's hand down behind the counter and held it, lightly squeezing it. Randy squeezed back.

CHAPTER TEN

The healthier Danny got, he became obsessed with finding the woman that stole his life from him.

The once-painful space that filled his mind that was now filled with anger and thoughts of revenge. The two most important things in the world were taken from him, and by a cheap whore, no less.

He saw the news reports of Madison being reunited with her parents. Thoughts of going after the girl again flooded his mind. A police sketch filled the television screen. Madison had given the police a description, and the police sketch artist had done a pretty good job.

"How hard could it be to draw a beard with eyes?" Danny said out loud.

He had not been to a barber in years, but now flipped through the yellow pages until he found one close by. It would be fairly easy to change his appearance; a good shower, a shaved face and haircut would allow him to walk around with impunity. Simply getting cleaned up would be his disguise.

He began plotting and planning. His mind filled with

revenge on the hooker that had upended his life. He had had Madison longer than he had had any other girl. The stolen money was more than he had ever had at any one time in his life.

For a short time in his life, Danny worked as a private investigator. He tracked people for a living. He usually had more information to go on that he did now, but it was never impossible to piece together enough information to find someone. Gathering information is like a snowball rolling downhill, gathering more and more snow as it moves.

He sat on his couch using a TV tray as his desk and began writing down everything he knew about Platinum. He glanced down at the still-littered floor and saw the blood that he had not taken the time to clean yet. He saw the remnants of their struggle. He saw all the filth.

Danny recounted the day he called Platinum, it was around 11:00 A.M. and she arrived roughly an hour later. Taking into consideration that she sounded groggy when they spoke, he decided that she probably needed some time to wake up, get dressed and ready. He surmised that she probably lived within ten to fifteen minutes of his trailer. The area code that he called was the next county over, but Danny lived close to the county line, so he figured she lived on his side of the county. She had a Southern accent. Specifically, she had what he called a "hill accent." Nothing in her accent or speech had an inflection of Creole in it, so she wasn't from one of the parishes in Louisiana. Most likely she was originally from the central part of Mississippi or Alabama. She looked as if she were around forty or forty-five, but more than likely she was closer to thirty-five. Danny knew these women lived hard lives, and it aged them rapidly. Jaimey was certainly no exception.

"There was something different about her," Danny

thought out loud. She had an air about her, as if she came from money. From the way she spoke, he could tell she had a good education. Her grammar was correct, and her accent sounded as if she came from privilege.

So often, the girls he had used in the past were part of the stripper circuit, a network of sorts, traveling from city to city to strip and make money. Some of them were also call girls, so Danny knew those girls were transient.

When he called her, it seemed to be a direct call to her personal line, so he didn't think she had a pimp. Danny made a note to find the number in his mess of a home.

He made a list of the local strip joints. He scribbled a star by number three on the list "Mike's Girls." It was close to his trailer, and he knew it well. The girls knew to stay clear of him or at least from the old Danny.

He jotted down other notes: yearbooks, property taxes, health department. AIDS was running rampant through the sex worker community. He was sure, like most were, that she was getting regular checkups. He covered all the bases. He gave himself no timeline to find her. In his mind, she took everything from him, so he would take his time and spare nothing to find her.

CHAPTER ELEVEN

Russ carefully drove behind the club house and parked at the end of the road near the maintenance shed. A pond built to catch drain water, full of bedding bream, sat on the edge of the fairway.

The two remained, as they had for most of the morning, quiet. It was difficult to find words. Neither really knew the other. They had very little in common. The last four years had been spent living under a cloud of dysfunction. Of alcohol fueled rage. Of tears. Of screaming. Of dodging each other after hurtful words were spoken in anger.

They sat on the edge of the water next to each other and threaded a hook through the middle of a cricket. The water boiled in the middle of the small pond and held a rotten, musty odor. Randy lobbed his cricket toward the rolling water. His red cork disappearing into the black water. He stood as he freed the fish from its bed. The bream fought its way out of the dark hole as Randy brought it toward him and released it from the hook. He watched Russ's face become flush with excitement. Their eyes locked, both smiling at each other.

Russ watched as his cork hit the water beside his father's and quickly disappeared. For close to an hour, they caught fish, throwing some back that weren't big enough to keep and came away from the pond with three quarters of their stringer full of Bluegill and Chinquapins.

"Thank you," Randy said. "I would have understood if you didn't want to do this with me today. It says a lot about what kind of person you are. It takes a big man to accept an apology and move on."

Russ stared out at the only fairway he could see. He watched as a ball bounced and then rolled toward the pond. Soon he saw golf carts appear and players exit and hit their second shot. He longed to be on the course playing, but he wouldn't trade what he was doing right now for anything. "He's trying," Russ thought to himself. He turned back toward Randy as he pulled another fish out of the small pond. He still had a smile on his face.

They left with a stringer full of fish and a promise from each to come back and do it all over again. Russ was bursting inside. It had finally happened. He had prayed for his father to finally stop drinking and hang out with him- and here he was.

Jaimey was standing in the kitchen as Russ and Randy walked through the garage door. They were laughing and talking about their morning as Russ walked in carrying a long stringer of bream. The look on her face turned from anger to shock.

"Mom look!" Russ shouted. "Dad and I went fishing!"

The excitement in Russ's voice broke Jaimey's heart. She could only imagine it would be short lived. Russ took the fish outside and added them to a bucket and began running water over them.

"If you break that boy's heart, it will be the last time," she warned Randy.

"I'm so sorry for how I've acted Jaimey, I'm so sorry."

Jaimey left Randy standing in the kitchen by himself staring at the refrigerator, knowing what was inside.

CHAPTER TWELVE

Cappy stood on the number eight fairway, in the turn, on a tight, claustrophobic dogleg left. He was contemplating his second shot when Russ appeared to his right. He stood out because nobody walked the course at Beau Chene.

Cappy watched the boy tee up and drive the ball with a fading hook on a par three and put it right on the green six feet from the hole. He picked up his ball and drove over to talk to the boy. Russ saw Cappy approach out of the corner of his eye, threw his cigarette on the ground, and stepped on it to drown the smoke.

Cappy watched as his demeanor changed. The sly confident kid that had the golden stroke quickly became a shy little boy.

"How's it goin', son?" Cappy asked as he exited his cart and lumbered toward the boy to shake his hand.

"Fine," Russ said, never looking up from the ground.

"I've been watching you play out here," Cappy said. "You're really good."

"My grandmother's a member, I have permission," Russ said quickly, as if he were about to be kicked off the course.

"I knew your grandmother and your grandfather. Noel was my banker for years and a friend. We played tournaments together. He wasn't as good as you are, though." Cappy said as he watched a slight sheepish grin cross Russ's face. "I just wanted to tell you that you have a great swing. You really strike the ball well."

"Thank you," Russ said, still staring at the ground.

"What's your name?"

"Russ, Russ Crawford."

"How old are you, Russ?'

"Fifteen," Russ said proudly.

"Well, Russ, would you like to play a couple of holes together?" Cappy asked.

"Well, my mom will be here at exactly 10:00 to pick me up," Russ said, picking his eyes up from the ground toward Cappy.

"Well, why don't we play number nine and ten and then head back to the cart sheds, and I'll have you back to meet your mom before 10:00?"

That made Russ feel better, and he agreed. Cappy strapped the pull cart behind his cart, and they arrived on the ninth tee box. Cappy watched as Russ was first to tee off, and just like clockwork, he sailed one right down the middle.

"Man, fantastic shot," Cappy said, heaping praise on him.

A smile came over Russ's face, and Cappy got the feeling that he didn't hear compliments often.

"Thanks."

The two played through the last hole, and Russ birdied both.

"Russ, I want to show you something," Cappy said as he began heading toward the cart sheds.

"Well, my mom will be here at ten o'clock exactly, and I have to go to work," Russ said nervously.

"I know, but it's twenty till, and I promise you I'll have you there on time," Cappy said with a broad smile, showing all of his straight white teeth.

"You know your grandfather has a cart and cart shed out here, right?"

"No, sir, I really didn't know my grandfather that well. I did play with him a few times, but the cart was always at their house. We haven't always lived here, I grew up on the coast outside of Biloxi. We moved back here only a few weeks ago," Russ said.

Cappy pulled up beside number 25 and handed Russ the key.

"Open it," Cappy said, noticing Russ was a little hesitant as he looked toward the parking lot watching for his mother's car.

Russ opened the sheet metal door and walked inside. Cappy flipped the light switch on, and Russ's eyes lit up.

"This was Papa's?" he asked in disbelief.

Russ's eyes followed the old pictures and the caps and shoes lining the walls.

"Boy, he really kept everything neat and clean." Russ said. Cappy chuckled, thinking of how much work he had done cleaning the place.

Cappy handed Russ a key to the golf cart and Russ crawled in to look it over. He slid his hand across the seat and it was smooth and oily from having been cleaned.

"Can I really use this whenever I want?" Russ asked.

"Absolutely, it's yours. I'm sure Noel left it to you anyway. I thought you might be able to get around the greens a little faster and get some more play in before your mom picks you up from now on."

As soon as Cappy said that, Russ heard a horn; the excitement left Russ's face.

"I've got to go," Russ said, almost sprinting toward the door.

"Here, take the key," Cappy said as he quickly handed it to Russ.

"Thank you, Mr. Capstick; I'll see you in the morning," Russ said as he ran off toward the honking car.

The next morning was clear and the warm air was thick and humid. It was the time of year between spring and summer when mornings can't make up their minds to be cool or warm. Cappy stood on the chipping green under Ol' Red, staring up through the massive limbs draped in green leaves that were fresh and new. The chipping green is where he met "the boys," as he referred to them, every morning. Cappy wondering how Russ would fit in with this tight knit group of boys that had grown up together.

The boys, under Cappy's tutelage, have been coming to this course their entire lives. Their parents all knew each other. They all attended the same school- the same school that their parents went to. Golf is what they did when they were at Beau Chene. They only spent time at the pool when they needed to take a quick dip to cool off or irritate some group of girls that usually placed themselves strategically on the side of the number eighteen green.

They always traveled in a pack. When you saw one, you saw them all. They were promptly dropped off around 7:30 in the morning and picked up at 5:00 in the evening. All day they played and all-day Cappy coached them.

The boys were good. Each playing on the school's golf

team. Cappy was sure they would one day win a state title. A couple of the boys had scholarship potential.

One by one they began to appear, joining Cappy on the chipping green. Some not fully awake, they yawned and stretched. Fatboy arrived with a biscuit in his free hand and a chocolate milk between his legs. Curtis jumped out, excited to show everyone his new driver, and Cappy told him to tee it up and show him what he had. He did and sailed the ball over the highway, watching the white ball as it disappeared it the clouds.

"Everybody signed up for the Scramble?" Cappy asked. The boys hadn't missed this tournament in the last three years. It was the highlight of their summer. For some, it was the highlight of the year.

"Everybody got a partner?"

"I don't, Cap," Fatboy said while he unwrapped his second biscuit and took a bite.

"Don't worry; I've got someone in mind for you," Cappy said as he stood on the edge of the green leaning on a lob wedge. He kept looking toward the parking lot waiting for the station wagon.

"Hey, Cap, when are we gonna start playing?" Spanky asked in a bored whine.

"Let's go," Cappy said as he hopped into his cart and lead the boys to the number three tee box.

Cappy rarely played in these "practice" rounds, he just sat in his cart and watched the boys play. One by one they walked up to the tee, teed up their ball, and flew it down the fairway. Spanky was the last to tee off.

"All right, Spanky, let's see what ya got, son." Holding to the name Cappy gave him, he "spanked" the ball straight down the fairway.

He replaced the driver in his bag, high fived a couple of

the boys and in a single line, they headed toward their balls. Cappy pulled up the rear. As he left the tee box, he looked one last time toward the parking lot for the rusted station wagon... it wasn't there.

Under the watchful eye of William Capstick, the boys lived by certain rules while on the golf course. They couldn't cuss, they couldn't drink, they couldn't throw a tantrum when they hit a bad shot, and they had to follow the dress code for Beau Chene, collared shirts and golf shoes, no flip flops or regular sneakers.

Cappy wanted them dressed properly and he wanted them to be respectful on the course. He preached the same sermon about maintaining their composure every day.

You're going to hit bad shots and miss easy putts, he would say, *but allowing your emotions to get out of hand isn't going to help your next shot. History should be a word that you repeat after a bad shot because that's exactly what that shot is, history. It's over. Think about the next one. Don't shave off two points on one hole because you're mad about making a bogey two holes ago.*

The boys fanned out like the blue angels in an air show as their carts ambled down the fairway making their way to their balls.

While the boys continued playing, Cappy drove straight to the number 25 cart shed and opened the door; the cart shed was just as he last left it, nothing out of place.

He looked one last time toward the parking lot, still nothing.

CHAPTER THIRTEEN

Danny Crabs' investigation was hitting roadblocks. The only name he had was Platinum, Jaimey's working name. As far as he could tell, she had no pimp. She didn't run with any other girls. She worked for herself. It was hard getting information from call girls. Prostitution is not a career choice that necessarily breeds trust. In the last week, Danny had spent over four hundred dollars paying prostitutes for nothing more than information yet getting nowhere.

They spoke to him more easily since he was clean cut and clean shaven but information was still slow coming. Many of them were hesitant because they didn't trust strangers. Money seemed to help. Twenty or thirty dollars made them more willing to talk, even though the information was rarely helpful. Many of the girls took his number down and said they would spread the word but so far nothing.

Danny personally knew Queen who was a "Bottom Bitch" to a pimp known as "Johnny Dollar." In a corporate environment, she would be the Vice President of Sales and

Acquisitions. He knew she knew the players in the game. She would know the girls working just off of the beach, near the air base, which is where Danny thought Platinum's territory might have been.

Danny knew the rules of the street. Permission would have to be obtained from Queen's pimp. If not, speaking to her would likely result in both of them being beaten.

Johnny Dollar had an enterprise that rivaled and often exceeded many small businesses in the Biloxi area. Information, like girls, was sold on the street, and Johnny Dollar never missed an opportunity to make a buck. Danny knew where he headquartered. His legitimate business was a laundromat in the back of a fifteen-room motel built in the sixties. He rented the rooms to his girls and their tricks and used the room off of the laundry area as his office.

He was a Gorilla Pimp, often using force, he beat his girls to keep them in line. He ruled with an iron fist. The girls knew better than to go against him. Arriving at the laundromat, Danny found him after wading through a sea of girls who were working hard for a date.

Danny was shocked when he entered the small room. Johnny Dollar sat in an ornate gold chair positioned atop a platform, allowing him to be above all that came in his presence. Danny suddenly felt like a court jester performing for the king.

"Johnny Dollar?" Danny asked as he approached the pimp with his hand out.

"Who the hell is you?" Johnny Dollar said as he spoke from his perch.

He raised a cup to his mouth and took a quick sip from it. The cup was gold and encrusted with jewels. His initials set on the front and back. The hand holding the cup was covered with gold and platinum rings, some with diamonds in them. His hair was straight with a wave on the top. His shirt sleeves had long wavy cuffs that stuck out well beyond the cuff of his coat. His shoes were shined, his shirt was starched and his pants had a crease so fine you could cut butter with it. He looked like a million dollars... and he had a million dollars.

"Tell me what you want; we jus' like Baskin Robbins, we got 31 flavors, anything you want, white girls, colored girls, Chinese girls, skinny girls, hell, we even got big-legged girls."

"Just information today, sir," Danny Said.

"I'm looking for a hooker that stole from me, and I think your bottom bitch, Queen, may know the girl. I would like to have your permission to talk to her," Danny said reading Johnny Dollar's face.

"What she steal from you? This bitch work for me?" Johnny Dollar asked, his voice rising.

"No, I think this girl works alone. She stole my little girl from me."

"Damn, she stole your daughter?" Johnny Dollar asked, shocked.

"No, she wasn't my daughter, I just had her," Danny said, suddenly feeling as if he had given away too much information. There would be no mention of the missing money for fear that it would come into play for payment for information. He figured a low-life pimp wouldn't give a shit about him being a pedophile.

"What you mean you jus' had her?" Johnny Dollar asked cocking his head, waiting for an answer.

"Well, she was mine, I kidnapped her... a year ago to keep," Danny said, wishing he could take it back immediately. He could have told him anything, and here he was telling the truth, which was something he never did.

Johnny Dollar smiled and sucked his front gold tooth, "How old?"

"Six, seven," Danny said, feeling more at ease after seeing the smile come across Johnny Dollars face.

"You mean you've been tryin' a seven-year-old girl for a year?" Johnny Dollar asked, his eyes widening.

"Yeah," Danny said with a smirk on his face, imagining there was an unspoken fraternity among those in the sex trade.

Johnny Dollar leaned down to the right side of his chair and picked up an ornate cane topped with a round sapphire ball held in place by intricate metal lattice work.

"One hundred dollars," Johnny Dollar said as he played with his cane, moving it in a circular motion in his hand.

"All I have is a fifty," Danny said, lying.

Johnny Dollar held out his hand as Danny stepped forward to give him the payment. As he did, Johnny Dollar brought the cane down on Danny's head splitting open his forehead. He swung again splitting his right cheek open. He immediately jumped down from the chair and punched Danny in the face repeatedly until he was unconscious and no longer moving. Just for good measure, he planted the end of his cane squarely in Danny's crotch hoping he would never have the desire to molest again.

Johnny Dollar bent down and started going through Danny's pockets, pulled out two hundred-dollar bills, and immediately kicked him in the ribs four times, hearing a quiet gasp coming from Danny as he did.

"Nothing I hate more than a pedophile. Only thing that's worse is a lyin' pedophile," Johnny Dollar said, thinking of his eight-year-old daughter at home.

Johnny Dollar called Baby Girl and Pretty Lil' Dino into

the room. "Drag his sorry ass out the back, and put him in one of the box cars."

Another plus to the location of Johnny Dollar's business enterprise was that it backed up to the tracks. Trains moved through several times a day. It was a convenient place to dispose of people who disrespected him or his girls. He never killed anybody because that would bring too much heat. He just beat the shit out of them and placed them in a box car sending them who knows where before they woke up and realized they weren't in Biloxi any longer. It was very convenient, he had never heard from anyone that "rode the rails," as he called it.

CHAPTER FOURTEEN

It had been years since Cappy had been to Noel's house. The last time was the day he told his friend goodbye just before he died. He knocked on the front door that was in need of a fresh coat of paint. He got no response and walked to the back of the house. The station wagon he had seen at the golf course was parked just off of the drive on the grass. A lawnmower handle protruded from the back and the strong stench of gas filled his nose. A small number of boxes from the move were stacked in the garage with some of them having been torn open to retrieve this or that. There were clothes on the line that looked as if they had just been doused with the rain that moved through earlier in the day.

He knocked hard on the screen door, sending loose flakes of paint to the ground. He looked through the screen as he waited and noticed an old Rex Air vacuum cleaner in the entryway, sitting in front of the door, like a watchdog. No one came. He knocked again and rang the doorbell.

"Hello!" Cappy called, but no one answered.

He turned to leave when he noticed the woman he had seen at the golf course walking toward him.

"Hello, Ma'am,' Cappy said as he removed his hat.

It startled her, and she stopped dead in her tracks. She rarely received visitors at her house.

"Hello," she said. Her eyes glanced downward and darted into the house at the same time.

She was wearing a large pair of sunglasses and no makeup. She was a small woman. Her skin was wrinkled in places it shouldn't have been and looked leathery from too much sun. Her blonde hair had course, grey strands peppered through it and hung down just below her ears. She was wearing shorts and a t-shirt that were two sizes too big for her, no bra, and flip flops. She was carrying a liquor box from a shed in the backyard into the house that contained an assortment of cheap sour mash and Vodka.

"My name is William Capstick," Cappy said as his lips parted into his signature million-dollar grin. His huge hands extended to take the box from her, but she pulled back.

"I've got it. Thank you though," Jaimey said sheepishly.

"You're from the Country Club?" Jaimey said as she sat the box on the ground beside her.

"Yes Ma'am," Cappy said, shocked that he was looking at Noel Mitchell's daughter. He had known her as a beautiful little blonde-haired girl. Noel constantly talked about Jaimey through her high school years and especially about her years at Ole Miss. He often recounted stories about her sorority and was so proud of the grades she made. He had talked about her starting a career and getting married to a boy who came from a good family from the Delta. He had a great real estate business, and then, one day the stories about Jaimey stopped, and now Cappy understood why.

"Rusty told me about you and what you did for him. Dad would love knowing he was using his old cart; thank you." Jaimey said, embarrassed, hoping that William Capstick wouldn't really remember her growing up, but, deep down, she knew he did.

"Hey, you're welcome! He is a great kid and a fantastic golfer," Cappy said noticing that she kept looking around nervously.

"You know Dad really loved to play, and he was good too," Jaimey said trying to be polite and make conversation.

"Oh, I know; I played for years with Noel after I retired from the service and moved back home," Cappy said, trying to make a connection. "And he was the best banker a man could have too," Cappy said, watching her, trying to read her face through her sunglasses.

For a minute her body language seemed to ease and she appeared calmer, but soon became fidgety again when she realized she thought she heard a noise from inside the house.

"Well, what can I do for you?" she asked, lighting a cigarette with a trembling hand.

"Jaimey, we're having a tournament at the club, and one of the boys that I coach that doesn't have a partner, so I wanted to see if Russ could play; the entry fee has been taken care of; all he has to do is show up," Cappy said, hoping she would agree.

"Oh, I don't...... "

"You know, Russ is a great golfer, and has a lot of talent. I've watched him play," Cappy interrupted Jaimey before the word no could be heard.

"I don't think his dad would approve," Jaimey said still looking around nervously.

"Well, is he here; could I talk to him?" Cappy said peering toward the door.

No, he's gone. I don't think this is a good day to talk to him," Jaimey said, hoping Randy wouldn't wake up and embarrass her.

Cappy followed her eyes behind him and realized he was overstaying his welcome. She was anxious. He wasn't sure why. He complimented Russ again and thanked her for her time.

"Please think about it; we'd love to have him."

Jaimey waived as Cappy backed out of the driveway. He watched her as she picked up the box of liquor and disappeared into the house.

CHAPTER FIFTEEN

F atboy was laughing so hard that Coke spewed from his nose. He and the rest of the boys were laughing at Effie Mae Hunt and making fun of her considerable backside the usual stupid stuff fifteen-year-old boys find funny that most other people don't understand.

Effie was round from head to toe. Her skin was smooth and soft, buttery almost, the color of coffee with cream, and she smelled like Johnson's baby lotion. Her breasts were generous, well-supported, and pointed just as if she had stuffed two orange highway cones into her dress.

She had worked at The Nineteenth Hole for 23 years, long before any of these boys now laughing at her were even born. She treated them as if they were her own, caring for them as if she were their mother, which was the case for most of these boys. In the summers, she saw them more than their real mothers did, and if, the boys were ever honest about it, they loved Effie but would never admit it-especially if asked in front of the others.

She meandered through the lunch crew of mostly old

retired men. She knew them all. Her cooking was legendary, and most members ate there daily.

Lemon icebox pies covered the length of her arm. She slid them onto a table as she made her way toward two customers that had just walked in the door. She stopped and grabbed the two-dollar tip from the last table she had waited on and stuffed the bills into her bra.

She moved toward the new customers and handed them a menu then took their orders. Two specials and two pecan pies, and Effie disappeared into the kitchen.

She reappeared with plates spread along her arms singing a quiet version of "Jesus Saves," only stopping long enough to speak to the mayor. People came to The Nineteenth Hole for the food, but mainly they came to see Effie. They wanted to hear her sing and eat her homemade pies and drink cold beer.

She began singing a melodic "Amazing Grace" as she disappeared again into the kitchen with a stack of dirty dishes only to catch Fatboy with a pie and Junior stealing beer from the cooler.

They quickly replaced the items and ran by Effie dodging her towel as she slapped toward their backsides and made their way back to their table. As Fatboy and Junior finished the rest of their lunch, they heard Effie in the back talking to Ray Ray.

"Ray Ray, here, take this beer to number four green for Mr. Dickey." Effie shouted to her youngest son and delivery boy.

"All that nasty cigar smoke makin' cotton in his mouth," Effie muttered under her breath.

Ray Ray quickly headed toward number four in the "beer cart" and met Spanky and Curtis on number one tee box under the big oak tree. They exchanged the beer and Curtis tipped Ray Ray as usual.

"Just make sure to charge that to Dad and date it for last Saturday," Spanky said, signing the ticket in the best forged handwriting Curtis had ever seen.

"He nails it every time," Curtis said to the rest of the boys.

"Sure does, I seen his daddy sign before and he don't even write it that good," Ray Ray said in utter disbelief.

Just as Ray Ray was leaving, Fatboy pulled his cart beside the others and pulled out a six pack.

"Where the hell did you get that?"

"Effie left it on the bar and went in the crapper and I grabbed it; nobody saw me," Fatboy said, elated. He had finally done something that was cool in the eyes of his peers. High fives came from all directions as the boys rose out of their carts and sat back down like the wave in the stands of a football game.

"All right, everybody has two beers a piece with two left over that we'll all split," Curtis said, instructing the boys.

The green they were waiting on finally cleared, and the boys one by one struck their ball. Everyone except Fatboy was straight down the middle of the fairway. They finished the hole with two birdies, two pars, and a Fatboy bogie and were off to the next tee box.

Russ stood on the tee box as the boys arrived and offered to let them play through.

"Naw, that's O.K. There's one of you and five of us," Duckhead said as he walked around Russ's cart.

"Nice cart ya' got there," Duckhead said as he turned to the others for their snickering approval.

"What kind of clubs are you hittin'?" two of the boys asked in unison.

"Some old Pings, they were my granddaddy's." Russ said proud to have the newer clubs.

"So, you're playing with hand-me-down clubs?"

"Yeah, I guess so."

"What's your name?"

"Russ Crawford."

"Hey!" Fatboy said with a big smile and bits of peanut butter crackers blowing from of his mouth. "You're my partner in the scramble; yeah, Cappy told me about you! This guy's good!" Fatboy said as he turned to the other boys.

"Come on and join us; want a beer?" Junior asked.

"No, thanks."

"Ok, everybody, pour your beer into an empty Coke can so we don't get busted."

They did and hid the empty beer cans in their golf bags. One by one they struck their balls, flying them straight down the middle. Just as they arrived at the tee box, they left in the same manner. They fanned out on top of the hill, found their balls, selected their clubs and stood waiting for the green beyond them to clear. They waited, disgusted by the slow play in front of them. Each took a hit off their beers as Curtis began choking from taking too large a gulp.

"Y'all feelin' anything yet?" Spanky said as he sipped from his "Coke" can.

"Hell no... shit, we just starting drinking! Damn, give it time to take effect, shit!" Fatboy said as if he were now a seasoned drinker.

"Hell, Fatboy, it would take at least four or five beers for you to even feel anything, you fat bastard," Duckhead said as he stung Fatboy's newfound confidence like an angry wasp jolted from its nest.

The green before them finally cleared, and they all

parted out of Fatboy's way as he was further back and the first to hit his second shot. He bent over and removed a blade of grass from the top of his ball. He looked down the fairway and adjusted his stance, lined up his shot. Right in the beginning of his back swing, the still, muggy, afternoon air erupted into total chaos.

The boys turned to find the commotion behind them. Effie was barreling toward them in the beer cart. She wore a look on her face that the boys recognized. The wind moving her large lips all over her face blew into her mouth, extending her cheeks into round mounds on the side of her jaws. Her dyed red hair looked like hell's fire waving with each gust of wind. She had the cart at top speed, and her large breasts bounced up and down as she hit each terrace. Her elbows flared out of the side of the cart. Her dress and apron flying wildly in the wind. Cooler tops bounced up and down with pieces of ice and pearls of water spewing from them. Effie was out for blood. Men from all over the course stared in her direction. She had interrupted several putts, drives and chips, and the boys were terrified.

"Fatboy Walker, you keep your thieving ass right there! You ain't gon' steal from me, boy!"

Hearing this the boys all hopped into their carts, knowing that somehow Effie discovered the stolen beer, and the chase was on.

"Split up!" one of the boys shouted. But, it didn't matter, she was after Fatboy and his cart was the easiest to spot in the crowd since all of the springs on the driver's side were utterly exhausted and had given up long ago.

Fatboy's cart was the slowest, and as soon as Effie's cart hit level ground, it was a fair chase. Fatboy was scared; Effie was someone you didn't cross, and when he turned and looked at her, he was sick to his stomach from fear. She was mad as hell. The flames of Hades waving from her head made Fatboy wet himself.

His clubs clanked ferociously as they beat against each other, and he began to weave and pitch trying to throw her off his trail, but she kept up matching each of Fatboy's moves like a sheepdog herding cattle.

Russ stood on the tee box and watched this and laughed out loud for the first time in a while. He looked around, but the others were not to be seen.

Fatboy kept looking back at Effie with tears welling in his eyes. His beer was sloshing from its Coke can, so he grabbed it and began pouring it out.

"Pour it out, go on! I know you stole that beer, I don't need any evidence!" Effie shouted as she stayed on course with Fatboy still matching his every pitch and turn.

He saw a garbage can and decided to get rid of the evidence anyway. He veered the cart toward the can and hung himself halfway out of the cart, planning to throw the can inside and keep moving, but he misjudged and ran over the garbage can, throwing himself out of the cart. His clubs jolted from their resting place and balls spilled out all over the ground around him.

Effie was on top of him immediately. She grabbed him by the back of his collar, brought him to his feet, grabbed him by the back of his shirt, and led him to the beer cart. With one motion, Effie had Fatboy across her lap spanking him. Men near them, watched as Effie began whaling away with the leather strap that she used to sharpen knives.

"I know your momma taught you better! I'm hittin' you six times! One for each beer you stole!"

With every lick, Fatboy wailed as though he were being tortured in a prison camp.

"You're payin' for that beer, Fatboy; you're fixin to give

Ray Ray a break from washin' dishes is what you're fixin' to do," Effie said, still shouting, trying not to cuss as she had just passed and recognized the new pastor from the First Baptist Church.

The beer cart slowly inched its way back to The Nineteenth Hole. The weight from both of them was almost too much for the little cart. They were both out of breath and sweating. Fatboy's eyes were swollen from crying. He quietly whimpered all the way back. A trickle of blood flowed from his nose, and he thought he was bleeding to death, begging Effie to take him to the emergency room.

"Shut up, you ain't dying!" Effie said as she held the back of his collar and led him into the kitchen.

CHAPTER SIXTEEN

Randy Crawford finally rose from the couch at 10:45 A.M. His head was pounding from too much whiskey and all of the shouting. His neck was stiff from sleeping wrong on it, and he was nauseated. He lit a cigarette and sat on the side of the bed holding his head. He looked as if he were twenty years older than he actually was and this morning he felt it.

As the cobwebs in his head began to clear, he looked at the knuckles on the back of his right hand. They were bleeding. He had knocked off the scabs that had formed there from the last "argument" he had with this son and wife.

As he continued staring at his hands, they shook, and he swallowed hard, fighting back tears, trying to understand why he did it. The small, sober parts of his days always brought with them sorrow and remorse.

The same cycle played out most days. The ringing of his wife's voice telling him he was just unhappy with himself and his own failures, and that's why he did it. He knew it, but he couldn't stop. He had failed so many times and finally gave up. He had nothing left, nothing but the power that came from the hitting and the spewing of hateful words forced on the people that he should be loving. They were the only people that he had left in the world.

The bedroom door slowly creaked open; Randy and Russ locked eyes. As soon as he saw Randy awake, Russ retreated closing the door behind him.

"Russ," Randy called out. The door slowly opened again.

"Yes, sir?" Russ said sheepishly, almost in a whisper.

"Come here."

Russ opened the door completely, now standing fully in the doorway. His eyes cast down toward the ground, unable to look at Randy. The emotions would come and go for Russ. He knew he should never believe Randy when he says he wants to change and stop drinking because his father never did. It was nothing more than a cycle- a vicious cycle. Randy rose from the bed and walked the few steps toward him and cupped his hand on his cheek as Russ pulled away from him.

"I'm so sorry; I don't know what gets in me sometimes," Randy said as he moved in to hug Russ.

Russ grimaced and pulled completely away from him. He had not completely healed from the previous beating when the same play unfolded. He continued standing with his hands by his side numb, unfazed by the words, but wanting to believe them at the same time. Wondering if he could feel anything at all for his father again. Wondering if he could ever love him? Wondering if he really meant what he was saying right now? Sure that, later tonight, he would get drunk again and repeat it all over again. The fishing trip wasn't real. He wasn't serious about changing.

It was rare that Randy ever woke up to anyone in the house. They were usually out of the house early in the morning.

"Did you need something?" Randy asked attentively.

"Mom just wanted you to know she cooked breakfast if you're hungry," Russ said still unable to look Randy in the face.

"Sure; I'll be right there."

The last big blowup landed Randy in court; and if any of the blows had landed on Russ's face then, instead of his gut, he would have spent some time in jail. Russ spent the majority of his days worried and fearful of Randy, and the times he had gone to jail were the most peaceful times Russ had spent on this earth. The only other times of peace came when he was on the golf course. Golf had always been his sanctuary.

Randy lit another cigarette, his fingers, teeth and mustache all yellowed, stained from one Camel after another. He smelled of alcohol, cigarettes, and the absence of soap. He stood and put on a pair of wrinkled board shorts and a printed floral shirt. He walked into a pair of flip flops and put on his sunglasses before his eyes hit the sun. Duran Duran was singing "Hungry Like The Wolf" on MTV and he cut it off. He preferred The Doors, but these days they were even too depressing for Randy.

He walked into the den and over to the answering machine and listened to two messages- one from community counseling, rescheduling his missed appointment, and one from the employment office telling him he needed to come in to reapply.

He stopped to get a couple of Tylenol from the kitchen and noticed the plate with his breakfast on it. The back door was slightly cracked. He looked outside; the station wagon along with Russ's bike and lawnmower were all gone. He saw the truck with the driver's side door still opened from the night before. He closed the door behind him and plopped down in a chair at the breakfast table.

Randy was tall and skinny. What used to be a fit, muscular good looking, successful man had turned into a skinny, slight man with no muscle tone at all. The constant smell of stale beer seeped from his pores.

He drank because he had become unsuccessful and lost everything. He did great as long as his business was doing well, and he was making good money; but, as soon as he hit the slightest bump in the road, he folded. He just gave up and quit. There was nothing in him to know how to keep going, to not quit, to take his licks and go to the next thing, to keep trying. He built a multi-million-dollar business once; certainly he could do it again. But, he chose not to; instead he chose to create a life of poverty for his family, turn his wife out to prostitution, working only as her pimp. He lost everything, the beach house, the boat, the yacht club membership, the cars, but, most importantly, his self-respect. That went away quickly; it all just happened so quickly. He gave up so fast and, for too long, made nothing but bad decisions.

Randy sat on a lawn chair just outside the backdoor in case the phone rang and burned off one last cigarette. As he took his last drag, he flicked the butt into the yard and watched it burn out. He went back inside, retrieved the keys, and stumbled to his truck. He was about as sober as he would be all day, but that was about to change.

In his sober hours, he felt the conflict of knowing what he should do and not being able to do it consistently. That set off waves of anxiety and the only thing that relieved the overwhelming fear was to drink.

Randy returned from the store and took his place again by the door outside. He tried to make himself smoke slower so he could make the cigarettes last as long as possible; he had only scraped enough money together to buy one pack.

Most days presented a major decision for Randy-should he buy beer or cigarettes with what money he had that day? Cigarettes usually won out in the mornings because the nicotine helped with the nausea; but, then, later in the day, he needed the beer to keep his hands still.

When he and Jaimey were first married and living in Lewiston, they socialized with a couple that lived two houses away. He remembered they always had a refrigerator full of beer. He slowly stood from his lawn chair and slipped through the backyard that connected their two houses. As he approached the house, he heard kids splashing in the pool. He turned and walked back home.

Randy's hands started trembling again, a clear indication, if not an excuse that he needed a drink. He immediately went to the refrigerator and looked for a beer, but there was none. The phone rang again, but he ignored it even though he had waited most of the day for the call. He went to the truck, and, after searching under the seat, he found one, a hot beer that had been rolling around for a few days occasionally hitting him on the heel of his foot. He drank it and rifled through the ashtray and the seat looking for loose change, but there wasn't anything left from his search two days earlier. He went back into the house and searched through every conceivable place that one could find money; and, after several minutes, he had managed to find a grand total of sixty-five cents. He went into Russ's room and looked through his drawers, nothing. He looked under his bed, nothing. Finally, in the top of his closet, he found an old shoebox. Inside was a picture of Russ's grandfather, some baseball cards from Chipper Jones' rookie year and some old coins that had been left to Russ. Under all of the coins, Randy spotted green paper, two brand new two-dollar bills, and he slid them from their place in the box. He had enough for a six pack.

CHAPTER SEVENTEEN

Danny Crabs lay flat in the box car, pine tree bark prickling his back. His sense of smell was the first to awaken. The scent of pine filled his nose and slowly woke him from his semi-comatose state. He gasped for air; as pain shot across his ribs, he tried rolling over onto his side. He heard what sounded like the low hum of large equipment close by. He brought his hand up to feel his nose, and he could tell it was swollen and broken sitting slightly off to the side of his face. Dried blood flaked off of his cheek as he checked there for swelling. He couldn't see out of one eye.

He tried to roll over to help himself up and immediately collapsed from the sharp pain around his torso. He had no strength to move and couldn't catch his breath. He felt around his mouth; as much as he could tell, the teeth that he still had were there, although a couple felt loose. He looked at his hands through his one good eye; they were clear. No scrapes, no blood, no cuts. He hadn't participated in a fight, he just had his ass whipped.

He lay there fighting the pain, thinking, looking around,

trying to remember how he had gotten in this shape, and then realized he was in a rail car. It started to move, but only momentarily. He pulled himself to the door and found the source of the strong scent of pine. He was in a lumberyard. As far as he was able to see, pine trees were stacked toward heaven, ready to be sawed into lumber.

His pain wouldn't ease. He forced himself to sit upright on the edge of the box car, but the compression on his rib cage was too much to bear. He lay back down. He lay there and tried to clear his mind and remember how he had gotten here.

"Johnny Dollar, that son of a bitch!" Danny Crabs said as he grimaced from a hard cough.

"Genius," Danny Crabs mumbled out loud as he lay still thinking about how smart the pimp was. He didn't know how long he had been knocked out and didn't know how far he was from home but he did know he admired Johnny Dollar even though the pimp had beaten the shit out of him.

"He put me on a damn train," he mumbled.

As his brain started clearing, he realized he must still be fairly close to home. He was at a lumberyard. Lumberyards were a dime a dozen all over south Mississippi. If true, he just needed to figure out how he would get back to Biloxi.

Danny forced himself to sit up again. He was slowly able to get to his hands and knees. From there he stood, holding on to the side on the box car. There was no way that he could move that didn't hurt. He made his way to the door and started looking out, realizing that standing didn't put as much pressure on his ribs; breathing was much easier. Looking out of the door, Danny saw fresh-milled pine lumber being loaded three cars down. L&N was painted on one of the doors.

Two men appeared to the left of the box car wearing overalls holding walkie talkies. They stared at him in shocked horror. He was cut and swollen, bruised and bloody.

"Fella, you're not supposed to be in there," the older man said motioning for him to get down.

"What in hell happened to you?" said the younger of the two.

"Where am I?" Danny Crabs asked, ignoring their attempts to get him down from the box car.

"Ocean Springs," said the older man as he stared at Danny, still in disbelief.

The two men had seen their share of young people who called themselves train hoppers and the old bums who rode trains from place to place, but it was rare to see a man that had the hell beaten out of him and smelled like urine and feces and didn't know where he was or what day it was.

Danny was relieved that he was close to home. Ocean Springs was where he had kidnapped Madison. His mind raced back to the day that he took Madison. He remembered how easy it had been. How quickly it all happened. He was so close to her now. That memory ended as Platinum's face surged back in his memory.

"Where is the next stop?" Danny said in a pained broken voice.

"Biloxi," said the older man. "It came from Biloxi last night and will stop back by there on the way to Louisiana. Where you from; where did this happen to you?"

"I'm from Biloxi. I was jumped the other night and thrown onto this train, I guess. I have no other way to get back home. How about just letting me stay on this box car until I get back to Biloxi, and I'll get off there?" Danny asked, hoping the men would feel some sympathy for him.

Considering that they would have to help this man that smelled of urine and feces, they easily agreed.

Danny watched as they loaded the last of the lumber in the box cars. He found a piece of rope dangling from the ceiling and held onto it tightly, bracing himself for the pain he would surely feel when the train started moving.

CHAPTER EIGHTEEN

Cappy stood on the edge of the number nine green and watched as each one of the boys teed off, critiquing their stance, swing, and rotation.

"All right, Fatboy, if you're not too sore from being captured and slapped around by Effie, get over here and tee up," Cappy said sarcastically.

Fatboy and Russ were shooting in the mid 70's scrambling. They were all approaching the last hole and were glad; it was a grueling hot day.

"You boys want to go to The Nineteenth Hole when we finish and get a burger and something cold to drink?" Cappy asked, watching for Fatboy's reaction.

"Y'all go ahead; I need to get home anyway," Fatboy said, sadly thinking about missing one of Effie's cheeseburgers.

"Come on, Fatboy, you're gonna have to face her sometime; let's just go ahead and get it over with, son," Cappy said.

The carts arrived at The Nineteenth hole in a cloud of dust.

"Everybody grab your beer, cause here come the beer thief," Effie said as she bounded toward Fatboy grabbing him and pulling his head into her chest. "You know I love you, baby."

Right at that moment, Fatboy wanted to tell on Spanky and explain how he had ordered the beer, signed his dad's signature, and had done it a hundred times before; that was kind of like stealing, but he saw Ray Ray and thought better of it. Effie would kill Ray Ray. He would have to go to a funeral. Plus, that was the only way they had to get beer right now because he wasn't up to stealing more anytime soon.

"What y'all want, Cappy?"

"Effie, I think we will all have one of those wonderful cheeseburgers of yours with some fries and Cokes," Cappy answered.

"I want two cheesb......,"

"Naw! You ain't getting but one. You don't need two. You're big enough as it is; you keep on an' one day you gone look like me," Effie said laughing at the expression on Fatboy's face.

The boys finished eating, and Cappy laid two twenties and a five down on the table.

Effie followed the boys to the front door as they were leaving and grabbed Fatboy.

"Come here, baby," Effie said as she took his head and again buried it in the large crater between her massive breasts. Fatboy's cheeks were squeezed together, his lips poking out, and he winced as he felt his teeth biting into the sides of mouth.

"Fatboy, you know I love you. Don't you ever steal from me again, you hear?"

"Yessum," Fatboy said as Effie wiped a streak of flour from his forehead.

CHAPTER NINETEEN

The boys met again the following morning. By 9:00 A.M., they were clustered together on the putting green, semi-comatose waiting for Cappy's instruction. Fatboy was finishing the last of the two biscuits his mother cooked him for breakfast. Duckhead was curled up on the seat on his golf cart making sure he finished his eight hours of sleep. When Curtis finally showed up, the group was complete except for Russ. Cappy watched the boys arrive in their usual BMWs or Cadillacs, but the rusted station wagon had yet to show.

"You boys go ahead and start playing; I'm going to pick up Russ," Cappy said, hearing a series of groggy "Yes, sir's" from the boys.

He made his way to Russ's neighborhood and noticed the truck pulled up in the yard with the front bumper inches away from a pecan tree, no sign of a bike or lawn-mower. He continued through the neighborhood until he noticed Russ on his bike way ahead of him, the lawnmower was strapped to the back of his banana seat. A gas can attached to his handle bars slowly swayed back and forth and periodically threw off his balance. His long lanky, tanned legs were struggling as he pumped up and down ascending the small hill trying to reach the crest.

Cappy pulled up beside him; his face was flush and wet with sweat. The temperature was already hitting the mid-eighties by 9:30 A.M.

"Hey, you need a ride?" Cappy said leaning toward the passenger window.

"That's okay, it's not much farther," Russ said out of breath.

"Come on, get in," Cappy said as he let down the tailgate on his Bronco.

"Where you going?" Cappy asked as he loaded the lawnmower, bike, and gas can in the back.

"To Spring Street, Mrs. Frank's house."

"You mean Mrs. Bill Franks?" Cappy asked considering how large her yard was.

"Yes sir."

"How many yards do you cut, Russ?"

"Six, including ours," Russ said quietly.

"Six, so when do you get them all done?" Cappy asked, wondering how he had time to play golf.

"Mainly in the afternoons, some in the early morning."

"Well, it's good to earn some extra spending money."

"Well, most of what I earn goes to my mom for groceries; my dad's out of a job right now."

Cappy looked over at Russ. He looked tired. His head rested on the door frame, and his eyes were closed as he spoke.

"Well, you need any help?"

"No, sir, but thanks anyway."

Cappy arrived in front of Mrs. Frank's house, and, just as he let the tailgate down, he heard the unmistakable sound of a muffler dragging the ground. He looked up just in time to see sparks flying under Noel Mitchell's truck as it turned onto Spring Street.

Cappy looked over at Russ and saw a wet spot growing on the front of his shorts.

"You better go, Cappy; I'm sure he's already drunk."

"I'm not going anywhere. Will he try to hurt you?"

"I don't know," Russ said with exhausted anxiety. He was anxious and too tired to care anymore. The bridge connecting his ability to rationalize and hide his darkest secret was slowly collapsing, disintegrating and falling away.

The truck came to a stop behind Cappy's Bronco, and Randy stumbled out of the door.

"Who the hell are you?"

"William Capstick, just gave your son a ride, hot day already," Cappie said as he stuck his hand out to shake Randy's.

"You can go now; I need to talk to my son in private," Randy said, his words slurred.

Cappy looked at Russ; the wet spot growing larger now, and his face looked defiant as Cappy noticed Russ setting his jaw. Cappy didn't want to go.

"Russ sure has done a good job cutting Mother's grass this summer. Russ, I'll be in the garage if you need some water," Cappy said as he winked at Russ.

Cappy stopped in the middle of the long driveway. He watched the two in his rearview mirror. He got out and leaned on the passenger door and watched.

Russ hung his head, staring at the ground. Randy's arms flailing all over the place. His long, skinny finger pointing in Russ's face. A slight push to his shoulder. His face contorted in anger as he spoke. The volume of his voice rising and falling. His eyes moving around from house to house as neighbors were looking for the source of the commotion. He was grabbing at Russ's pockets, shaking his shorts. It appeared he was looking for money.

As Russ continued to stare at the ground, Randy caught his chin in his hand and jerked Russ's head up. His face now inches from Randy's and Russ stared directly into Randy's eyes. Like a switch had turned on inside Russ a slow rage was growing in him. He stood rigid against Randy, tensing his body, readying himself for the blows. His fist curled into a tight ball.

Cappy moved out from his truck and started toward them. Randy was holding Russ' chin firmly with his right hand while he was slightly slapping him with Russ's fists still held tightly at his side. He hoped for his own good that Russ would hit him. Get the frustration out. Cappy picked up his pace and started running toward Russ.

The commotion attracted more neighbors and a small crowd formed. Randy was so involved in what he was doing, he never noticed the crowd forming around him.

One little slap after another, over and over again. Quiet tears streaming down Russ's face, standing there, taking it, like he always did, unsure of what he should do.

As Cappy continued moving toward them, he could hear the drunken vile that spewed from Randy Crawford's mouth. The slaps got harder and harder. His hand came back for the hardest one yet, but the motion was stopped.

"If you want to hit somebody, hit this big man behind you," Cappy said as he braced himself.

Randy turned and swung all at the same time, losing his footing and fell. As quickly as he could, he got back to his feet, squared off in front of Cappy with an around the world swing, missing his target.

Cappy waited for the next swing, and just as a snake would strike its prey, Cappy jabbed Randy square in the mouth. It stung him hard. Blood began trickling from Randy's nose.

After another wayward blow from Randy, Cappy targeted his midsection. After three hard and fast punches, Randy doubled over and began vomiting. Each punch felt good to Cappy. He had wanted to punch him the first day he met him.

"If I ever hear of you laying one more hand on this boy's head, you'll be getting more of what you just got, you sorry son-of-a-bitch."

Turning to one of the neighbors, Cappy asked through tight breaths to call the police and report what had happened.

"Ask for Jimmy, tell him his brother is involved," Cappy said referring to his younger brother. James "Jimmy" Capstick was the local police chief and had recently been reappointed for his third term as chief.

Neighbors that were lining the street were now slowly going back inside their homes. A group of younger boys who knew Cappy from the golf course stood legs spread balancing their bikes.

"Wow, Cappy, you kicked his as..., butt," they said, careful not to cuss.

Randy was still hunched over, dry heaving, and Russ looked on his father with disgust, hate, and embarrassment. All of this humiliation in front of so many, and those boys from Beau Chene saw it too. But, of course, it was like this everywhere they had ever lived.

"I guess everything you said when we went fishing was just a lie. I guess you really don't want a relationship with me or mom!" Russ shouted.

Jimmy arrived within a few minutes and steered through the small sea of onlookers to find Cappy standing with a young boy. His eyes turned and saw a man lying on the ground in a pool of his own vomit, not making any effort to move or get up.

"Hey, brother," Jimmy said nonchalantly.

"Chief!" Cappy said as he shook Jimmy's hand.

"Can you put him in for a while?" Cappy asked quietly as he saddled up beside him.

"I can make it last longer if you want to file charges. Right now, I can get him for public drunk, disturbing the peace and driving while intoxicated. That will keep him in for a little while," Jimmy said.

"What about child abuse?" Cappy asked hoping to pile on more charges.

"You'll have to get the boy involved for that to stick, he'll have to testify in court," Jimmy said, figuring the boy had already been through enough. He steered Cappy away from that for now.

Jimmy walked over to Russ and shook his hand.

"You must be the superstar golfer my brother has told me about," Jimmy said as he tussled Russ's hair.

"I'm Russ; I don't know about the superstar part," Russ said as he dried his face.

Jimmy patted him on the back and walked over to the trunk of the patrol car to look for a towel. He stood Randy to his feet and walked him over to his car, handcuffed him, wiped his face off and read him his rights.

Russ watched as his father was handcuffed and placed in the back of another patrol car.

CHAPTER TWENTY

Although he had never seen it from this side, Danny Crabs began to recognize the outskirts of Biloxi, as the train slowly made its way back toward the city. He knew the city limits began as soon as they passed the sound between there and Ocean Springs. He didn't know what the back of Johnny Dollar's motel looked like. In his condition, he didn't need to be walking down the streets of Biloxi, Mississippi, even if he was in the bad part of town.

The pain remained unbearable. It was becoming harder to breathe and almost impossible to move. He worried that his ribs were broken, and he couldn't imagine how he would get down off of the box car.

The train slowed and sped up as it approached curves and crossings. So far, all Danny Crabs had seen was over-grown fields and dilapidated shrimp boats. Trailer parks dotted the landscape along the tracks, occupying the least desirable parts of town.

After several minutes, he began to notice faded signs on the backs of buildings. He made out a portion of the words "five and dime." Paint on buildings slowly fading after years of neglect and salt water and baking in the sun. A red dragon appeared, seeming to be propped up, leaning against a wall, a bygone remnant of an old Chinese restaurant.

He knew he was getting close after seeing Shoney's Big Boy floating in the air. He remembered it wasn't far from the motel.

The train's rhythmical clanking began to slow as the train prepared to stop. After several screeching minutes it did, and Danny stood there knowing this might be his last chance to get off, but the pain was too severe. He imagined jumping would make him pass out.

As soon as the train stopped, it slowly started backing up and Danny panicked. He blindly jumped and landed on a pile of discarded railroad ties, knocking the air from his lungs again. He writhed in pain on the ground unable to find his breath.

Fire ants quickly moved on him, forcing him to sit up and try to get to his feet. Unsteady, he was able to get on his knees. He slapped at the ants and immediately felt his ankles, waist and face begin to welt and swell. Unable to breathe, fighting through the pain, he finally stood and looked around, knowing he needed to travel west. He began walking, following the tracks. Still slapping at ants, he soon noticed what had to be the backside of Johnny Dollar's motel and laundromat.

He watched, planning his next move, when two girls appeared at the back of the building. They lit a joint and Danny closed his eyes and inhaled as if he were smelling a fragrant rose in a garden. Soon, the ladies were met by two men slipping around the corner of the building and they passed the joint, and then the ladies began to work.

"Making some money off the books," Danny whispered to himself.

The twenty or so yards between them made him want to take a hit so badly, and then he remembered he had a joint in his shirt pocket and reached for it, but Johnny Dollar had taken that too.

He moved to a nearby light post and stood with his back against it. This seemed to ease the pain and help with his breathing. He stood there watching the sun eventually dip behind the cityscape. The round orb melting, turning the horizon into a dark orange glow.

Under the cover of dusk, he made his way toward the parking area. He spotted his truck under the only light in the entire lot. He was parked directly under it, and he could see that someone had taken a bat to it. His windshield was shattered, and dents covered the driver's side from front to back.

"Hopefully, the keys will still be where I left them," Danny mumbled in a pained whisper.

He meandered quietly through the other cars in the lot and finally reached his truck. He heard a woman's voice behind him ask if he wanted a date. He ignored her and went directly to the gas tank, opened it, and relief spilled over his entire body.

When he opened his door, he didn't recognize his truck. The seats had been slashed and his radio had been stolen. He didn't care; he just needed it to crank, and it did. He pulled out of the lot and drove toward 143 1/2 Waterway Road.

CHAPTER TWENTY-ONE

C appy arrived at the Beau Chene cart houses at his usual time of 6:00 A.M. It was Saturday, his favorite day of the week. He had already eaten breakfast at The Dixie Café, his usual Saturday morning breakfast haunt. Crispy bacon, two eggs sunny side up on wheat toast, real hash browns, grits and an extra coffee to go. He had done this every Saturday for the last ten years. The same table. The same conversation. The same men, telling the same stories.

The morning was clear as he neared the golf course. The sun's rays exploding over the tops of the trees in a broken sunburst. He heard the rumble of a far-off mower. The smell of freshly cut grass replaced the bacon that remained in his nose from breakfast. He inhaled deeply.

Cappy watched as the sun continued to rise, trying to punch its way above the pine trees that lined the fairway by the number three tee box. He knew this day would be a scorcher. As he approached his cart shed, he heard the familiar slow groan of metal rubbing against metal from a slight breeze, and noticed the door was slightly ajar on number twenty-five.

He was excited that Russ had already made it out so early. He made his way toward the shed to close the door and latch it. As he peered through the door, he noticed a form in a red shirt curled up in a tight ball on the cart seat.

"Russ?" Cappy asked in confused disbelief.

Cappy opened the door fully and saw Russ curled in a tight, bean shaped form. On the floor beside him Jaimey lay on a makeshift bed made from beach towels. They both woke to a large silhouette framed by light filling the door.

Jaimey scrambled to her feet and stood by her "bed" as if she were a little girl in trouble for some terrible infraction. Cappy's eyes fixed on her. She was holding her dress together between her chest and shoulder. The hand that held it was red from blood and blue from bruises. The skin had been scraped off of her knuckles. The forearm that now blocked the light from her eyes had blocked blows from the previous night. Her matted, blonde hair looked as though it had not been combed in days. Bloody scabs formed in the spots where hair had previously been. Faint lipstick was smeared across her chin, and her right eye was cut and swollen. She wore no shoes, and her feet were dirty. The stench of beer and cigarettes and rape permeated the thick, hot air around her.

Cappy moved his large frame in the door to block the light, allowing their eyes rest. Russ began gathering their things as if he had intruded into someone's home.

He was in no better shape. He stood in front of Cappy with only a pair of shorts on. He had a black eye and his chest was red and purple the remnants of old and new bruises. When he turned to grab his shoes, Cappy audibly gasped. The belt that Randy had used as a weapon had landed mainly on Russ's back as he had attempted to shield his mother from yet another beating. Randy landed several blows that included the buckle and its outline was clearly visible. Welts and open sores covered Russ's back. He was unable to wear a shirt because the pain was too severe.

Cappy's eyes reddened, filling with tears. He felt responsible. After Randy had been released from jail, things had improved, according to Russ. Randy had apologized to them both over and over. He even showed interest in Russ's golf game, but the regret hadn't lasted.

Cappy thought his threats had done the trick, but they hadn't. His first opinion of Randy was that he was just an asshole, but monsters are far worse than assholes.

Russ turned back toward Cappy. His face told the story of fear and exhaustion, looking as though he had lived more years than he had. He looked as if he were tired of life, period. It looked as if all of the love and hope and motivation had left his body. It looked as if his soul was depleted.

"You two wait here; I'll be right back with my truck," Cappy said as he gently pulled them close and hugged them, careful where he touched. Cappy made his way toward the Bronco, his heart heavy and sick.

He returned and found Russ and Jaimey standing in the same spot waiting to be told what to do next, like soldiers in a training exercise. They were numb and said nothing. The drive toward Cappy's house was quiet. He took the side streets and backroads so they wouldn't feel anxious about being seen.

As he headed north out of town, Jaimey asked Cappy to pull over, and she quickly opened the door and vomited. She was unsteady on her feet, and Cappy rushed over to help her back into the Bronco. She laid back in the seat, her face blank, void of emotion. She looked as if her spirit had left her as well.

Cappy continued north, and soon the hum of the tires on pavement gave way to the crunch of gravel. After a mile on the gravel road, he turned at an old church. Jaimey stared blankly out of the window as they made their way toward Cappy's house. His neighbors' yards were manicured, and the houses were spread out far apart from each other. There were people on front porches, sitting calmly with flyswatters in their hands and passing time with conversation. The smoke from weekend grills swirled in the air. The aroma of steaks and chickens and hamburgers wafted through the valley.

Children moved away from the road as Cappy's truck approached. They all waved. Cappy waved back. Rows of corn outlined by a sea of other vegetables dotted empty spaces between houses.

Cappy turned off of the main road onto a long, narrow, pinched trail. After a quarter mile, the road opened up into a beautiful pecan grove surrounding a large rustic cabin. He pulled around to the back under a spacious airy carport.

They made their way inside through a large mud room. Each wall covered with a variety of fishing rods, golf clubs, and framed photos of Cappy with various friends spanning a lifetime.

The trio made their way through the kitchen and into the den, and Cappy walked Jaimey to a large plush recliner and eased her down into it. She winced as she settled into the chair. A huge bull moose stared at her from its spot over the fireplace.

Cappy left to fetch pain relievers and water. Russ sat beside Jaimey, holding her hand. They looked blankly ahead. The large house felt like a fortress. Its location alone gave them both a sense of safety and security.

Cappy returned with pain pills and glasses of water. They downed both not realizing how thirsty they were. Cappy guided Jaimey to her room, helping her along the way.

"This will be your room for as long as you need it, Jaimey," Cappy said, showing her where the towels were located in the bathroom. He pulled a large terry-cloth robe from the closet and hung it on the back of the door for her.

"You can wear this when you finish with your soak, and we'll get some clothes for you as soon as we can. I filled the tub for you." Cappy said as he stacked the towels and bath cloths on the vanity for her.

"Mr. Capstick, thank you so much for this; I don't know how we'll ever repay you," Jaimey said as she began crying.

"The only thing you have to do for me is call me Cappy."

He left her there and arrived back in the den to find Russ asleep. He hated to wake him, but knew he needed a bath and some clean clothes.

"Come on, Sport," Cappy said, reaching gently under his arm to steady him. He showed him upstairs to his room. He started the bath for him and gave him the smallest t-shirt and shorts he could find. He left Russ to bathe and soak.

CHAPTER TWENTY-TWO

Danny Crabs sat in the middle of the filth that was his tiny travel trailer. He watched television as he continued healing from his run in with Johnny Dollar. With every day that passed, he felt himself getting stronger, the pains subsiding. It became easier to breathe and his face was close to looking normal again.

He flipped through the channels as he waited for his monthly government check to be delivered. Down to his last twenty bucks, he watched for the mailman. Since Platinum had stolen his money, he was back to sitting by the door, waiting for the mail to arrive.

As he stared toward his mailbox, he heard the news reporter murmur the words *kidnapped, girl, back home*. He turned his focus to the screen. A short video of Madison and her parents filled his television. The video was shot in the kitchen in her home. It was large and well decorated.

Danny's pulse quickened as he looked into Madison's face. He never noticed the sad look she wore. He never noticed she never smiled like most other girls her age did. He only saw something to use, something to exploit and eventually throw away. Her sadness never entered his mind.

Madison's mother recounted the day that a mysterious woman dropped her off at their house. They never saw her, but knew from Madison that she wasn't the one who took her.

"She's an angel," Madison's mother said through tears of appreciation. "We are just so thankful for her and the gift that she has given our family."

Danny listened intently to the interview. Madison said nothing. She shyly hid behind her mother. Even though she was home and protected, fear permeated every minute of each day. When they were together, almost daily, Danny threatened to kill her and her whole family if she ever told anyone about him.

His fickle mind then shifted gears. He no longer thought about money, he was enthralled with Madison again. She was just a few miles down the road. The memory of taking her and how easy it was constantly filled his mind. It wouldn't be that easy again. He couldn't do anything, though, until he got his money back and kill the bitch who took it. He stood and looked into a small, cracked mirror that hung crooked on the wall. He rubbed his hand lightly over his face and dabbed medicated cream on cuts and gashes.

The news story shifted to the search that had been ongoing for the last year. The detective talked about how relieved he was that Madison was back with her family. He referenced "new information" they had on the abductor and a description.

The police artist's sketch of Danny filled his screen. It was a good sketch of what he used to look like. With his haircut and beard shaved, he looked nothing like that now.

He was confident enough, that he felt he could walk into the police station, and even they wouldn't know who he was.

He figured that eventually Madison would be able to tell them where he lived, if she hadn't already. The risk was too great. He had to leave. He had to hook up his home and move on. Another location along with his new disguise, no way he would be caught.

A knock on the door startled him. Plans of moving and moving quick drew his attention away from his mailbox. He turned quickly to see a mailman standing at his door with a shocked look on his face. Danny's face was still bandaged and bruised.

"Sorry to scare you, is this 143 1/2 Waterway Road?" the young mailman asked as he pushed a handful of envelopes toward Danny.

"It is, thank you," Danny said as he opened the door and retrieved the mail.

"Bad fall," was all Danny said.

"The door is off of your mailbox... take care," the mailman said, before he quickly made his way down the skinny path past the barking pit bull that apparently didn't hear or see him when he first arrived.

He gave a wide berth as he ran by the dog. Danny stood at his door watching his dog snarl and growl at the man. Pulling hard against the chain. Hungry for blood and hungry to run. Hungry period. Danny had not fed the dog in days and that reminded him he needed to pick up some dog food.

CHAPTER TWENTY-THREE

Russ and Jaimey sat at a large round table staring at a Lazy Susan slow in its rotation. They had both been awakened by the smell of bacon cooking and the clanking of silverware and plates. They eased into their chairs to find orange juice and coffee waiting on them. On the Lazy Susan sat a mound of fruit of various kinds along with small boxes of cereal, in case they didn't like what Cappy was cooking.

"Everything smells so good, Cappy. Thank you again for everything," Jaimey said as she took a sip of her coffee.

"Can't beat the smell of bacon," Cappy said through his ever-constant grin.

Cappy brought huge plates of bacon, eggs, toast and hash browns and placed them on the Lazy Susan.

Russ quickly, but respectfully started filling his plate and immediately started eating. He was starving, unable to swallow well after Randy's fist missed his cheek and landed on his throat.

"It's been so long since we've had a cooked breakfast like this," Jaimey said as she took another piece of bacon.

"My favorite meal of the day," Cappy said as he twirled the Lazy Susan for more hash browns.

Cappy wiped the corners of his mouth as he finished eating and relaxed, sipping fresh french pressed coffee.

He made small talk. Picking subjects that were light and fun and had nothing to do with Randy or their current situation. He told them stories of hunting in Alaska. Shooting bear and Moose and Ptarmigan, birds the same color as the snow. His exploits hunting the small bird were almost as interesting as shooting the large bull moose that hung on the wall above them. He watched Jaimey's eyes grow wide as he told the story of meeting Hemingway in a bar in Idaho on a pheasant hunting trip. Russ asked who Hemingway was.

"I think the two of you need to be looked at by a doctor. I hope you don't mind, but I've asked my personal physician and good friend to make a house call. He'll be very discreet," Cappy said.

Before either of them could accept or deny the offer, the backdoor opened. Dr. Jim Spencer walked into the kitchen. He was a specimen of health. He stood 6'6" and was muscular and fit for his thirty-seven years. His body was formed early on at Ole Miss as the one of the best wide receivers that had ever walked on the field.

Since college, he had run marathons and more recently participated in Ironman competitions to stay fit.

Cappy introduced Russ first and then Jaimey and noticed Jaimey kept her eyes cast down, staring at the ground. The blood returning to her cheeks. A look of embarrassment washed over her face.

"Nice to meet you," she mumbled.

Dr. Spencer turned to Russ who was now staring at him as if he were a god.

"Cappy tells me you're a good golfer," the doctor said breaking the ice.

"I really like to play," Russ said through an embarrassed grin.

"What's your personal best, Russ?" Jim asked as he placed his stethoscope around his neck.

"I shot a 68 at Weeping Oaks back home," Russ said proudly.

"I know that course; it's not an easy one," Jim said as he looked at Cappy. His eyebrows raised in impressed shock.

"Russ, why don't you come with me so I can examine you," Dr. Spencer said as he grabbed a piece of bacon.

Russ stood slowly, fighting the pain, and walked with Dr. Spencer.

As they disappeared into the back of the house, Cappy watched as the embarrassment and anxiety remained on Jaimey's face. Cappy had no way of knowing how she was feeling. Dr. Spencer obviously stirred a definite reaction from her. She hoped Jim Spencer didn't remember her.

Jaimey was aware how she looked. She wondered if she had really changed that much. Her memories returned to Spencer's days playing football at Ole Miss. How could he not remember the homecoming queen? She had met him so many times at his fraternity house at swaps and after parties. She wanted to talk to him about the upcoming football season and ask if he ever ran into any of their old friends. She was suddenly reminded of her good friend Poppy Turner, who was a Sigma Chi fraternity brother of Jim's.

Here she sat penniless. Her young, perky, beautiful, homecoming queen face had turned into the face of a hard life lived as a prostitute. A face now wrinkled with the added years from constant worry and now bruised with the worst decision of her life.

Her self-confidence had left her a long time ago. She allowed herself to be led by Randy, her body to be sold by Randy. She never asked questions; she just did everything he ever told her too. Unable to reason, unable to have discernment. He had beat it all out of her.

The same thoughts and rationalizations plagued her. Constantly she thought of her parents, her mother moreso, and how they must have been so disappointed. She came from a good family, an old family. A family that doesn't breed prostitutes. With every transaction, the old Jaimey slowly disappeared, any self-respect she ever had chipped away over time. Time that would never return to her. Time that will forever be gone. Time that she can't return to, to change the past. No time traveling machine to take her there could erase it, or erase what has happened to Russ. She couldn't go as far back to the marriage and erase that. She couldn't lose Russ but the other, the other she wished so hard to make disappear.

Jaimey sat alone, frozen still with thought, when Jim and Russ walked back into the room.

"How is he?" Jaimey asked as she walked to Russ and softly kissed him on the forehead.

"Nothing broken, but he will need time for his wounds to heal," Jim said, really unsure of what to say. It was the worst abuse he had ever seen.

"Jaimey, why don't you come on back and let me take a look at you?" Dr. Spencer asked with a comforting smile.

As Jaimey made her way toward the bedroom, her mind was flooded with thoughts. The cuts and bruises on her face showed just how stupid she felt, how dumbed down she thought she had become.

Since seeing Jim, she started feeling a stronger, pissed off even. Seeing Jim reminded her of who she had once been. She stood at a crossroads in her life. There was no better time to take the right road. To change her life for the better. To jump on the time machine in her mind and ride it and sweep all the bad away. Fix Russ.

But then, those thoughts left just as quickly as they came. She accessed all of her old memories of them. She struggled with the idea of telling Jim who she was. She was unsure if Cappy had told him. She was unsure if she should introduce herself. She was unsure of everything.

Her mind spoke to her. Convincing her she was ashamed. She was poor and lost. She had failed at every-thing since leaving school. She was one of those dumb blondes that excelled at being the typical professional student, but failed miserably at life.

She yearned to talk to him about football season and the team's chances this year, but she oddly didn't feel as though she had the right. She sat broken of spirit and beaten emotionally. Her pretty "queen" face gone, replaced with wrinkles and bruises. The lines on her face told the story of a life lived with abandon. Now she stood in front of "Mr. Ole Miss," and the memories came flooding back.

She watched as Dr. Spencer prepared to examine her. He rifled through his bag looking for the tools of his trade. She noticed his tanned long legs and the way he was dressed. He was on his way to play tennis after the exami-nation and his white shorts and shirt were in stark contrast to his muscular and tanned arms and legs.

As Dr. Spencer retrieved his tools and turned to Jaimey, she had already removed her robe and stood in front of him completely nude.

"You can put that back on, Jaimey," Dr. Spencer said. "I can examine you with your robe on."

Dr. Spencer sat her down in a chair and placed a stethoscope on her back and asked her to take several deep breaths. She did and felt the cold metal against her skin as he listened to her breathing from various places on her chest and back.

"Sounds good," he said as he moved to her eyes.

He moved the small beam of light back and forth to be sure there was no permanent damage to her bloodshot eyes.

"I'm Jaimey Mitchell." Jaimey timidly blurted out. She waited for the shocked response from him, but it didn't come.

"I know... I would know those crystal blue eyes anywhere. You really haven't changed that much since school," Jim said trying to ease her anxiety. He could feel it hanging in the air.

"I'm just so embarrassed," Jaimey said, drying her eyes and smiling at his sweetness.

"I understand, no need to be embarrassed around me."

"There's so much you don't know about me," Jaimey said feeling as if she were ready to purge her life onto Jim Spencer all at once.

"Well, what I do know is bad things happen to good people, and it's never too late to change the course of your life and fix what is broken," Jim said.

He continued checking for broken bones. He felt inside her robe and worked his hands along her ribs on each side. He ran his hand down her spine asking her if his pressure created any pain. He felt around her cheekbones, careful of the cuts. "Have you spit up blood since this happened?" he asked her. He took her arms in his hands and felt up and down her forearms softly, then around her upper arms and around her neck.

"Jaimey, have you ever spoken with a therapist? It might help to talk to someone. Tell them what you've been through."

"I haven't. It seems like this all came on so quickly; I've just never taken the time. I've been more focused on Russ and how this was affecting him."

"Well, it might be good for both of you to see someone. I've got a few people I would recommend for you when you get ready."

"Thank you," Jaimey said.

After more questions about where she hurt, old wounds, etc., he left Jaimey to change into the t-shirt, jeans, and tennis shoes his sister sent to her. The jeans, faded and worn fit perfectly. The t-shirt had been washed and smelled of detergent. She stood in front of a full-length mirror and fixed her hair, pulling the back tight into a pony tail and ran her hand over her face softly paying close attention to smooth the bags forming under her eyes. She dabbed on lipstick, careful around the split in her lower lip and softly rubbed them together. She applied base to the bruises around her cheeks and right eye until they disappeared, and then added some color around her eyes. The transition from call girl to stay at home mom was complete.

"Well?" Cappy asked, hoping for some positive news.

"Have you seen that boy's back, Cap? What kind of sick bastard does that to a kid, much less his own son?" Dr. Spencer said, his anger growing by the second. "Jaimey's in no better shape."

"He's a sorry son-of-a-bitch, Jimbo," Cappy said through gritted teeth.

"Cap, legally I am obligated to report this; I'm here off

the books, so I'll do what you want me to. You really need to get social services out here and let them create a report," Jim said.

"Jim, please don't mention to anyone that they are out here. I don't want that bastard finding out and putting them in more danger."

"I won't tell anyone, but social services needs to be called. Think about it," Jim said as he started for the door.

"The last time I got involved, this happened. I don't want to make anything worse," Cappy said as he shook Jim's hand thanking him for coming.

Their conversation was interrupted as Jaimey walked into the room. Jim looked up at her. She looked like she was getting ready to head to class at Ole Miss. For him, she hadn't changed. He still ached for her.

CHAPTER TWENTY-FOUR

J im Spencer arrived at his office the next morning at 7:30 sharp, just as he had done for the last fifteen years. He cherished the time he had to himself before the barrage of patients started showing up for the day.

He needed quiet before the litany of bitching and complaining from his nurses about their jacked-up lives had to be heard. It was exhausting. If these nurses who had great families, good jobs and mostly okay husbands could hear Jaimey tell the story of her life, they would quit complaining about all of the mundane shit in their lives and be thankful he thought.

He immediately started the coffee pot and made his way to his office. He walked down a long hall adorned with team photos of all four of the teams he played on at Ole Miss. Seeing them made his mind retreat to the previous morning, and seeing Jaimey, and how shocked he was at the whole situation.

As he sat, he grabbed an Ole Miss yearbook behind his desk, and turned to the homecoming section and found her.

"Damn, she's gorgeous!" he said out loud.

"Who?" A high-pitched, nasally voice that he knew all too well, broke his morning tranquility.

Jenna, his head nurse and office manager, stood in the door. Bald-headed, she was 5'6" tall, but with her hair teased to heaven she stood 6'. She was a wanna-be rock star, who dreamed of being on MTV. Jim constantly stayed on her about keeping the top button of her nurse's uniform buttoned. He caught her constantly showing the patients her Rolling Stone tattoo. She was their number one fan.

She switched to them after Elvis died, although she kept a special place in her heart reserved for "The King" and had a Walkman dedicated to nothing but Elvis's songs. Jim heard her tell the stories a million times-where she was the day Elvis died and how she got backstage to meet Steven Tyler that time.

"There's a man outside. I was on my way to Mickey D's and saw him standing at the front door, thought it might be an emergency, said his name is Cappy; he's a real cute older man."

"OK, please send him back and ah, please button...," Jim said pointing at his chest seeing a portion of the famous lips and tongue that was synonymous with the Stones.

"Okay," Jenna said exasperated, stretching a two-syllable word into four as she rolled her eyes.

Jim heard Cappy's booming voice talking to Jenna as they made their way toward his office. He could tell she was flirting with him.

Cappy walked into the room and closed the door in Jenna's face.

"That will be all, Jenna," Jim shouted through the door sure she was listening on the other side. Jim heard her feet scurrying as she rushed away.

"That is the one you *don't* want knowing what's going on at your house," Jim said pumping his finger toward Jenna.

"Jim, I think I want you to call the social worker that you know. I've talked to Jaimey and apparently, they have a file with social services. She said this could help her with a future custody battle and continue to show a pattern of abuse."

"Great; I'll make the call this morning," Jim said. "If anything else happened and the authorities found out I made a house call, it could mean a lot of trouble legally for me."

"What are you looking at, there?" Cappy asked picking up the yearbook in front of Jim.

"That's her," Jim said pointing to Jaimey's photo.

Jaimey stood on the fifty-yard line at Vaught-Hemingway stadium. It was a beautiful fall day. The sky was clear and blue, and she was surrounded by the band. She stood gracefully, wearing a white dress, her arm locked into her father's. He stood beside her, unable to be prouder of his daughter. The bottom of her dress had been swirled around her feet by her lady-in-waiting. The crown that was placed on her head was outlined by a large, blonde bouffant. She wore her mother's pearls. White gloves covered her arms just above her elbows. She held a large bouquet of red roses as she waved. The rest of her court stood behind her, creating a blurred array of white and red. She was stunningly beautiful.

"Is that Jaimey?" Cappy asked, shocked.

"That's Jaimey!" was Jim's excited response.

"Look how proud Noel was," Cappy said.

Cappy looked at him in utter disbelief then glanced back down at the page. Her bio was listed below her photo.

Jaimey Lynn Mitchell
Ole Miss Homecoming Queen
Phi MU Sorority
Sigma Chi Little Sister

The office grew quiet. Cappy continued staring at Jaimey, shocked. He had only known her as a little girl. He remembered hearing Noel talk about her being voted homecoming queen. Now seeing this photo, knowing how her life has turned out, he was increasingly sad for her.

"You know I was in love with her; hell, I still am," Jim said feeling exposed as if he had told a stranger his deepest darkest secret.

"You knew her?" Cappy asked, his voice now almost a whisper.

A heaviness came over the two of them.

"I always held out hope for one day, Cap. One day that she might reappear in my life, and we might reconnect. I knew about Russ, and I imagined she probably had more children, and that was okay; I could accept them as my own and raise them. Yeah, I've always loved her and here she is coming back into my life as I'd always hoped, just under different circumstances."

"Is she why you've never married?" Cappy asked.

"She is. I just always felt she was the one for me. I never wanted to one day have the opportunity and be married myself and have a decision to make, so I just never entertained the idea." Jim said, laying his heart bare.

"I understand. No one could ever replace Margaret for me. The heart wants what the heart wants, bud." Cappy said with a toothy grin. "She needs a man like you in her life; Russ needs a man like you too."

"Russ has you in his life."

"Right now, he does, but I'm old. It sure would make me feel good knowing he had someone taking care of him... and Jaimey too."

CHAPTER TWENTY-FIVE

The drive was farther than Susan Shaw had imagined. The directions were precise. She was amazed that the mileage from one landmark to the next was so exact. William Capstick was very precise with his instruction; indeed, there was no question that he had given them before.

The terrain would rise and fall with every curve she rounded. The first hay bales of the season began dotting the landscape like breadcrumbs leading her to William Capstick's home.

As the miles clicked by, Susan asked herself why anyone would want to live so far out of town, so far from a grocery store, so far away from a hospital. What would happen if there was an emergency? How could anyone get to a doctor on time? Her brain raced, worry occupying her mind as it always did.

Deep in thought, she suddenly noticed the static coming from the radio. She turned it off instead of changing stations. The dreaded drive was turning out to be a relaxing one. The cobwebs in her mind were quickly disintegrating along with all of the troubling cases she was currently working on.

Looking to her left, she passed a group of elderly women sitting in a carport around a large washtub. They shelled peas and butterbeans. They rocked slowly as they shelled, laughing at a story, swatting at flies.

She glanced down at her directions. A right turn was approaching, but she saw nothing that closely resembled a road.

She looked at her notes. *The road is almost hidden* it read.

She continued reading. *Look carefully,* her note said. She spotted the road, and just as he had said, it was well-hidden. She turned and was soon driving through a grove of pecan trees. As she topped a crest in the road, the rustic cabin with the green metal roof that Capstick described came into view.

As she approached, she saw a young boy leaning on a golf club. He had the build of a golfer, she thought, tall and lean. She also spotted the man who had to be William Capstick standing in front of the carport waving at her.

"Miss Shaw, thanks for coming," Capstick said, approaching her with meaning in his stride.

"You gave great directions. Never got turned around once," Susan said, prouder of herself than in Capstick's ability to give precise directions.

Interviewing abused women and children was something that Susan Shaw had been doing for the last ten years. She met her husband her junior year at Iowa State, and they had moved back to his hometown after they both graduated. After her husband told her about the need for social workers in Mississippi, she was all in. She never considered or prepared herself for the culture shock. She looked more like a buttoned-up librarian than a social worker. She was straight-laced, always punctual, always professionally dressed. She spoke proper English with a nasal midwestern accent. Her accent was so foreign to her clients, they rarely understood her.

Soon Russ joined the two, and after a quick introduction, the three of them went inside. It was obvious to Cappy that Russ had been through this before. He looked as if he knew the drill.

Inside, Susan Shaw introduced herself to Jaimey. She noted the same far off look on Jaimey's face that she had seen countless times. The look that seemed to say *all hope is lost*. The women with that look usually had every ounce of confidence beaten out of them. They were not only physically abused, but also told they were nothing so many times, they eventually believed it. Susan asked Cappy if there was a place she could interview them both separately. He took Susan into the hallway and showed her to a room at the end.

Inside, Susan got straight to work. The bad thing about Susan Shaw was that she was all business. She had no bedside manner. She was stoic and didn't know how to relax and let her hair down a little.

Jaimey sat quietly with her legs and arms crossed and stared blankly at Susan Shaw. She stared at Susan's hair which appeared to be "fixed" at a beauty parlor by an old woman. Curled and sprayed and heated under space alien dryers that sat in rows along a wall full of gossiping women. Jaimey noticed Susan's blouse was buttoned clear to her chin. It was tight around her neck, the bottom tucked into the waist of a skirt that hung below her knees. Her legs were covered in dark panty hose. Her shoes laced and were dark brown matching her skirt, shining. Jaimey traced her way up from the social worker's feet and watched her push her glasses higher on her nose.

Susan kept her paperwork neatly stacked in front of her. The interview was painstakingly slow as Susan Shaw wrote every word carefully. She wore a wedding ring below an engagement ring on her left hand. The diamond so small Jaimey squinted to see it. She wore no makeup and her fingernails, slight and narrow, were cut short and unpainted.

"How long have you been married?" Jaimey asked.

"A while," she said, guardedly.

Jaimey could tell she was uncomfortable talking about herself. Maybe her life at home wasn't all that great either. Maybe her perfect hair, and perfect skirt, and perfect blouse and shined shoes were just a front. Telling the world all was good but maybe it wasn't. Maybe she was just like the rest of the world, screwed up. Maybe she had a bad marriage, too.

"I'm not going back to the beginning," Jaimey said, defiantly. She made her mind up she didn't like this social worker the second she met her. She wasn't sure why. It might have been the way she looked, how she dressed. She would have been made fun of at Ole Miss, walking across campus like that, prim and proper, no damn personality.

Jaimey felt herself despising Susan Shaw. *Was it the woman herself or her profession?* she wondered. A familiar mean streak raised it's head and flowed through Jaimey, and she felt it boil. She knew it was wrong, and now she watched Susan squirm in her seat uncomfortable.

"I assume you're going to get our files from the coast?" Jaimey asked. "Cause I'm not reliving all of that shit over again. I'll tell you about the other night, and that's all. So, how are things with you and your husband?"

The social worker was taken aback by the question. "I'm sorry," she sputtered and looked at Jaimey, unsure of where the question came from... unsure of the tone.

Jaimey's face turned darker, became expressionless.

"You're sitting here talking to me about my life. Tell me about yours. Everything perfect at home? I bet not. If you would unbutton the top three buttons on that blouse it would probably be better. Don't you think?"

"Jaimey, I'm here to interview you, not the other way around."

"That's right, spill my guts. Tell you all my deep dark secrets so you can sit there in judgment of me; you don't know me."

"You're right, I don't, that's what I'm trying to do. Get to know you."

"I bet you go home at the end of the day and bore the hell out of your husband with one story after the other. Making yourself feel better about your life, about your marriage... talking about all of your clients who can't get their shit together."

Jaimey heard herself getting louder and she stopped talking.

"I'm sorry...I don't know why I said all of that, Jaimey said reticently. "I usually don't treat people the way I just treated you. I'm so sorry."

"It's okay; I understand. You're right. I don't think any of us are as perfect as we want to be or think we are. The world only sees what we show them. Including me."

A long, awkward silence filled the room. Susan Shaw sat straight, her wispy hands folded across her lap waiting for Jaimey to speak.

"I suddenly feel like I'm in a shrink's office. Should I lie down on the bed?" Jaimey asked sarcastically.

"Look, I know you've been through this before. I'm sure you get tired of talking about it, having to relive it. I just need to make notes for the record, so just tell me what you what me to know."

Jaimey stood and started unbuttoning her shirt. She laid it on the bed. She unzipped her jeans and let them fall and stepped out of them. Susan audibly gasped and slowly placed her hand over her mouth. Tears flooded her eyes as she bent down and pulled her camera from its case. She began shooting photos.

"The 'D' mark is from his belt buckle. If you care to measure it, the belt is an inch and a half wide." As Jaimey spoke, she turned in a slow circle. Susan gasped a second time and started shooting. Her camera clicking, the shutter keeping a rhythm as she moved the lens from Jaimey's neck to her feet. Her entire backside, colored, streaked in different shades of blues and purples. Strap mark after strap mark. Some ending with the buckle making a clear imprint on her skin. Purple handprints on her thigh below her rear end.

"He beat us both because I got a job. I made the mistake of telling him about it. Said I was trying to show him up."

Jaimey turned, stoic, fully facing Susan again. Her arms flat against her sides.

"He raped me with a flashlight in front of Russ. Russ ran to his room and came back out with a baseball ball and knocked him off of me. We ran out of the house and slept in the cart shed...that's all."

Jaimey's face was drawn and tired. The years of abuse. The years of telling the stories over and over piled up. She told herself this was the last interview with social services for her and Russ. After she finished her account of her own abuse, she started to tell Susan about Randy beating Russ.

"I'll need Russ to tell me that directly," Susan said in her monotoned voice.

"I can't believe Russ has to go through this all over again," Jaimey said.

Jaimey felt sick. This would make the third time.

Russ wasn't as forthcoming as Jaimey, and Susan had a hard time pulling information from him. After he listened to several of Susan's questions, he quietly opened up.

"Can't you just get our files from Biloxi? Most of my stories are in there."

"What kind of stories?"

"Please just get those files. It's too hard to relive those times. We've left Biloxi. We've left dad for good. As far as I'm concerned, that part of our life is over. I'm done with him."

"Okay, I'll request the old files, but I'll need to make a report about what happened last week."

Russ recounted the day that Randy followed him to Mrs. Frank's house. How he started slapping him and how Cappy stopped it.

"That was the day he was arrested," Russ said. "He was in jail for a few days. We were nervous about him coming home, but for a few days, he was nice to us."

Russ grew silent and stared straight ahead. His eyes were fixed, not blinking. He looked like he was reliving the memory. He continued, telling Susan Shaw about Randy coming home that night.

"I was excited to see him. It was the longest period of time that he had gone without drinking. The house had been quiet. We actually sat down at the dinner table and had supper one night, together. It was nice."

Russ stopped and wiped his nose. Thick tears started falling down his face. He continued, telling her about meeting him in the garage the next night and he knew. He knew he was drunk again.

"Mom had dinner cooked again. She was actually excited to see him. He had talked about looking for a job. I think Mom thought he was finally making an effort. She was doing everything she could to help him, support him. Everything was fine until mom told him she found a job."

Russ bent over and planted his face into his hands. Susan handed him a Kleenex and placed her hand on his shoulder. He recoiled from the unintended pain.

"Oh, I'm so sorry."

"That's okay; you didn't know. It's still very sore. I've got an open wound on my shoulder."

"Do you mind if I see?" Susan asked.

Without saying anything Russ stood and slowly, easily took off his shirt. Susan Shaw audibly gasped. Russ's back looked as though it was painted with various shades of yellow and purple. Susan counted eight darker purple, almost black marks in the shape of the letter "D" across his back.

Susan held her hand to her mouth. As much as she had seen in her short career, this was by far one of the worst.

Russ looked up at Susan. "He was hurting mom..."

"It's okay; she told me, you don't have too..."

"He used a flashlight."

Russ looked up from his lap directly into Susan Shaw's eyes and held them there. She stared back into his eyes, red and floating in tears. "He made me watch. Told me... this was how you handle a wife who gets out of line. I hope I never have to lay eyes on him again."

CHAPTER TWENTY-SIX

Three weeks had passed since Cappy had found Russ and Jaimey in the cart shed. Their visible scars and bruises were healing and Russ was able to move without grimacing. The open wounds on his back had closed and were no longer sore. He could wear a shirt without it hurting, and most important for Russ, he could swing a club with no pain.

Russ stood on the number eighteen tee box, playing his way in to meet Cappy at the clubhouse for lunch. It was his favorite hole because the fairway sat directly beside the pool, and today the pool was full of girls his age in bikinis.

He teed his ball high and lined up his shot to land as close to the pool as he could. His plan worked. He was 125 yards from the green. He gladly had to wait for the three-some just ahead of him to finish the hole. The threesome included the oldest, as well as the slowest, members of the club. He leaned against the chainlink fence and lit a cigarette. He felt the row of blondes watching him out of the corner of his eye. He took a long, deep drag and blew smoke from the corner of his mouth. Mothers disgusted by

Russ' smoking sat protectively by their young daughters. Girls embarrassed to sit with their mothers sat beside girl-friends on the side nearest the green. Young children ran and splashed around the pool. The men who didn't play golf sat by their coolers all day and gawked at the women. They strategically sat at the end nearest the gate so they didn't have far to walk to the men's room when the beers filled their bladders full.

With the green clear, Russ winked at the blonde nearest him. He flicked his cigarette as coolly as he could into the fairway and stepped up to his ball. He took a couple of prac-tice swings. He stole a look behind him and saw one of the blondes still watching him. He took a few more practice swings, lined up his shot, hovering his club over the ball and looked at the flag one last time. Finally, he struck the ball, topping it. The ball crippled and rolled ten yards into some thick grass on the edge of the fairway. He quickly made his way to his ball, keeping his back toward the girls, unwilling to show his reddening face.

As he approached his ball, he saw Cappy waving him into the clubhouse. Focused again on his game, he struck the ball and placed it inches from the flag. He kept his eyes toward the pool the whole time he was driving to the green. The girls never looked his way again. Embarrassed, he parred the hole and headed inside for lunch.

The smell of frying bologna filled the kitchen as Russ walked in the back door.

"There he is. There's my baby!" Effie said, almost shout-ing. She left her duties at the stove and hugged Russ.

"My whole church been prayin' for y'all, baby," Effie whispered.

Russ pulled back from her and looked confused wondering how she knew.

"Cappy told me. It's alright, I ain't breathin' a word," Effie said, assuring Russ his secret was safe with her.

"Thank you," Russ said as he asked for a bologna sandwich.

He made his way over to Cappy's table and sat down with him and Bubba Stewart.

Soon, Effie brought them their lunch, just as Fatboy walked in, announcing his arrival with his order.

"Two cheeseburgers, please," Fatboy said as he made his way beside Russ.

"You can have one, and you ain't gettin' no fries today either."

"Yes, ma'am." Fatboy said in a defeated voice.

As Fatboy started another argument for fries, Bubba Stewart watched a bright red Porsche lead a line of dust toward the clubhouse.

"Who in the hell just bought a Porsche?" Bubba asked as a tinge of jealousy crept into his psyche.

"I'm sure that's Bill," Cappy said, rising from the table followed by Fatboy and Russ.

They all watched as Bill Turner exited his car. It looked like a Polo commercial was being shot right at Beau Chene Country Club as he unfolded his 6' 3" tanned frame out of the driver's side. His silver hair framed his aviator sunglasses.

"Whoa," Fatboy moaned as he walked around the car slightly rubbing it, his eyes wide with wonder and excitement.

"Have a seat," Bill said as he threw Fatboy the keys.

Fatboy squeezed into the driver's side. He had forgotten all about the extra burger he was trying to talk Effie out of, and he watched Bill and Cappy make their way back into the Clubhouse.

Bill Turner was dressed neatly, a crease in his pants and a shine on his shoes that would blind in the right light. His white shirt accentuated the perfect tan that came naturally to him, with the help of a combination of sun rays from the course and his boat. His chiseled face was outlined by silver hair that was combed carefully away from his face. He was fit and lean, the perfect golfer's body, the perfect athlete's body. He didn't look close to his seventy years and didn't act it either. He came from old and new money. His father had left him a small fortune partly from ill-gotten gain as a moonshiner in his early days, and later more legitimately as an oil man. Bill made the majority of his money in the stock market, but also traveled to far off places and did extraordinary things like mining for gold in Alaska. He was a lifelong bachelor who loved adventure and had no problem finding a lady to hang from his arm. Even Effie was not immune to his charm.

"Hey Mr. Bill," Effie said, showing the expanse of space between her two front teeth. Effie had not smiled in so long that Cappy had forgotten about her gap.

Bill immediately rose from his chair as if he were greeting the queen herself and took Effie's face in his two-long, tanned hands.

"Effie," Bill said as he kissed her on the forehead.

"Y'all can't tell, but my face red, my head hot." Effie said, fanning herself.

"Mr. Bill stop! Ray Ray gon' see you and we gon' have to tell him you his daddy!" Effie said, the table erupting in laughter.

"Thank you for letting us sit in it, Mr. Bill," Fatboy said, handing him back his keys.

"We'll go for a ride after we play if you want to," Bill

said offering the Porsche for some late afternoon entertainment.

After lunch, the boys made it out to the number one tee box flanked by Cappy and Bill Turner. They rode together, watching the boys play, keeping a special eye on Russ.

"You know, for so long, I've been out here working with these boys. I realized lately I've been shining too much light on Russ. I've got to hold back with the public praise, but watch this kid. He's next level, Bill. He's just a freshman in high school. Mainly self-taught, looks like. He's got a couple of bad habits, but not many."

One by one, the boys all teed off. Russ teed his ball low and sent it sailing down the left side, lining it up beautifully for his approach shot.

"Damn, Cap, that was at least a 310-yard drive. He's set himself up for his second shot." Bill Turner almost whispered to Cappy.

"You see what I mean. He's like clockwork!"

The boys were all on in two strokes. A couple of birdies and the rest pars.

The next hole was a slight dogleg left with pines on both sides of a narrow fairway. Everyone was center of the fairway except Russ who placed his right in the center of a group of pine trees.

"This next shot will show us a lot," Bill said.

Cappy and Bill hung back in the fairway as the rest of the boys made their way toward their balls ahead of Russ. He pulled up and found his ball sitting on a shiny layer of fresh fallen pine needles.

"That's going to be tough hitting out of that pine straw," Cappy said.

Cappy and Bill watched as Russ walked out in the fairway, stood in the center and jumped a few times trying to see the flag on the green. It was surrounded by water on the backside forming a small horseshoe. The front had a hard slope back to the fairway as the green was elevated. Azaleas and Crepe Myrtle trees lined the right side while also serving as a border between the green and the next tee box.

Russ would have to pull the shot just right. Too much and he would be in the water, not enough and he would be yelling "Fore!"

He lined up his shot, adjusting a couple of times. He turned over his body movement in his mind, reminding himself to turn his shoulders hard to the right. He stepped out on the fairway one more time and jumped, looking to the right side finding a marker to line up with. He reapproached the ball and scraped the pine straw from under his feet. After a couple of practice swings, he struck the ball. It rose high and turned in midair as if God had blown on it. It landed on the green rolling to a stop, inches from the flag.

The air erupted in claps and whistles and hollers. High fives flew in the air. Russ immediately ran from the trees to watch his ball, jumping all the while. He saw the product of his shot, and as if he hadn't done anything great at all, walked back to his cart, placed his club back in his bag, and drove toward the green.

Bill Turner looked at Cappy as if he couldn't believe what he had just seen.

"Let's get this kid over to Waving Pines soon, Cap. Let's see what he can do on a PGA-level course."

CHAPTER TWENTY-SEVEN

Bill Turner took the drive that led to Cappy's house without slowing much. The little green man showed himself again as it did every time he rose from the bottom and crested the hill and the log cabin came into full view.

Bill Turner didn't covet much, but he coveted Cappy's house. He loved everything about it. The pecan grove, the lake, the boat house, the house itself. He coveted Cappy's shooting houses during deer season. He coveted the fact that he could walk out of his front door and be hunting or fishing in minutes. He coveted the fact that he could take a leak in his front yard and not worry about neighbors seeing him.

Bill announced himself loudly when he walked through Cappy's backdoor. He walked around the fireplace calling when he saw Russ and Cappy on the deck sighting in a rifle. He made his way to the sliding glass door and onto the deck.

"Mr. Turner, watch this!" Russ said as he leaned over Cappy's 30.06 Weatherby.

Cappy handed Bill binoculars.

"Remember to breathe," Cappy said as he placed the tips of his fingers in his ears.

Russ clicked off the safety and took a deep breath. He allowed the air to escape his lips slowly. "Boom!" the shot echoed through the hardwood bottom.

"Center Bullseye!" Bill shouted. "Doesn't get any better than that!"

Russ pulled up from the scope and smiled at them both.

"Fantastic shot, Russ!"

"What are you doing out here so early?" Cappy asked.

"I've got something I would like for us to do today if it's okay with you Cap," Bill said as he glanced at Russ.

"Yeah, sure, what have you got on your mind?" Cappy asked.

"Russ, why don't you go get dressed and ready to go spend the day with these old men?" Bill said.

Russ quickly disappeared into the house.

"Want a cup?" Cappy asked as he walked to kitchen for the coffee pot.

"Cap, I almost hate coming out here because I want this place so bad. I know it's wrong, but I get so jealous every time I see this place. You've done a great job out here."

Cappy filled a cup with hot coffee and handed it to Bill.

"You know you don't need an invitation to come out here! Let's do some huntin' this fall."

"Be careful, I never will leave!"

"So, what's the plan?" Cappy asked as he blew on his coffee and took a quick sip.

He turned and leaned on the rail and watched a flock of wood ducks rise from the lake. Bill joined him on the rail.

"I noticed Russ was playing with some older clubs the other day. Let's take him to Jackson and get him fixed up with a new set and a few outfits, balls, tees, new bag, the whole nine yards."

"Bill, he will love it!"

"We can run by the Dixie, have breakfast and head out, make a day of it. We can eat lunch at the Piccadilly, and head on back home."

"Let's do it, sounds great!"

Russ slid open the door. His hair was combed, and he had put on a fresh shirt. Jaimey fell in behind him. She was fully dressed and made up. Fresh makeup covering old bruises that hadn't disappeared yet.

"Why are you so dressed up?" Russ asked as he turned to see his mother behind him.

"I am going with Dr. Spencer to Oxford today. We're just going to go ride around campus for a little while and head on back home."

Russ hugged Jaimey and whispered in her ear.

"Good, I'm glad."

Jaimey looked visibly relieved.

Bill bent down and kissed Jaimey on the cheek and greeted her and said goodbye, all at the same time.

"We'll take good care of your boy today."

"Thank you."

Jaimey hugged Cappy.

"Have fun," Jaimey said as they walked through the door.

Russ was slightly disappointed when he saw the four door Mercedes instead of the Porsche. The breakfast at the Dixie went down fast. Russ ate in anticipation of the day's unknow plans.

The Mercedes' speedometer read 90 when Bill glanced at his dash after he saw the blue lights.

"Cap give me that wallet in the glove box, please."

Cappy opened the box, lifted a few envelopes and pulled out a small leather wallet and handed it to Bill.

Bill lowered the window and flipped the wallet open and showed it to the patrolman.

"Enjoyed the ball last month," Bill said as he smiled at the patrolman.

"Thank you for your support, sir; have a good day."

Bill handed the wallet back to Cappy, and after several seconds, he was nearing 100 miles per hour again.

"Wow, no ticket! That was awesome." Russ said as he watched the patrolman through the back glass.

"Where'd you get this?" Cappy asked as he opened the wallet and stared at the badge.

"Governor."

Russ leaned toward the front seat as Bill parked the car in front of the golf shop.

"What are we doing?" Russ asked.

Cappy looked at Bill, allowing his friend to answer.

"We thought it was time you have a fitted set of clubs and some new duds Russ," Bill said, as he stared at the boy in the rear-view mirror.

"Really?" Russ asked quietly.

Russ jumped out of the backseat and walked through the door as Bill held it for him.

"Mr. Crawford?" the store manager asked.

"How does he know my name?" Russ asked as he turned to Bill.

Russ followed the manager toward the long row of clubs. He was measured from head to toe. He tried several drivers finally choosing a Callaway. He chose Titleist irons and a Ping putter. He was fitted with a sand wedge.

While the shafts were cut and the clubs were being

built the manager helped Russ pick out several shirts and shorts.

"Am I supposed to be getting this much?" Russ asked Bill wide eyed.

"The manager knows what to do," Bill said, smiling at Russ.

Russ sat in a chair in front of three pairs of golf shoes and tried them on. He stood and walked in them making sure they were comfortable. He picked out three bags of tees and four boxes of balls. He tried on a glove for fit and the manager added two more for a total of three. He chose a visor and two regular hats with golf brands emblazoned across the front.

The last thing he chose was a golf bag.

"Do you have a nickname?" the manager asked.

Russ thought for a while and sheepishly answered, "Country Club."

"Wow, great nickname!" The manager said.

Russ smiled.

"What else?" The manager asked.

Russ stared back at Cappy and Bill with his palms thrust toward the heavens and hunched his shoulders.

"I think that's it," Russ said.

"Great! If you gentlemen would like to go get lunch, we will have everything ready for you when you return," the manager said as he walked over and shook everyone's hands.

Bill slipped the manager his credit card and left it with him while they went to lunch.

They sped off to the Piccadilly and enjoyed a long slow lunch. They took their time getting back to the golf shop. When they walked in, Russ's packages were sitting near the door. His clothes were in bags. The balls, tees, gloves, and clubs were already in his bag. His shoes were in a compli-mentary shoe bag. Russ walked to the clubs immediately and noticed his name embroidered on the bag "*Russ 'Country Club' Crawford.*" He turned to Cappy and Bill and pointed toward his name.

"Just like the pros," Russ said excitedly.

"Might as well get used to it now," Bill said.

The manager handed Bill his card with the receipt folded around it.

"Thank you, Bill," Cappy said.

"Hey, thank you for taking such good care of him."

"Before you go take out your driver and pitching wedge. Let's go back here and take a few practice swings. Make sure we've got those cut right for you," the manager said to Russ.

The car was loaded. Handshakes were exchanged and the three of them were soon headed back down Lakeland toward Lewiston.

"Mr. Turner, thank you," Russ said. "This was very nice; I don't how I'll repay you."

"You don't owe me a thing, Russ; promise me you'll let me know when you need something else."

Russ pulled a pile of new shirts form a plastic bag and ran his hand over them feeling the softness of the material. The brand was one his father used to wear. A brand Randy could no longer afford.

CHAPTER TWENTY-EIGHT

The shadows of mailboxes clicked by less frequently in the ditches as Jaimey rested her head-on Jim Spencer's car door. The paved city driveways soon gave way to county gravel and slag as the scent of turned dirt wafted through the fresh air. Farmers were turning the soil that would soon stand white with cotton. Colonel Reb sparsely greeted their arrival at the homes that supported the school to the north.

Jaimey and Jim had made this pilgrimage before, trudging back and forth from home to school. The ride made Jaimey feel young again. Imagining she was headed back to school to a swap or to The Gin or The Warehouse, to eat at Pasquale's, or just hang out on the Square before the police would shew them away.

The Square was alive with people, and tulips and azaleas in full bloom. Jaimey glanced over at Jim, staring at him, asking herself why they never got together. The constant murmur of people everywhere filled her ears. It brought her back to a simpler time when Oxford, Missis-sippi and Ole Miss were her entire world. When the headiest decision for her was figuring out what she would wear to the next swap or which boy would ask her out, or who Ole Miss played next.

This particular Saturday was as close to a fall gameday feeling as you could get in Oxford, Mississippi. The Spring Scrimmage was an excuse to tailgate before the season started. A sea of blue and red dots filled The Grove as friends caught up with each other. They lived for the mass of time between August and November. The scrimmage did nothing but make that desire for fall grow stronger.

Jim drove slowly along fraternity row. The houses were buzzing with horny fraternity brothers nursing a hangover from the night before while simultaneously working on their next one. Girls in short skirts and big hair teased to Heaven hung on their arms like a boll weevil to cotton. The men of Kappa Alpha were dressed in polos and khaki shorts their boxers hanging just below the bottom seam providing an air of aloofness and privilege, boat shoes were tied loosely on sockless feet. They were double fisting beers with an extra in their back pocket.

A huge Confederate flag slowly waved in front of the KA house with two brothers dressed as Confederate soldiers standing guard on either side. They each held a sword in one hand and a scotch in the other.

Jaimey stared at the house and watched them. She watched a couple sitting on the steps and remembered the first time she met Randy. A game day. She remembered being impressed that he was from the Delta. She always wanted to marry a boy from the Delta. Move there and live in a big plantation house and host parties.

Her mind stayed on that day. He was good looking. He had a confident smile and she remembered he looked directly into her eyes when he spoke to her. She remembered what he was wearing that day. As her mind's eye recounted how he was dressed, she also remembered he had a bottle of Jack Daniels in his hand. It never left.

Jim pointed his convertible toward the stadium, and they inched their way through traffic surrounded by a sea of humanity in lawn chairs nursing their fourth Bloody Mary of the morning, others mixing orange juice and vodka, planning for the fall and catching up on everyone's family.

Jaimey leaned over and kissed Jim.

"What was that for?" Jim asked, a broad smile coming across his face.

"Thank you for this day; you don't know what this has meant to me."

Her heart was full; the day was perfect and sweet. He brought her here because he knew how much it meant to her, and, if he were truthful with himself, he was living out a dream he held on to, always hoping would happen... a date with Jaimey Mitchell.

They sat in silence, his mind quickly moved to a book he was reading, *Sorties: Journals and New Essays* by James Dickey. Recently enamored with Dickey and his poetry and essays, Jim read his first novel *Deliverance* and had already seen the movie by the same name. The novel and movie were okay, but Dickey's poetry is what he appreciated. *Sorties* was the last thing he read. In it, Dickey described the best women to marry.

The best of all wives is the country girl and the next best is the prostitute who manages to get married, and who must work hard all the rest of her life at recovering the love and the sensuality that she spent a number of years losing for money.

He hoped Dickey was right. Even so, he didn't want Jaimey working so hard to recover the love and sensuality that surely, she *had* lost. She had paid enough with her life as it was. He was willing to pick up that slack. She wouldn't owe him anything. The only thing he would require from her would simply be for her to one day say "yes."

As the road returned them from cotton fields to pine plantations, Jaimey sat with her head resting on Jim's shoulder and her arms wrapped tightly around his. They rode all the way to Lewiston not saying another word.

Finally back home, Jim pulled into Wilson's Quick Stop. The shop was a more modern take on the old general store. Everything could be purchased inside. Cigarettes, beer, chips, motor oil, Playboy magazines. The smell of biscuits and sausages and scrambled eggs filled the early risers. Plate lunches full of fried foods were cooked in the back and ready for the noontime crowd. Gizzards and livers sold by the bagful fixed late night drunk cravings. Pinball machines were lined up against the outside wall; the poker machines were in the back. No one played poker unless Wilson knew them.

Jim read a sign near the cash register. *Tina Turner, Humphrey Coliseum. Tickets on sale now. Twenty-five dollars each.* He asked for two.

Jaimey waited for Jim, reclined, her head back on the headrest, her eyes closed. She opened them at a light tapping on her window. Randy stood beside the car staring at her. His eyes gaunt almost black. Sunken deep. He was thinner than the last time she saw him. She drew back hard toward the driver's seat expecting violence.

Jim rushed out of the store walking quickly toward the car. He stood near Randy, waiting for what Jaimey's estranged husband might do next. Waiting for him to attack. Waiting for him to scream, to say anything. He just stood staring at Jaimey on the other side of the window. Jim slowly made his way toward the driver's side and sat down. He cranked the car. Randy and Jaimey locked eyes. A single tear fell from Randy's eye. He never moved. He remained wobbling; his hands beside him. His eyes begging forgiveness. Again.

CHAPTER TWENTY-NINE

As usual, Effie was heard long before she was seen. Her car was no different; the "hooptie," as she referred to it, was a Cadillac from the early seventies. The paint job resembled that of a calico cat, not standard for a Cadillac.

The original color had been champagne, a soft gold color, but after much needed Bondo in several places, added primer and whatever paint was available at the time, it most closely resembled a calico cat.

The shocks had long been shot; when she hit a rise in the road, the muffler dragged and sent sparks flying. The glass packs her son had installed, told of her impending arrival to many of her usual haunts- a blessing to some, a warning to others.

As she made her way toward Cappy's house, her mind became occupied with Jaimey. Effie questioned how she got into the situation she was in. She thought about Jaimey's father. Noel Mitchell was one of the few bankers who loaned black people money in the sixties. It was years later that she learned most of the time he wasn't loaning money from the bank but from his own pocket. She was glad to be able repay him by taking care of his daughter and grandson.

The sound of Effie's car had become a source of comfort to Jaimey over the last few weeks. She met Effie at the back door, unlocking it. The fear that Randy would somehow find her haunted her constantly. Even so far out in the country, she was afraid he would find her. His recent tears meant nothing. Just as his fishing trips with Russ meant nothing. Just as his apologies meant nothing. They were only results of his bipolar personality.

"Hey, Baby!" Effie said as she gently pulled Jaimey to her. "How you feelin' today?" Effie asked as she moved a single strand of blonde hair up and back, folding it behind Jaimey's ear.

"Much better," Jaimey said while nervously looking out of the window to see if Effie had been followed.

"Ain't no sense in lookin', ain't nobody followed me out here from the projects," Effie said with a light chuckle.

Jaimey gave Effie a sheepish smile and stared toward the driveway just the same.

"Well, you sure look a sight better. You just looked like plain shit the other day when Will brought you home." Effie said unapologetically. "The girl jus' looked like shit," she breathed, mumbled in a whisper as she walked toward the bathroom.

Effie's body moved rhythmically through the kitchen. Some parts moved well before others. As she started breakfast, pots, pans, and sheets were filled with eggs, and parts of pigs and dough. Effie stopped to squeeze on an apron and asked Jaimey to tie it, unable to reach the strings in back. Normally, she would just let it hang and cover what it would; but today she had a new church dress on, and she couldn't afford to get grease or flour on it.

Effie refused to measure, as she threw ingredients into mixing bowls. She stopped and pulled a hairnet from her apron and covered her hair. Her bottle red hair still showed through the thin material.

"I know y'all don't want any surprises while y'all eating this morning," she said while she carefully tucked the last hair under the net.

Jaimey smiled watching Effie. She had never learned to cook. She was so impressed with the ease in which she worked, never hesitating as she threw ingredients in the bowls mixing and cutting and finally cooking.

"So, what are we having? Can I help?" Jaimey asked, unsure really of what she could do.

"Can't stand havin' nobody in the kitchen while I'm cookin' gir; you jus' sit there and look pretty. Will knows he not 'spose to be eatin' this bacon because of his cholesterol," Effie shouted.

Jaimey was sure she saw spit from Effie's mouth fly into the pancake mix as she laughed.

"So, how long have you known Cappy?" Jaimey asked, taking a piece of bacon.

"My whole life. Willie and I are the same age. My momma worked for Willie's momma, and we grew up playin' together. We're about as close as a sister and a brother can be."

With breakfast cooked, Effie went into Russ's room to wake him. He felt a tug on his right big toe and eased one eye open enough to see a large creature draped in gold standing in front of him. She stood looking down at him with one hand on her hip. She was dressed in gold taffeta, her matching stockings gold with a vertical silver stripe in them. Her shoes looked to be two sizes too small for her. They were pressing into the two corns on each of her big toes. The pain making her shift her weight from side to side as she moved. She looked like a walking disco ball as light reflected from her dress.

"Wake up, baby! You goin' with me this morning," Effie said as she made her way from the foot of the bed to the closet.

"EeeeWeee, where did you get all these new clothes?" Effie asked.

"But this is Sunday!" Russ said, rolling over to go back to sleep.

"Don't I know it is, and it's a beautiful day, my favorite day of the week. Now get up and get dressed so you can eat and we can go," Effie said tired of arguing.

"Where are we going?"

"You are going to church today, Mr. Russ."

"Church?"

"That's right, you gon' be the only white boy up in Mt. Moriah M.B. Church," Effie said with a big grin.

"M.B, what does M.B. stand for?" Russ asked, his jolted brain beginning to work.

"Missionary Baptist."

"Missionary? Y'all feed poor people there or something?" Russ asked.

"Jus' people starving for the Lord, baby."

Effie threw a shirt and pair of pants down at the foot of the bed.

"Put this on, and I'll go get one of Willie's ties."

Russ had learned to do what he was told when it concerned Effie. He somehow knew that under her rough exterior she loved him.

After breakfast, Russ and Effie made their way to church and arrived early. A young girl in a long white dress met them at the door.

"Hello, Tameka," Effie said, patting the girl on the back.

"Please follow me," she said as Russ and Effie fell in behind her.

As they made their way down to the front row, heads turned and looked at the visitor. Several heads nodded with quiet greetings. The usher led Effie and Russ to the row designated for visitors.

Before the service started, many from the congregation made their way over to welcome Russ.

"He's one of Willie's boys," Effie would explain proudly.

"Who is Willie?" Russ asked confused.

"That's what I call Cappy," Effie said.

"Why are all those girls wearing white and standing all over the church?" Russ asked.

"They the ushers, baby. They seat us, and then take up all the offering money, and then take it back to the counting committee."

His eyes were darting all over the room. More well-wishers stopped by and quietly extended a hand and a welcome.

Soon the quiet of the church was interrupted as Reverend Charlie Hightower burst through the door from a side entrance followed by a line of elders.

Russ' eyes continued watching around the room; he focused on the band. The electric guitar player and drummer kept a slow Blues beat as the reverend and the elders found their seats. The beat continued for another minute, and then abruptly stopped. Within a second of stopping, the organist's hands flew down the length of the keyboard and was quickly joined by the guitarist. Out of nowhere, a tall man appeared on stage and began thumping a bass guitar. The tempo slowed and quieted as the backdoors of the church were opened simultaneously by two of the girls in white. A melodic hum filled the room as the choir started stepping toward the choir loft. The female choir members were dressed in white while the men were dressed in black trousers with white shirts and black bow ties. Everyone in the congregation stood keeping rhythm with the choir.

The two rows of choir members stood behind the double doors waiting direction from their leader. Russ stared at the choir director as if he were waiting on his next instruction. His hands lifted and hung in the air like humidity, and then with a nod of his head, they moved in a slow side-to-side motion, his fingers pressed together and extended straight in front of him. Russ watched the choir, their bodies moving in a slow rhythm matching the director's hand movements. The members all stepped in time with the rhythm of the band. The director sang out, "We've come this far by faith," and, on cue, the choir began singing.

> "We have come this far by faith,
> Leaning on the Lord.
> Trusting in His holy Word,
> He's never failed us yet.
> Singing oh,oh,oh can't turn a-round,
> We've come this far by faith."

Soon the entire congregation joined in, and the small church was pulsating.

The choir's rhythm was perfect and well-rehearsed. With each step, their bodies moved in unison, and, with all their weight on the same foot, they pumped twice, standing in the same place, still moving slowly toward the front. From left to right their bodies slowly flowed into the choir loft.

Russ was mesmerized, he had never witnessed such pageantry. His grandparents' church was much more subdued, much more boring.

The choir stopped. The organist continued for the reading of the church announcements. Mrs. Hattie McDaniel stood and after thanking the choir, gave instruction to the congregation as to upcoming events. BYW would be having a meeting next week at her house; the youth would be having a carwash to raise money for back-to-school items for the less fortunate. Lastly, she gave a call for anyone who wished to testify.

Mrs. Coleman began to rise but was quickly pulled back down by her daughter. Suffering from dementia, it was uncertain what she would say. She disrupted church for a minute as she admonished her daughter for stopping her but soon quieted down.

Russ noticed the gold sequins in Effie's dress reflecting on the back wall as Revered Hightower made his way to the pulpit. Her hat was so big Russ wondered if the people sitting behind her could see and he turned around to find them leaning to the side to see around her. A sea of similar hats dotted the congregation.

Reverend Hightower was a large man. His voice was deep and rich, and he made an extra effort to slow himself as he pronounced his words very succinctly. His speech pattern was slow, and he used that for effect to make a point. At times, he would speak softly only to follow that up with a booming voice that would shake the walls. His message this Sunday was on forgiveness. Russ wondered if Effie planted a seed with the good reverend. He wondered if this message was just for him. He thought about his father and forgiveness. Forgiveness for Randy was hard to consider.

The service ended after an hour and a half. Russ was exhausted but invigorated. Praise, compliments, and well wishes were heaped on him as he and Effie made their way to the door.

"You know a lot of these people been prayin' for you," Effie said bending down to whisper.

"Really, but they don't even know me."

"Don't matter, God know who they're talkin' about."

Effie and Russ walked next door to the convenience store to pick up a few things for lunch. Russ reached for the door and heard a voice that quickly made him forget about forgiveness.

"Where the hell did you and your bitch of a mother go?"

Russ turned and saw Randy standing behind him propping himself on his grandfather's truck with one hand and holding his pants up with the other. A six pack in his free hand. Effie quickly moved to Russ.

"Who the hell is this darkie?" Randy asked spurting hate mixed with spit.

"Who am I? Who the hell are you?" Effie asked, now standing in front of Russ.

Effie easily outweighed Randy by two hundred pounds. She stood defiant, her hands on her hips slowly working the strap on her purse tighter around her hand.

"I'm that little bastard's father," Randy said slurring every word.

"Daddy! Please, stop!" Russ said begging Randy to leave them alone.

"Daddy, Stop," Randy said mocking Russ in a high-pitched tone. As Randy said that, he placed the six pack on the truck and lunged toward Russ. As he did, Effie stepped back and swung with all of her weight landing her purse against Randy's head. He quickly went down. Her foot found his mid-section. Her weight behind the kick. A crowd from the church soon formed from across the street. Effie smiled at the crowd and worked Russ in front of her and through the door of the store. Russ turned and looked back toward Randy, who was now rocking on all fours trying to get to his feet. Men from the church picked him up and threw him into his truck.

"How are you supposed to forgive someone like that?" Russ said, his chin quivering, fighting against tears.

Effie was surprised that he had listened so closely to the sermon. She wanted to tell him something spiritual, but couldn't find the words. She agreed with Russ. "*Parents shouldn't exasperate their children;" that's in the Bible.*"

CHAPTER THIRTY

Danny Crabs continued to heal from his run in with Johnny Dollar. He made a mental note not to mention his love for underage girls to anyone ever again. Apparently, there was no crossover in the sex trade when it came to pedophilia.

He took a broken deep breath around the pain that still existed in his torso. He reached a hand in his mouth. Two teeth were still loose and needed to be pulled. He ripped a band-aid off and applied more antibiotic cream on a wound and reapplied a new band-aid. The stitched cut was closing up and healing.

He walked into the bedroom and stared where his money had been before it was taken. He had stared at the same spot a thousand times as if it would magically reappear. Hoping he had just missed it all the other times. Hoping something may have fallen on it and covered it. He moved the corner of a shirt that had at one time laid on top of the bag. Still nothing.

He fell hard onto the bed after standing to be sure the money still wasn't there. He winced at the pain and sucked in hard to absorb it, then took out the pistol from the bedside table. Quick shots of pain found his head again, and he took a drink from the bottle that sat on the floor at the foot of the bed. He spit it out. Still unable to drink the brown whisky. Still unable to take the burning of the open sores that had yet to heal inside his mouth. He worked his way through the trash, stepping over broken bits of glass and remnants of dog excrement and made his way to the kitchen. He opened and slammed kitchen cabinets and finally found a used straw and pulled it from a bottle of coke. Sliding the straw into the bottle of Jack Daniels, he slid the straw as far back into his mouth as he was able without choking and suck down as much whiskey as he could stand. He placed the pistol under his chin again and squeezed his eyes shut anticipating the pain. He pulled it away and drew himself into a clump of sobbing mass and stuck the straw into his throat again, pulling in the medication.

His memory of the day he retrieved the money pounded in his head since he realized it was gone. It was the easiest money he had ever made. The man lay dead in his recliner. Hadn't been dead long. His trailer empty. He snooped around, Madison trailing behind him. He held her hand tight, dragging her mostly. He took a coin collection. He found a receipt on top of the old man's wallet. A cashed retirement check. Under it the cash. He placed it in his pocket. He found women's jewelry. A diamond ring that he hoped was real. Loose pearls that looked as if they had just fallen from an oyster. A gold pocket watch in a small box that sat in red velvet. He took it out and looked on the other side searching for initials or personal markings. There were none.

He grabbed a plastic garbage bag from the kitchen and

walked back to the man in his recliner and spun him around.

"You stand still," he said to Madison.

He grabbed a corner of the back of the man's recliner and pulled. The Velcro that held the false back pulled off and cash fell to the floor.

"Help me," Danny said to Madison. They both bent to fill the bag. He replaced the back on the chair and looked around the trailer.

He took the man's belongings home and hid them. He locked Madison in her room and returned to the man's trailer, called 911, and waited for the police. The ambulance arrived along with city authorities. He gave them his statement.

The police only asked if he had disturbed anything. Of course, he had not. He completed his statement. A pained expression and a wipe of the nose alerting the police to the sadness of his friend's passing.

He stared at the pistol again. He couldn't do it. Maybe there was money left. There were always other girls whose parents weren't keeping a close eye on. He could get money other ways. Go to the casinos. Watch the old people win and follow them home. Just as he had done in the past. Just as he had been taught.

He purchased a brown seersucker suit, a white shirt, and a striped tie from a thrift shop two streets over from where he lived. He found a pair of old wingtips in his closet. He blew the dust off of and shined them.

The following day at noon he took a shower and shaved. He dressed in his suit, clipped on his tie, tied his shoes and went to a barber for a high and tight. For the first time in close to twelve years, he saw himself in a full mirror.

"I could pass for a detective," Danny quietly thought as he stared at the reflection.

He walked around the corner to a nail salon and left with a fresh manicure. Danny visited the same doctor behind the Chinese restaurant. He had his photo made and after some cutting and pasting, he had a badge and identification. The transformation was complete. It was now up to him to say the right things and get in front of the right people.

He pulled the list of strip joints from his new suit coat pocket and stared at it, running his eyes over the names. He wasn't sure where to begin, so he decided to start at the top and work his way down.

He parked his mangled truck far away from the entrance each time. The fake badge and I.D. cost him fifty dollars, and, so far, it had been working. Many of the girls talked to him. He had been through the top five on the list; and so far, no one knew anyone named Platinum save for one stripper at The Purple Pony, but that Platinum was a black girl.

There were two more locations left on the list, and he began thinking this was another dead end.

Danny exited the next-to-last club feeling defeated and decided to just give up. She could be anywhere in the world. With absolutely nothing to go on, there was really no way to find her. He thought of the pistol again.

Out of habit, he started in the direction of his old trailer and pulled up into the parking lot beside Mike's place to turn around. He stared at the door and looked around the parking lot.

He walked in thinking he would give it one last shot. He flashed his badge to the bouncer who actually wasn't a bouncer. He was Mike's teenaged son who was really there to take up the cover charge, half of which he pocketed when Mike wasn't there.

"I need to speak with the manager," Danny said with authority in his voice, flopping the fake ID in front of the boy just like he had seen on television.

"Sway!" the boy called out and Danny saw a man dressed as a woman walk toward him. The walk was Sway's best impression of Mae West with bad feet. Her blonde wig was large and framed with a feather boa. For a man, Danny thought, she wasn't bad looking.

He pulled his badge from his coat pocket just as he had all day and asked Sway if she could sit and talk for a minute. She agreed and sat Danny at a table before leaving to get them a couple of drinks.

Danny looked around the room. He was shocked to see three girls that he knew. They had given him lap dances before. No one recognized him.

Sway returned with a beer for herself and a water for Danny.

"What can I do for you?" Sway asked in a deep voice.

Danny had repeated his story enough that he sounded much more convincing, even to himself.

"I'm sure you have recently heard about the death of one of the working girls run by Boogie Corleone."

Sadly, Sway nodded her head.

Danny continued, "We've discovered another girl is missing by the name of Platinum; you know anyone by that name?"

Shaking her head, Sway said no and called a few of the other girls to the table. Danny began getting nervous, worried he could be recognized.

"This is a cop looking for a girl named Platinum; any of you know anyone by that name?"

They all shook their heads in unison except China Doll. Something didn't feel right about this to her. She had just talked to Jaimey. She knew where she was, and she knew she was on the run from someone down here. Was this the man? Shrugging, China Doll shook her head, no one named Platinum.

Danny struck out again. His fickle mind returned. If these girls didn't recognize him, would Madison?

CHAPTER THIRTY-ONE

Randy woke with the first slow sensation of cotton in his mouth. His head was pounding as if he had stood in front of a six-foot speaker at a Metallica concert, and he smelled himself. He was still wearing the same clothes he had put on three days ago when he last remembered consciousness. His efforts to wash away the blood and vomit were lazy at best, and his pants were soaked with urine and soiled with his feces.

He lay quietly, dazed, stretching his brain to think of what day it might be. Slowly, images of Russ and a large black woman filled his memory. He tried counting the days since the woman hit him with her purse but soon gave up the math and began the effort to get out of bed. As he stood, his waist no longer held his pants up. He tripped as they fell to his ankles. He assumed his former position and gathered his pants, squeezed them at the waist, and started toward the kitchen.

He opened the refrigerator. The stench of rotting food permeated the room. The electricity was disconnected soon after Russ and Jaimey left. He held his hand to his mouth then bent over a garbage can, but all he could muster was a dry heave.

Going to the refrigerator was a habit. His beer was in a cooler out in the garage.

The mail was the only thing that had not been cut off. He hadn't checked it in several days. He made his way to the mailbox, shuffling his bare feet on the driveway, patting himself for a lone cigarette.

"One cigarette, and no match...no lighter," he mumbled incoherently.

Randy neared the mailbox. A neighbor drove slowly as she approached him, a look of disgust on her face.

"Got to hell, bitch!" Randy shouted around the unlit cigarette hanging from his mouth.

He opened the mailbox. It was full, mostly of junk mail. There was an old past due notice from the electric company and a small package addressed to Russ. He stared at the package immediately recognizing the handwriting. It belonged to Randy's sister who lived in Batesville. *"Happy Birthday, Russ"* was scribbled on the front in large letters with balloons and stars drawn on it in bright, brilliant colors.

He quickly tore into the package and tossed two tickets to the Bellsouth Classic in Memphis to the ground. He moved around two head covers and a Calloway glove and grabbed the envelope on the bottom of the box.

He ripped it open and read the note inside.

Happy Birthday! The classic is in two weeks. Come stay with us, I'm sending a little spending money for the tournament.

Love you and happy birthday,

Aunt Lisa

"I'm sending you a little money for the tournament,"

Randy mocked in a sarcastic, high-pitched voice as he repeated the partial note in jealous disgust.

A crisp new one-hundred-dollar bill crinkled in Randy's fist as he reached again to adjust his pants and bend over to pick up any evidence that there was ever a package in the mail for Russ's birthday.

"Thanks, sis!" Randy mumbled around his cigarette as he made his way back toward the house.

He tossed the tickets and the rest of the mail in the garbage as he stumbled to the cooler for his last beer. His day was made- a beer in one hand and a one-hundred-dollar bill in the other.

His closet was bare. One pair of pants hung on a wire hanger. He looked around the floor for a shirt that looked to be the cleanest and scooped it up. From there he found the bathroom looking for soap and shampoo. It had been weeks since anyone had gone to a store of any kind, and there was none. He remembered seeing some dishwashing detergent in the carport storage room after Russ had used it to wash the car.

Noel Mitchell designed the house in the late fifties. He built the house after the war when he was able to save the down payment. On one side on the garage, were two large storage rooms. It had now become Randy Crawford's headquarters for drinking, and smoking, and sitting, watching the hours tick by. A place to sit and feel sorry for himself.

Randy made his way toward one of the storage rooms and began rifling through the leftover items from a lifetime lived by Marjorie and Noel Mitchell. Old tools, lawn chairs, coolers, boxes of tax receipts from the 1960's. Above him were a line of six leather dog collars that served as memorials for Noel's birddogs. Most had died from old age except for Lulabelle. She died after getting bitten by a rattlesnake on the trip to Texas. The loss was hard for Noel. He tried so hard to get her to the vet that day, but they were too far from town.

Seeing the collars brought back a flood of memories. Years of quail hunting with his own father and Noel. As a kid, he spent time on his uncle's plantation in Rolling Fork; and when they weren't working, they were hunting either quail or ducks.

He was with Noel on the Texas trip. Always impressed with how much Noel cared about and for his dogs. Lula-belle's death hit Noel hard; he always felt responsible somehow, although he couldn't explain why.

Unable to find what he was looking for, Randy took one last perusal then made his way into the next one. This one looked more promising. He saw many of their things from the hasty move. He looked on the wall at several shelves and finally saw what he was looking for.

"Well, the little shit finally did something I told him to," Randy snarled as he reached for the dishwashing detergent. He quickly found an old sponge and looked around for a small cooler he could mix the detergent and water in. He saw a cooler beside their boxes from the coast and grabbed it. As he turned to leave, the corner of a green army duffle bag caught his eye. He had seen Noel with a similar bag on every hunting trip he ever went on.

He grabbed it, ready to take another trip down memory lane. He pulled it from under the myriad of boxes and other items that had been heaped on top of it. He unzipped the top and was immediately shocked and elated and confused all at the same time as he stared at the bag full of cash.

Even in his drunken stupor, Randy knew the cash wasn't Noel's. He knew Noel was a stickler about keeping his money safely in the bank for fear of losing it or someone stealing it.

He picked up the bag and headed inside the house locking the door behind him. His heart beat wildly as he stared at the cash. His mind crazed with thoughts of the money and what he would do with it. He thought about using it to start over, reinvest it in a property and slowly build his way back up just like he did before. The thought of all the hard work and failure creeped back into his mind. He thought of the long hours and hard work and instead focused on a much faster way to make money. One that didn't require as much work and was much more fun. It was located thirty minutes down the road, and they had food and free drinks there.

Randy had been the only one near the house in weeks except for the utility workers that disconnected the water and electricity, but still the paranoia kept him from thinking logically. He made his way to the farthest room in the house and locked the door behind him. He threw the duffle bag on the bed, turned it over to dump it out. When he did, he noticed a name in block print on the side "WILLIAMS."

"Who in the hell is Williams?" Danny mumbled softly to himself.

His curiosity subsided quickly as he considered it may have been an old army buddy of Noel's. He finished dumping the money on the bed. Hundreds, twenties, and fifties poured out. He began counting. He stopped several times and started over, unable to focus for long.

He started over, organizing all the cash into stacks according to their denominations. As he picked up a small stack of cash, a small plastic bag full of a white substance fell from the stack. He picked it up and held it up close to his eyes.

"Cocaine?" he asked the empty room confused.

He realized this wasn't Noel's bag. It was near all of their stuff they had brought from the coast. *"Jaimey got this money somehow,"* he thought.

"How in the hell did she get this?" he asked. "The name has to be a trick's name," he spoke into the empty room.

He left the room to retrieve a pen and some paper. Returning, he tore the paper into strips and laid a strip on each stack as he totaled them. After counting several times, he was staring at $14,590. This was the most money Randy had seen in a long time. He had gambled more than this at one sitting so many times. His mind raced. The voice returned, telling him how to spend it. Telling him to gamble it all. Telling him it would double. Telling him he was someone different. Randy the drunk, Randy the loser, was now Randy the gambler again.

CHAPTER THIRTY-TWO

Danny Crabs returned to the trailer park and pulled up to the row of mailboxes that balanced on a rotting 2x6. The support post in the center rotted causing the center to sag. He retrieved his mail and stopped by the store located in the trailer park's office. He walked in and straight to the beer cooler and grabbed a case of Milwaukee's Best. He placed it on the counter. The owner handed him an overdue bill for lot rental refusing to sell him the beer until it was paid.

"Your first month's rent is past due; you're not buying beer from me until you get caught up."

Danny tore into the case of beer and started throwing the full cans of beer at the man, hitting his landlord. He cracked the glass on the meat counter. He walked to the owner, grabbed him by the collar, and punched him twice.

"You'll get your money when I get mine."

He grabbed the rest of the beer and headed to his trailer. Once inside, he began tearing the place up. Anything he could find, he picked up and threw, drinking beer between tantrums. He grabbed one end of the small loveseat and turned it over grabbing the cushions and throwing them.

He stopped long enough to grab another beer and catch his breath. As he opened it, he looked down at the floor; and, in the middle of the mess, he noticed a card. He reached down, picked it up and flipped it over in his hand. A Mississippi Driver's License- Jaimey Mitchell Crawford. He looked at the photo in the corner. A blonde woman smiled at him.

"Platinum, found you, bitch!" Danny said chugging another beer.

Danny immediately jumped into his truck and headed toward the address on the license. He began thinking of what he would be able to do with his money back. He would get the landlord off of his back and pay him a year in advance. He reached into the glove compartment and took out his KA-BAR knife. He stuck it behind him in his belt. He switched the handle facing to the right so he could easily reach it.

Following a city map, he drove to the address.

"All this time, she's only lived two and a half miles away," Danny said, almost shouting.

The unpainted townhomes weathered by the salt air showed their age. They sat in the middle of a development of low-income housing. The units stood in quads, reflecting the Spanish influence of the coast.

He glanced quickly at his badge and adjusted the KA-BAR so it was now hidden by his suit coat. He was still sweating from his outburst and the speed at which he drove to the Palm Breeze apartment complex.

He sat still, parked near the unit for several minutes, watching, trying to calm himself. He made his way to the door and knocked, readying himself to force his way in. He placed his hand on the handle of the KA-BAR as the door slowly opened. He looked down at a small girl now standing in front of him after struggling with the weight of the door.

"Madison?" Danny asked, confused.

"No, sir, my name is Kelly," she said, smiling up at the man.

"Is your mommy home? I'm Detective Williams."

Danny stared at the girl. He could snatch her and be gone before anyone knew what happened. His heart started racing as he planned the abduction in his mind. His developing fantasies quickly cut short as a voice behind him asked if he needed help. He slowly turned toward the voice behind him.

"I'm Detective Williams with the Biloxi Police Department; how are you?" Danny asked, flashing his badge and managing a soft smile that covered his lack of teeth.

"Just fine," the lady said as she made her way between her daughter and Danny.

"You go inside and play," she said as she shut the door behind her.

"What could I do for you?"

"My department is investigating the disappearance of a Jaimey Mitchell Crawford, and this was her last known address."

"Yes! She moved out just before we started renting here. She left a few things; I've been meaning to throw them out. Would you like them?"

"That would certainly aid in our investigation, ma'am; thank you," said Danny.

She vanished into the apartment and returned with a small shoebox and a piece of paper.

"Was this all, ma'am?"

"That's all I seen in here. They left this place a damn mess, they was shit everywhere; hope you find her," the lady said as she closed the door in Danny's face.

Danny quickly made his way back to his truck and started to go through the box of items. The piece of paper still wadded up in his hand. In the box was an Ole Miss Alumni magazine, three Bob Seger tapes, one mixed tape, an overdue electric bill, and an eviction notice from the property management company.

Danny sat there after hitting one more roadblock, ready to give up again as he flipped through the Alumni magazine. It fell open to the center. A young lady dressed in a white evening gown, a crown sitting on her head and a large bouquet of flowers draped across her arms, Jaimey Mitchell Crawford, Homecoming Queen, University of Mississippi.

"Holy shit! She was a homecoming queen at Ole Miss," he said out loud, confused.

He began reading the short blurb. Jaimey was among a group of former homecoming queens that the magazine revisited. Then his eye landed on the sentence that he had been looking for. *Jaimey Mitchell Crawford, originally from Lewiston, Mississippi, was currently residing in Biloxi, Mississippi.*

As Danny read, he realized the paper was still wadded up in his hand. He unfolded it. It read *M&D 662-555-5629.* He quickly drove to a payphone and turned to the first page of the phone book. A list of all area codes for the state were listed, and he followed his finger down the list until he came to 555-Lewiston.

"That's it. She's gone home."

CHAPTER THIRTY-THREE

The image of Jaimey and Russ in the cart shed played heavy on Cappy's mind. It was no longer safe for Russ to be working by himself in town. The commute alone from his house to town just didn't make sense as Russ's mowing times were so erratic. He didn't understand how Randy was able to still be walking around a free man.

He met Bubba Stewart on the number ten fairway as Bubba dumped a truckload full of dirt near the new green. Cappy recounted the story. He told Bubba about Randy. He described how badly Jaimey and Russ were beaten and how they spent the night in the cart shed. How he couldn't send him out to mow any longer. Randy had been released from jail again. It wasn't safe. Russ needed a job.

"Hell, I could use some help out here," Bubba quickly said. "The club could afford minimum wage; let's get him out here."

The expansion of the fairway and new green was needed. The number ten hole had been a pretty easy par four. It allowed a straight shot, and, as it sat, was just over three hundred and fifty yards. On a dry day, especially on the tail end of a long drought when the ground was rock hard, a well-placed drive could bounce its way onto the green leaving the ball feet from the hole.

In 1974, Hugh Jack Rives made a hole-in-one, an albatross, on number ten. Hugh Jack usually played by himself, but that day he was needed to complete a foursome. Without witnesses, a hole-in-one never happens. The plaque honoring Hugh Jack remains on the tee box today.

With the expansion of the hole, Hugh Jack's hole-in-one on a par four stands as the only albatross in club history. To commemorate the shot, Bubba had a new, more substantial marker complete with an etching of Hugh Jack's face made. It told the story in more detail than the original marker did. A dedication ceremony was planned. The only two remaining witnesses as well as Hugh Jack himself would unveil the marker as soon as the construction was complete. The annual Hugh Jack Rives memorial tournament has already been scheduled for a fall date in October.

Russ started the next morning. Cappy watched as Bubba walked him through the expansion. He showed him the extension of the fairway and where the new green was to be built. He started twenty yards behind the current tee box and walked Russ the roughly three hundred and sixty yards to where the fairway would turn and continue left toward the fairway.

"So, if a good shot is hit off the tee, it should land somewhere right about here." Bubba said as he planted a red landscape flag in the ground. From there, he walked Russ toward the woods behind a measuring wheel. Walking roughly one hundred yards, Bubba stood in a clearing beside an old live oak tree.

"We're standing in the middle of where the new green

will be. This used to be an old garden spot years ago. There was an old house place where my shop is now." Bubba explained to Russ as he planted four flags in each corner of where the new green was planned.

"We need to take out these trees." Bubba said, walking toward them and tying flagging tape around the ones that would come out.

He and Russ tied tape around sixteen trees total leaving a narrow opening around the turn of the dogleg toward the green. Outlined by the lake and shaded by the sprawling oak, the number ten green was destined to be the most beautiful on the course.

As Russ and Bubba stood in the garden spot, Bubba pointed out to Russ the elevation change. "We'll have to build this up slightly, hard to see, but there's a pretty good drop right here. My plan is to slope it from the back so the ball will roll back toward the fairway. If the shot is missed on the backside the ball is gone. Hell, it'll never be found if it rolls off the green down into those woods. It'll have to be placed just so. We'll make a lot of 'em cuss on this one, that's for sure." Bubba said smiling as they both stared into the abyss of a dense pine thicket.

Bubba had been working on a backhoe or a dozier the better part of his life. He sat beside Russ teaching him to work the machine. For two full days, he sat beside him moving dirt, digging stumps loading cut trees into a burn pile. Russ took to it naturally. He dug trenches for draining, buried the stumps, knocked over additional trees and spread dirt to build up the green. Bubba delivered load after load of dirt and Russ spread it. Slowly building up the green.

He used the backhoe and learned to run the dozier, smoothing and grading. Bubba taught him how to feather the ground, and how to create drainage away from the green and toward the pond.

Once completed, the work they were doing would add approximately one hundred and twenty yards to the overall length of the fairway. Russ added a nice, terraced slope on the green just as Bubba instructed.

On the backside, Bubba's lake came into play, adding an additional water hazard. Russ and Bubba added the number eleven tee box near the backside of the number ten green, moving it back twenty-five yards, as well as elevating it. They brought the lake into play for the first fifty plus yards on number eleven.

Bubba watched Russ plan the elevations and shots from all over the fairway and around the green. He watched Russ as he took his shirt off to escape the heat and felt the shock when he saw Russ's back. Faded but still present marks and wounds in the process of healing were still evident. Bubba wiped at his eyes quickly as Russ hollered a question his way. He cleared his throat to answer him and gave him a thumbs up. Anger replaced the tears, and his concentration for the day ended. His desire to continue working left him.

Bubba watched Russ grab the pitching wedge strapped on the side of the backhoe and play a few shots as he worked. He played shots from different places on the approach and watched how the ball rolled on the green.

They left the original green intact for the upcoming tournament, and Russ worked around the golfers as they paced through their practice rounds.

Dan Woodrow sneered at Bubba and Russ on his daily walks around the course. He was the oldest member on the board and probably on the membership roll, but he hadn't voted for the new work on number ten. He didn't vote for the new sprinkler system either, sure that it would increase the water bill and the club would go broke. No way they could pump enough water from the four lakes on the course to supplement the city water supply into the course. He hated the new color they recently painted the clubhouse, and he especially disliked seeing women on the course.

He was the only member who didn't use a cart, claiming he walked for exercise. He walked because he knew it pissed off the other golfers.

The old man walked the entire course twice a day with two balls and a five-iron playing his way around all eighteen holes. Rarely did he allow anyone to play through, especially if the group were women. He enjoyed watching them squirm and become more impatient as he dragged out his shots and took longer finding an errant ball.

Russ didn't like the old man. He reminded of Randy. Never a kind word to say to anyone.

Russ made a larger than usual turn on the backhoe and ran over the old man's ball, burying it in the ground. He and Bubba sat in the wood line and watched as he looked for it for several minutes, slowing his play, causing the golfers behind the old man to play through, further infuriating him.

Many times, at the end of the day, Russ and Bubba sat in the edge of the woods and watched golfers play.

"You can learn a lot about people by watching them play golf," Bubba told Russ. "When people think no one is watching, their true colors come out."

They watched men kick balls out of the rough to play from a better lie. They saw dropped balls out of the line of sight of those they played against. They watched as men and women would emerge from the woods adjusting their clothing.

They mainly noticed men who lived at Beau Chene.

Who spent more time at the course than they did at home. Who drank, gambled and shared golf carts with women who weren't their wives, and when Monday morning rolled around, they went back to their jobs as bankers and lawyers and construction workers and then did it all over again the next weekend.

CHAPTER THIRTY-FOUR

Beau Chene was typical of most golf courses you find in small towns across the South. Even though the name sounded as if it belonged in Greenwich, Connecticut, it was the antithesis of a snobby country club located in some wealthy suburban enclave. There were a group of women who thought being a member of Beau Chene in Lewiston, Mississippi was the ultimate proof of wealth and prestige.

Monthly dues were sixty-five dollars. The golf course had no sand traps. The club house was nothing more than a renovated ranch style home. They built two additions onto it, since the new lumber mill came in to town, bringing more members.

It had a pool and two tennis courts that were somewhat neglected and always in need of maintenance and upgrades. The board was rarely interested, allocating the majority of the funds toward the golf course.

There were two types of memberships. The regular membership was a one thousand dollar buy in with a sixty-five dollar per month fee. This allowed voting privileges and made the individual a full-fledged member. The second was the Junior membership program. That buy in was for three hundred dollars with a thirty-five-per-month membership fee that would automatically upgrade when they turned thirty-five. To remain a member, the balance of seven hundred dollars was due; and the monthly fee increased to the sixty-five dollars. Junior Members were not allowed to vote.

Suzie Ward and her husband were junior members, and could barely afford that. She sat in the drive-thru line at the bank and asked the teller to give her her balance. It was close to the end of the month and she was overdrawn. She flipped through the calendar on her checkbook, three more days until payday.

Suzie flew into the 'Cutz and Curls on Main' salon and walked straight to the cash drawer and hit a button and took out two twenties. With a deft motion, her husband's nimble fingers unfurled long blonde hair from a roller. He worked quickly showing experience and confidence in his work.

"What are you doing?"

"I'm meeting the girls at the country club today to start decorating for the Classic and I need lunch money."

Suzie stared at the woman in the chair and simply spoke her name.

"Jane."

"Suzie," the woman said as she rolled her eyes. "Suzie decorating for the golf tournament again this year?"

"Lord, yes, she can't wait for school to be let out each year so she can start on that classic. Makes me work too! The rest of the time she lives out at that pool. Her daddy didn't know what he was creating when he had her at the country club for all those years. It's all she wants to do. It's like it's the most important thing to her. I think she's on every committee out there. You know, I can't say this to Suzie, but those ladies at that country club are just taking advantage of her, just workin' her like a dog. She thinks it's just dumb luck that she keeps landing on all those committees, but they know she'll do whatever they tell her to. It's sad, really," Jeffery said as he ran the brush through the newly curled hair.

"I'm in the Junior League with Suzie, and those women do the same thing to her there too. It is sad to watch."

"Well, she does it to herself. You ought to see her at that Methodist Church, does the same thing. Everything her momma does, she does. In front of that congregation every time an announcement needs to be made. Pulled me up there last Christmas with her whole damn family. We each had to read something. Lord, Honey, you know that's not my..."

Jeffery was interrupted by the front door swinging open.

"Are y'all talking about me?" Suzie asked as she made her way to the back. She reappeared with a bottle of confixor. "Put this on Judy Nell's account."

"Judy Nell doesn't have an account, I don't sell on credit," Jeffery said.

"Well just write it down, she'll pay for it next time she has an appointment."

"I guarantee you when she gives that to Judy Nell, it'll just be a gift. She's just trying to get information about that Jaimey Crawford that just moved here. You heard about her? Her son is that hotshot golfer out at the country club, she apparently was a hooker down in Biloxi."

"A hooker?"

"Yeah girl! Can you believe that? A real hooker!"

A line of brown dust followed in a four-car caravan beside the number one fairway as Suzie led her committee toward the clubhouse.

Effie stood at the back door of the Nineteenth Hole wringing out a mop as she saw Suzie exit her car dressed like Madonna. Her red hair was teased high in a quasi-bouffant with a lace hairbow in the top. Her makeup looked as though she were preparing for a high school musical, and she wore leggings under a thin skirt with laced up black boots.

"That bitch looks ridiculous," Effie mumbled to herself.

Suzie loudly began directing her gaggle of hens to take boxes from her BMW for which she was two months past due on payments. The theme for the party was "Margaritas and Palm Trees." Four margarita stations were set up in strategic locations around the clubhouse. Each table had a palm tree centerpiece. Two large cardboard palm trees stood on either side of the front door and greeted the party-goers as they entered the clubhouse. A live parrot sat in a large cage at the end of the foyer. Seashells served as card-holders that she would freehand and try to seat everyone as her mother did for bridge. It never worked, and she never learned her lesson. People sat where they wanted to. She hired a seventies Jimmy Buffett cover band.

At Suzie's direction, the gaggle soon fanned out throughout the building placing decorations where they were told. Her plan was slowly coming together.

She made her way to Effie's kitchen to discuss the menu. She was apprehensive, deep down Effie scared her. She tried not to show it but Effie knew it the first time she met her, and it thrilled Effie. Effie didn't like Suzie Ward, and she didn't try to hide it.

The door to the kitchen flung open, and "Madonna" ran

through it with her arms reached out wide hanging in midair.

"Oh, Effie, it's so good to see you," Suzie said as she awkwardly lunged toward her, attempting to hug her without returned affection.

"How's Ray Ray?" Suzie asked, trying to sound much more familiar with Effie and her family than she really was.

"Ray fine," Effie said flatly.

Suzie pulled out a list from her purse to go over the menu with Effie when Fatboy and Russ came through the kitchen door. Effie immediately ran to each of them and hugged them completely ignoring Suzie.

"Cappy sent these to you," Russ said, handing Effie a bag of tomatoes.

"Fatboy, you don't have anything in your hand; you must want something?" Effie reached under a towel that covered freshly buttered cathead biscuits and gave one to each of them.

"Can I have one more?" Fatboy asked as he began to run away from Effie's playful attempt to hit him with the towel that hung from her shoulder.

"Was that the boy that's living with Mr. Capstick, Russ and his mother Jaimey?" Suzie asked, trying hard to glean information from Effie.

"Sounds like you know more than me," Effie said picking up the box of pineapples. "What you want me to do with these?"

"I heard she was a hooker down in Biloxi; is that true?" Suzie asked, hoping it was true. Before Effie could say anything, Suzie continued, "I mean how does someone go from homecoming queen at Ole Miss to hooker in Biloxi?"

Effie remained quiet and asked again, "You need to talk to me about the menu for Saturday night?"

Suzie was disappointed. This was the most scandalous thing that had hit Lewiston in a long time.

Suzie gave her instructions to Effie and left to join the other hens.

"Girls," she said, waving them to her. "I just confirmed it was true! She *was* a hooker down in Biloxi. Effie didn't deny it! That boy that was just here, the skinny one was her son, Russ. They are living with Mr. Capstick!" Suzie whispered, not wanting Effie to hear the words vomiting from her mouth.

Effie looked out of the kitchen door and saw the hushed conversation.

"She's goin' to hell!" Effie said as she ducked back into the kitchen.

CHAPTER THIRTY-FIVE

The Clubhouse Classic schedule was the same every year. Many of the local players took Thursday and Friday off from work and converged on Beau Chene and the town of Lewiston. The entire country club buzzed with excitement. The day was clear; the sky was blue and the course was lush and green. The atmosphere was electric. Everyone was looking forward to the long weekend filled with golf, food, drinking and gambling.

Suzie Ward showed up wearing a new Madonna outfit and looking as if she had used every can of hairspray available in Lewiston. She and Jeffery delivered the final decorations and a couple hundred pounds of crawfish to the nineteenth hole.

Jeffery followed closely behind her like a little puppy attending to her every command. With help, he unloaded four large coolers of crawfish and at least twenty bags of ice.

Suzie brought in two life-sized cardboard cutouts of a man and woman dressed in their finest luau attire with a hole cut out for faces. After she set them up, she handed Effie a Polaroid camera and asked her to take a picture of she and her husband as they stood there with their heads stuck through the holes smiling as if they were on a cruise ship.

"Here, Effie, you get in there and let me take your picture," Suzie said stretching every syllable in the sentence and creating some that weren't there to begin with.

"You're crazy as hell; I ain't doin' that. That's a white woman's body anyway," Effie said in disgust.

Jeffery quickly tried to herd Effie behind the cutouts.

"You better take yo' damn hands offa me if you know what's good for you," Effie said as she made her way back into the kitchen.

Jeffery stood there, all five-foot-eight inches, Hawaiian shirt, long khaki shorts that fell below his knees. The shorts starched and held onto his waist with a belt that had palm trees and pink flamingos embroidered on it. He wore stark white socks pulled up over his calves that constantly fell because he had no calves. His legs were the same circumference from top to bottom and almost as white as his socks were. He wore a new pair of white canvas tennis shoes. A whole new outfit just for the weekend.

When Jeffery spoke, he used his hands and waived them like most women do to make points they're unable to make verbally. He was very expressive. His fingernails were manicured and shining. His hands were slight and soft.

"You know that fool got a new outfit for everyday of this weekend. He don't even play golf, barely can play tennis." Effie said to Ray Ray, who couldn't stop staring at Jeffery.

Thursday was always practice day for The Clubhouse Classic. The original pin placements were installed for Friday's play. The beds were freshly mulched. Coolers were placed on each green ready for waters and ice. The greens were cut and the stage was set up for the band. Bubba and Russ took the rest the week off, the heavy equipment silenced for the tournament.

Cappy gave Effie a quick kiss on her cheek as he and Russ walked through the back door for lunch.

"You stop that, William," Effie said embarrassed but liking the attention.

"Can we get a couple of cheeseburgers and some drinks, Effie?" Cappy asked.

"Jeffery out there, and that Suzie girl too," Effie said as a warning to Cappy.

As they made their way through the swinging doors into the main dining room, Jeffery quickly made his way to Russ.

"Hello, Russ! Jeffery Ward," Jeffery said as he stuck his hand out, sheepishly introducing himself.

"I hope your sweet mother will be joining us this weekend," Jeffery said with a look of anticipation.

"Not sure if she will," Russ said.

"I would love to m..." Cappy interrupted Jeffery, calling Russ to their table.

"It's a good idea to stay clear of that fella, Russ; he's the biggest gossip in Mississippi. He's just looking for some fresh information to use as talking points at his beauty parlor next week."

Jeffery didn't golf; he had never picked up a club. He watched. He was all over the course, watching, listening, gleaning information. He watched couples, easing up on them straining to hear their conversations. Jeffery spent too much time in the men's room after he finished washing his hands craning, staring.

After lunch, Cappy had Fatboy and Russ playing as a

team practicing shots. Driving them to different spots on the course setting up shots and approaches on various holes. They played the center of the fairway, the edge of the woods, the edge of cart paths and sidewalks. He placed balls behind pine trees and in the pine straw. He placed a ball on the edge of the water. They practiced hitting left-handed. Cappy took them through the paces of what they practiced daily. He watched them, sweating through a grueling hot day.

CHAPTER THIRTY-SIX

The briny smell of the Gulf of Mexico eventually gave way to the scent of pine as Danny Crabs made his way north toward the central part of Mississippi. He put Madison out of his mind, knowing he could always get another girl any time he wanted.

He changed the channel on the radio and settled on a rock station. "Devil Inside" by INXS was playing, and Danny sang along with the lyrics, best he could keep up.

The lyrics fed that place inside of him that was already dark, cultivating his festering hate. He set his eyes on the knife, making sure it was there and patted his pocket to be sure he remembered the mace. He glanced in the rearview mirror at the Louisville Slugger that balanced on the gun rack behind him. The bat's logo was peppered with small droplets of dried dark blood. He pulled Jaimey's driver's license from his chest pocket and stared at her face, committing it to memory.

"You have no idea what's on the way to you," he mumbled out loud.

As Danny exited Highway 49 onto Highway 59 moving

north, he had no real plan. He had waited so long for this information, once he found it, he immediately took to the road. He did stop to shower and shave and grab weapons. Beyond that, however, he would just have to wing it. He didn't have a "next step" if she wasn't in Lewiston. He looked again at the card and her address. He reached under his seat and pulled out a map. There was no city map for Lewiston.

He pulled into a gas station and saw a billboard advertising The Golden Star casino. He made his way inside and to the tall, round carousel that held maps and *Gazetteers*. He flipped through a *Gazetteer* until he found the city of Lewiston map toward the back. He pulled out the torn sheet from the alumni magazine and read her address again and ran his finger down the page until he found the street name. The address looked to be just off of the highway. He folded the book, opened a button on his shirt, and stuffed it inside, smoothed it down, paid for his gas and drove straight to the casino.

The landscape changed drastically as the Indian reservation came into view. He left behind old faded stores, scarce city landscaping and drove into money, new money. The kind of money casinos generate. The kind of money that make boulevards plush and green, freshly weeded and mulched. Healthy flowers changed seasonally.

There were crews crawling the grounds like ants, raking and shoveling, sweeping and cleaning. The parking lots were full. He pulled into the first entrance he came to and drove around to the back until he found a place to park.

Once inside, he walked the floor watching and listening. He scoured the casino and waited, listening for bells to go off, for screaming, for celebration. He listened for shouts of joy and the sound of hands slapping together. Listening for someone to win.

He walked the floors. He played a slot machine here and there, keeping his ears opened, watching people's faces. The casino was full. Mostly older, retired couples. Men and women of advanced age sitting at slot machines for hours on end, killing another day. Cigarettes hanging from their lips and oxygen tubes stuck up their noses. They trudged from slot to slot pulling their tanks, holding their cigarettes and ashtrays in their free hand, their plastic cups of quarters shoved in their arm pits. Elderly people without anything to do until the casino came to town. *Weekend warrior gamblers*, he called them. Warriors unable to keep their cool when they won.

"They always want the world to know when they strike it rich," Danny grumbled out loud.

Danny favored the areas where the slot machines met the crap tables, met the poker tables. The TRIAD he called it. The best place to be in a casino. He stood as close to the center of the TRIAD as he could waiting and watching and listening. Using the reflection of the shiny steel of the slots, always mindful of the eye in the sky.

Cameras dotted the ceilings like clouds on an overcast day. Teams of people behind them watching for people just like him. Teams of security people glued to the cameras, watching for a slight of hand, signals shot across poker tables and watchers waiting to see who wins big so they can follow them home.

Danny picked through the casinos out west until he was caught and evicted from each one until he had run through them all. He hit the small truck stop casinos that handled justice in a more direct manner. He was thrown through the back door by a small group of large men that made sure he never came back again.

He came out of retirement when the riverboat gambling finally picked up in south Mississippi and Louisiana. Compared to Vegas, the smalltown casinos were on a reservation in the middle of nowhere. Unsophisticated as Vegas or even the riverboat casinos of the Gulf Coast.

He walked the TRIAD staring into the faces of the pit bosses and dealers, he scanned the pit bosses. Studying the faces of the men who stood behind them, watching their every move. They were large men, local. Not men of Italian descent. Staying away from the federally protected land of the Indian casino.

Danny stared into his slot machine his eyes drawing down becoming heavy when he was jolted by the sound of sirens and screaming and hollering from a slot two rows in front of him. He pulled the arm down for the final time and slowly made his way toward the sound. A husband and wife hugging each other. Well-wishers surrounding them. Handshakes and hugs from regulars. The both wore toothy smiles. The husband stood with the help of his walker held still by yellow tennis balls and kissed his wife on the cheek. His shaking hand patting her sweetly on the back, rubbing between her shoulder blades. The wife wiping tears of joy from her face handing what was left in her cup to a young couple.

The casino floor managers came to confirm their wins and walk patiently with them to the cashier's cage congratulating them along the way.

"We've been playing for years and have never hit," the woman said. They stopped at times so they could each catch their breath and the floor manager finally called for two wheelchairs to be brought to their location on the floor.

They finally arrived at the cashier's window and cashed in their ticket for ten thousand dollars. Danny walked to the nearest door and into the parking lot and to his truck. He sat and waited and watched as they were wheeled through the doors and to the handicapped parking near the door.

"Come on!" Danny shouted beating the palm of his hand on the steering wheel watching the process unfold too slowly. They both finally settled into their car. The walker and oxygen tank placed strategically inside the back seat, the couple finally placed the car in reverse and left.

Danny waited, letting them pull out of the parking lot before he fell three cars behind them. Their car moved along the street slowly, braking frequently, watching, looking as if they were searching for something. The car finally veered into a turn lane and sat for several minutes waiting for cars that were too far away. Impatient horns blared as they finally punched it and sped across the street dodging oncoming traffic and screeching tires.

The car bounced as it hit the incline to a convenience store finally coming to a stop near the gas pump. He pulled up and then backwards, repositioning his car straighter and nearer to a gas pump. Danny pulled up beside them. He watched the lady open her purse and slowly count the cash for the gas and the man finally exited the car. He retrieved his walker from the backseat and started toward the door. Danny placed his hand on his door handle when the man was halfway inside the store. As he opened the door, a motorcycle pulled on the opposite side of the old couple's car. He sat for a moment and slowly took off his helmet and hooked it on his right handlebar, straddled the bike with his wallet in his hand, and pulled out a credit card. He inserted it in the pump, and flipped the handle on the pump. He stepped off the bike and took off his gloves, then spoke through the window at the lady.

"Dammit!" Danny quietly said through gritted teeth as he strained to hear their conversation.

"My husband and I just won on the slots over at the casino, ten thousand dollars!" she exclaimed, smiling, proud.

"Congratulations!" the man said and opened door for the old man and offered to pump the gas for the couple.

The old man thanked him and offered him a ten. The offer was refused. Danny watched as the old man handed an ice cream cone to his wife. They waited for the gas to finish pumping. They thanked the man, cranked the car, and drove off. Danny stared at the man on the motorcycle as he drove past, and he fell in behind the couple again.

He followed them down a lonely stretch of road. The road was flanked on either side by swamps. Gravel roads ran perpendicular to the paved one they were on and Danny cussed himself as he watched his gas gauge fall deeper into the red.

He looked up from the radio just in time to see black shards from a rubber tire fly through the air almost hitting his windshield. The old man was fighting the steering wheel trying to slow the car and keep it on the road at the same time. He was soon forced off the road, rocks kicking up, finally stopping on a small gravel parking spot worn from fishermen and cars parking under the moonlight late at night. The red dust plumes settling on the green foliage around them.

The car shook as it came to a stop, and Danny could see the couple shaken, looking at each other unsure of what just happened. Danny pulled in behind the car and got out and looked up and down the road. He walked to the woman's side, his hands on his hips as he waited for her to gather her brain and motioned for her to roll her window down.

"You folks all right?" Danny asked. "Looks like you had a blowout.

"Hope you're okay," the man said. "It was flying up pretty good back there, hope it didn't hit your truck."

"No, I'm fine," Danny said.

Danny reached around and placed his hand on the handle of his knife just as a young woman in a car pulled up asking if the old couple needed help. He stood and waved her off, saying he would take care of it. He watched as the car picked up speed and disappeared over the hill. He looked in the other direction and pulled out the knife and bent back down and placed the blade under the line providing oxygen to the old lady.

"Give me the money."

The woman opened her purse and Danny reached in and grabbed the winnings. He replaced the line flat and withdrew his knife.

Danny tipped an imaginary hat their way. "Been nice doin' business with you. Y'all have a good day."

CHAPTER THIRTY-SEVEN

The garden hose was neatly coiled from the last time Noel Mitchell had used it. It was mildewed and embedded in fingers of grass holding it down to the earth. Randy unscrewed it from the house and began stretching it out in a straight line, pulling it from its grassy fingers and toward the neighbor's house, stumbling and falling several times as he did. The mildew left a black silky film on his hands, and he rubbed them in the grass to try and remove it.

He crept over to the neighbor's house and unwound their hose meeting the two in the middle between the houses and turned on the water. He pulled his end into the garage, closed the door, stripped nude and turned the hose on himself. The water was cold and it took his breath, immediately sobering him. For a second, he oddly felt good; he had a feeling of clarity that he had not felt in a long time. His stomach stopped hurting, although he was hungry. Hunger was a new sensation that he had not felt recently. He had craved only drink for so long, and now his body was telling him he needed food.

He grabbed the dishwashing soap and turned it up over his head. Using his fingers, he began washing his hair. He eventually washed his entire body, and repeated the process. It had been a while since he had bathed, and he needed it badly. When he finished, he stuck the hose back through the door, dried off and got dressed. He disconnected the hose and rewound the neighbors replacing it as he found it.

He made his way back into the house, packed his new change of clothes in his new suitcase, and headed south.

As Randy neared the casino, his heart raced. His pulse quickened, and it made him feel dizzy and weak. He had not yet eaten.

As he walked through the front door, his senses sparked. The sounds and colors and lights were like a drug to him, and he immediately forgot about eating. The "clanga clanga" of the slot machines drew him like a magnet to metal. He immediately had a fifty-dollar bill changed into twenty-five dollars' worth of quarters and twenty-five in tip money.

He quietly watched a group of old women playing the slots and patiently waited for them to stop playing and move to another part of the casino. He had a theory that slot machines were programmed to pay out after so many pulls. He thought it was smart to let someone else do all the work and he would swoop in and win the pot. Sure enough, after only a few more pulls, the women had done their job, and he hit the jackpot. The siren on top of the slot machine sounded, and, along with the constant clinking of quarters, it attracted everyone within earshot. Claps came from all over the floor. The women returned, shocked and amazed, wishing they had just stayed just a few more minutes.

Danny "Crabs" Williams slowly spun around and saw

the quarters flowing from the machine. Expecting to see the little old ladies who had just been there, he saw Randy instead, standing frail, smiling.

Randy fit the category Danny allowed himself for men. Randy looked weak. He was skinny. It was obvious to Danny that Randy had either a drug or alcohol problem. He easily outweighed Randy by one hundred pounds. Randy's hands trembled and he was unsteady on his feet. Randy won five hundred dollars. Danny kept his eye on him.

Danny had continued moving but had stayed out of sight of Randy. He now sat two slots down from him. Danny had only spent a couple hundred dollars from the time he arrived that included his winnings. As Danny was getting ready to call it a day and go to the buffet, he hit. His siren went off and the clanking started which attracted more attention his way. As usual everybody clapped and whistled.

Winning on the slots made him look like a normal gambler. To the eye in the sky, on the other hand, it drew attention that he didn't need.

Danny began extracting his quarters and filling up plastic cups. Randy came over to him, slightly intoxicated, and pulled out a wad of cash from his pocket.

"Can you give me twenty dollars' worth of quarters? My machine is hot, and I really don't want to get far from it," Randy slurred each word slowly as he handed Danny a twenty-dollar bill.

Danny noticed the wad of cash. Randy had flipped through fifties and a few hundreds to get to the twenty.

"Been playing long?" Danny asked, hoping Randy would begin to warm up to him.

"I used to be a professional, but I started losing; I'm

sure you know the rest of the story," Randy said, not answering the question and making little sense.

"I've been there myself," Danny said, hoping to form a bond.

Danny gave him the quarters and took the twenty and returned to his machine. For the next several hours, Danny watched as Randy had no more luck on the slots. He moved to the craps table and won. He nursed a pretty sizeable pile of chips. Danny stuck to Randy, waiting for him to tire, and cash out, and head home.

Danny watched Randy head toward the cashier's window and left toward the parking lot. He got in his truck and began watching. He soon noticed an older model truck slowly pull toward the back entrance. He watched as Randy exited his truck, and before he could get to the backdoor, he was met by the officials from the casino. As usual they made a quick perusal of the immediate area, handed Randy his winnings and sent him on his way.

Randy won three thousand dollars at the craps table and had a total winnings of roughly thirty-five hundred for the day. Danny watched a smile crossed Randy's face as he passed in front of him.

"I'll be wiping that smile off of your face pretty quick," Danny said out loud to himself as he pulled in behind him.

Randy took a right out of the parking lot and headed toward Highway 15 traveling north. It was easy for Danny to keep up as traffic was light in the small town. He became increasingly uneasy as the miles clicked by and Randy picked up speed driving farther from town. He noticed Randy's expired tag. It was from Leesburg County. He quickly gathered up the map from the floorboard. He glanced in short spurts until he found Lewiston. Under it, in scripted print, read *Leesburg County.*

"This couldn't be working out any better; he's taking me straight to Lewiston," Danny said out loud.

Another mile down the road, he saw a sign that read Lewiston ten miles. He glanced down at his fuel level, the needle was gaining on the red mark near "empty." A few more miles down the road Randy started slowing. His blinker began flashing, and he turned off of the highway. He made his way around a sharp curve, slowed down, put on his blinker again, and pulled into the neighborhood's entrance.

Danny slowed, creating more space between himself and Randy and watched as he pulled into the driveway of a ranch-style house on the right. Pulling up near the end of the driveway, Danny watched as Randy stumbled out of his truck and immediately started unzipping his pants. He began using the bathroom in his yard. Danny noticed the familiar drunk wobble. He knew how Randy felt. Randy zipped his pants and continued around toward the back of the house.

"He left the money," Randy thought to himself as he exited his truck and made his way toward Randy's. He slowly opened the door anticipating it to creak open, all the while watching through the front windshield for Randy. Seeing nothing on the front seat or floorboard, he looked in the backseat. He saw the corner of a green bag covered by wrinkled clothes on the passenger side floorboard and grabbed it. Still watching, he unfolded the bag to see what was inside. As he did, he noticed white block letters that had been spray painted when Danny entered the army fifteen years earlier... WILLIAMS.

Danny's heart began to race, but at the same time confusion took over his brain. That was his bag; and, as he looked inside, his money. That meant Platinum was here.

He grabbed the bag and the loose bills on the seat and hurriedly made his way back to his truck. Once there, he looked inside the bag again, and it appeared most of the money was there. His hands shaking, he grabbed the piece of paper with the address he had for Platinum. 101 Beau Chene Boulevard. The numbers on the house matched.

CHAPTER THIRTY-EIGHT

The Beau Chene residential neighborhood was two driveways beyond the entrance to Beau Chene Country Club. It was developed together as one of the first golf course housing developments in the area. Noel Mitchell's bank was the main lender for the development, and his house was the first to be built.

Many of the members lived here; they paid for the convenience to drive their golf carts the short distance to play. Trails were cut through backyards, eventually leading them to either the number nine or number eight fairways. Others rode along the highway to the cart sheds and then on to the number one tee box or pool or tennis courts. The clubhouse sat in the middle of it all, and the first tee box was a short ride from the front door.

Every house in the development was occupied, and there were waiting lists when they became vacant. When residents became sick, or a death occurred, ears perked up. Obituaries were read daily, and a list of their children with their last known phone numbers were kept at the ready.

The neighborhood was older with two-story houses

and long expanding ranch-style homes on either side of a boulevard. Old established oak trees lining both sides.

Considered to be the nicest neighborhood in Lewiston. The houses and yards were kept in pristine condition, except the house at 101 Beau Chene Boulevard.

Since Russ and Jaimey moved in with Cappy, the yard had not been mowed. The newspapers had piled up in the driveway, and were turning into a wet, pasty mush with every pass from Noel Mitchell's truck tires. The last time the house had been painted was when Noel did it himself six years earlier, not long before he died, and it was past time for a new roof.

Since the neighborhood was a part of the golf course, it was party central the weekend of The Clubhouse Classic. There was more than the usual traffic during the week. Everyone was buzzing around making last minute trips to the beer store and checking cart batteries for charge. They made sure they had plenty of cigarettes and cigars and most importantly, a concoction to relieve the pangs of hangovers. The boys knew the later your tee time, the more you could drink and the later you could party the night before.

Randy woke to a group of men shouting and talking loudly. He glanced out of the window and saw the commotion centered around some drunk that had tried to unload his cart off the back of his truck and slipped off the ramps. They were all arguing, trying to set the cart back up on the ramp and cussing the driver. They couldn't seem to make their bodies do what their minds were telling them they needed to do, and they eventually allowed the cart to fall to the ground.

Randy again went through the whole process of hooking up the garden hose to the neighbor's for another shower; more difficult since it was Saturday. People were home, and all of the extra buzz from the tournament made it almost impossible for him to slip around unseen.

In the distance, he heard men laughing and cussing, standing in circles in carports, drinking and telling dirty jokes with talk of the tournament sprinkled in. Conversation of strategy, type of balls and new drivers faded into the morning air. Garage after garage, yard after yard held men looking over new pitching wedges, new drivers, showing off new bags that were purchased for the tournament.

He was finally able to mend the two hoses together and took another sobering "shower" in the carport. Finished, he replaced the hose, cut off the water, got dressed and was in his truck heading south again. He wore the same clothes from the day before since he only had the one new set. He smelled himself and was satisfied he was ready for a day at the poker table.

———

Danny arrived early and parked in the line of cars at the end of the street watching Randy's house. He saw Randy leave and waited a short while to make sure he was gone. He imagined the reaction when Randy realized the money was no longer there. Regaining his money was the first piece of a three-piece puzzle. The second piece was about to be dead.

Leaving his truck parked where it was, Danny walked toward Randy's house. Satisfied that no one was paying attention to him, he darted onto the driveway and into the garage. He pulled his KA-BAR out of his waistband and held it at the ready. He tried the door, and was surprised to find it unlocked. He let himself in slowly and quietly, wincing at a slight groan of the door. He began to make his way around the house searching every room. Careful to close doors behind him, leaving everything as he found it. As soon as he closed a bedroom door, he heard the garage door make the same noise it did when he entered. He quickly slipped into the attached bathroom.

Listening for the door to close again, he was startled when the door to the bedroom he was in opened. Looking through the crack in the door, he squeezed his KA-BAR tighter. He anticipated seeing Platinum, but was confused to see a plump black woman enter the room. He watched as she began opening drawers and taking bras and underwear and placing them in a paper grocery bag. She moved through the house in a hurry. Danny noticed she held a small .38 snub-nosed revolver in her hand.

Hurriedly, she packed as much as the grocery bag would hold and left. Danny listened for the door to the garage to close, and when it did, he ran to the door and cracked it open just enough to watch as Effie got into her calico-colored 1976 Fleetwood Brougham Cadillac and slowly back down the driveway. He darted across the driveway and toward his truck. Effie made a large loop and turned two driveways down into the entrance to the country club.

Danny made the turn with Effie and suddenly found himself in the middle of a huge crowd of people who were staring at him. The condition of his truck forced every eye on him. Attracting attention to a stranger that didn't look like he belonged there. He felt exposed and realized if Platinum *were* here, there were too many witnesses anyway. He turned around as if he had made a wrong turn. He got back out on the opposite side of the highway, and turned his truck around so he had a view of the entrance. He turned the ignition off and waited.

He watched intently for Effie's car. Hours passed as golf carts and car after car, vehicles of all types, entered and exited the road. Trucks with tables and chairs in the back made their way toward the clubhouse. A van with "The Boys of Summer" cover band, painted on the side, disappeared in a cloud of dust. Danny worried that Effie was going to slip right by him. He finally saw the Cadillac turn onto the highway and allowed a few car lengths between them before he pulled in behind Effie.

CHAPTER THIRTY-NINE

J aimey's nerves made her reconsider going to the Calcutta. The party the night after would be even bigger. Two nights away, and she was already nervous. Two nights in the middle of all those people. As she spent more time alone, her mind began to wander. The stares, the gossip. The talk she imagined about Russ and how Cappy was involved. They would pick out the most negative parts, not the good that Cappy was doing. She was a prostitute, or rather former prostitute, as Cappy kept telling her. Regardless, she needed to be there for Russ. She had not been there for him for so much of his life, and she knew it was past time to start making up for that.

As Jaimey waited for Effie, she paced around Cappy's home. She re-read his name again and again: *William O'Brien Capstick*. It was written on citations, diplomas and commendations from the Army. They hung on the walls all over Cappy's home.

Margaret's photo was in every room. Cappy told her he felt comfort seeing her regardless of which room he happened to be in. He had never remarried after she died.

"She was my one and only true love."

Sleepless late-night conversations usually involved Margaret. Cappy would hear Jaimey up pacing the floors unable to sleep, and he would put on a pot of coffee and join her. She emptied her worried mind onto him, and he told her about Margaret and the war. He told her things he had never told anyone. The death. Seeing his friends die in front of him. He described their deaths and talked about the most evil and horrific things he had seen. She realized later he was trying to show her that her life could be worse.

"It's dangerous for people to be by themselves with nothing but their thoughts at particular times in their lives," he would say to her.

Story after story he told her.

"I met Margaret in a MASH unit in Korea. She was my nurse. She was the first person I saw after waking from surgery following a grenade blast. I fell in love with her the moment I opened my eyes. She sat up with me late at night, after her shift ended, and read letters from my momma, and we would talk. Over the next year, whenever we got some R&R, we met in Hawaii and spent the weekend together. She was only the second girl I ever kissed."

Jaimey stared at Margaret's photos and thought about the person she had to be to make a man Like William Capstick be loyal even in death for so many years.

Jaimey felt herself become jealous of Cappy and Margaret. She wished she could experience only half the love that he has for her.

In every letter Margaret sent a photo of herself and Cappy had them in every room of the house. Every room Jaimey went in, Margaret was there smiling at her, dressed in her nurse's uniform or fatigues. She felt better when she saw Margaret's photos, like she knew her intimately.

The night they both cried the most was when Cappy told her about the day Margaret was killed.

"She was leaving the base where she was stationed. She was finally on her way home. We were going to get married as soon as she got back to the States. Her chopper was shot down just as it lifted off. She and our unborn baby died instantly."

Jaimey was sure Cappy had attached himself to Russ and the other boys to replace the child he lost.

Lightning bugs started glowing as dusk began ushering in nightfall. She sat at the table propped on her elbows chin in hands waiting for Effie. She began wandering again seeing something new every time she walked around Cappy's Museum, filled with memories of good friends and those he loved.

Cappy engineered three log cabins that he tore down by hand and reassembled, tying them all together. He added the modern conveniences, electrical and plumbing, and added a kitchen off of the back of the house. The kitchen was the largest room in the house, complete with a built-in gun cabinet that held six shotguns. The interior was all heart pine that Cappy took from a local cotton mill and used for the floors and walls in the spaces where there were no logs.

From the kitchen, the house spilled out into a large den area. The staircase stood in the middle of the den with a double fireplace, one on the kitchen side, the other on the den side.

Jaimey walked in circles. She studied the photos. Pictures of Cappy on various hunting trips. Cappy and his army buddies in exotic places like France and Belgium during WWII. He had been involved with the liberation of two labor camps after the fall of the Third Reich. Photos of his time spent in Korea and later Vietnam. Pictures of his prized bird dog Pearl were in several of the photos from his days spent bird hunting when he got back home. Sprinkled in amongst them all were childhood photos of Cappy and Effie as they grew up. In one, they stood with a woman Jaimey assumed to be Effie's mother next to a huge washtub framed by a wooden clapboard house; it's paint bleached by the sun.

Catherine was a small, skinny woman. Her skin was black as pitch. She wore a sleeveless sundress that showed toned, muscular arms from a lifetime of hard work in the sun. Her hair turning grey was braided into tight cornrows, and she wore a smile on her face. Her life was hard, Effie told Jaimey; but she always had a smile on her face. Jaimey realized Effie must have gotten her build from her father.

Looking at each photo, Jaimey realized Cappy was a rich man surrounded by good friends- people that he loved and that loved him back. Wealth, she realized, can't be found in real estate, or the casino, or lying on your back for twenty bucks, it's found in the people you call friends.

She walked back into the den and sunk herself into the thick, leather sofa and sat under a huge bull moose mount. Cappy told her the story of killing the moose on a hunt in Alaska not long after his last tour in Vietnam, soon after the war ended.

She sat watching the sun as it made its final descent. The bright orange orb reflecting off of the lake that was Cappy's backyard. Wood ducks circled, cupping their wings before flopping down to start feeding. Their muffled feeding calls coming in through the glass windows.

As she waited for Effie, the sun moved slowly behind the pecan trees that dotted the lake. She caught movement close to the house from the corner of her eye as she slowly adjusted to the coming darkness, and she froze. Her throat constricted making it hard to swallow, and her pulse quickened. She could hear her heart beating. She sat unable or unwilling to move. Her pulse slowed, and she relaxed. A small herd of deer were making their nightly pilgrimage through the grove toward the garden ready to eat leftover peas and corn. She calmed herself, placing her still-bruised hand over her heart taking deep breaths as she closed her eyes.

Randy still controlled her. She had not seen him in weeks, but he still controlled her emotions; he still made her jump and this made her mad. In an instant, she had had enough. Finding a new source of strength, she jumped up from the couch and made her way to the kitchen where she waited for Effie to arrive. She was ready get dressed, get to the Calcutta and enjoy herself. She wouldn't cower to him any longer, she told herself.

Jaimey stood in the kitchen with a newfound sense of power and hope as she watched the headlights rise and fall and flicker in and out through the pecan grove. Effie's Cadillac needed shocks, and with every bump, her lights moved violently up and down. Jaimey could only imagine what shape the driver's side seat was in.

She watched Effie's car follow the driveway toward the house. Behind her, she noticed in the darkness of the trees a small trail of dust as if it appeared from nowhere. It was in a straight line not blown by the wind and was closing in on Effie.

Effie's car door slung open, and the car rocked as she hurriedly slammed into park. She moved from the car as fast as she could. Effie couldn't run, her heft wouldn't allow it, but she used the momentum of that heft to move her forward as quickly as she could. She made it up the stairs and into the back door and locked it as a thud hit the door.

"Oh, God, he's found us! Randy's found us!" Jaimey screamed frantically. As they stood in the kitchen, Effie opened the gun cabinet. Her hands shook as she pulled out a twelve gauge over and under and a box of buckshot. She handed the gun to Jaimey, then reached into her bra and pulled out a small thirty-eight Saturday Night Special.

"Is that loaded?" Jaimey screamed.

"I found my money, you bitch!" the voice from the other side of the door screamed.

"That's not Randy?" Jaimey said wide-eyed, her mind racing.

Jaimey took a second to think, and then it hit her, WILLIAMS. The name on the duffle bag popped in her mind.

"He's alive!"

"Who's alive?"

"How did he find it?" She said, her voice shaking. "How did he find me? He's going to kill me!"

A myriad of confused thoughts flooded her mind. It was hard for her to wrap her mind around the realization that he was alive.

"I shot him! I saw him lying there. He was bleeding! I was sure I had killed him!" Jaimey said.

"Who? Who is that?" Effie asked.

Effie looked at Jaimey and put her finger to her mouth telling her to be quiet. Effie took Jaimey's hand and quietly guided her to the bookcase just under the staircase and removed two books. She reached inside pulled a lever and the bookcase opened. She replaced the books and stepped inside. After closing it behind them, she turned on the flashlight in the small room they stood in and shut off the main breaker for the rest of the house. They could still hear Danny Crabs shouting.

"I've got my money back. Now all I got to do is kill you," Danny said as they heard the back door burst open.

They could hear Danny slowly walk the circle around the fireplace, the old heart pine floor creaking under his weight. He stood next to the bookshelf. Effie turned the flashlight off quickly but it was too late. Danny saw the light bleeding through the crack under the door. They heard him feeling around the bookcase trying to figure out how to get in.

"I see you," he said almost in a whisper.

Effie and Jaimey heard books flying off of the shelves. They heard glass breaking, Jaimey prayed it wasn't a picture of Margaret.

Effie slowly opened the door that went down to the basement. After shutting the door behind them, she handed Jaimey a flashlight kept by the breaker box. They made their way down the stairs and out of the back door. Once outside, Effie grabbed Jaimey's hand and led her through a row of pecan trees that soon joined a vast pine plantation. The strong scent of pine hit Jaimey as if she had run into a wall.

Danny's frantic hand brushed against the lever and the bookcase door popped open. He made his way cautiously into the small room. He noticed another door and slowly opened it and stood at the top of a staircase. He very slowly crept down the stairs and to the opened basement door. When he reached the door, he saw in the distance a faint light moving spastically side to side.

"I see you!" He sang into the night.

Effie stopped and turned the flashlight off. She took Jaimey's hand again, pulling her through a second pine stand, moving as fast as she was able, maneuvering through the dark from memory toward the lake. She stopped again, bending over, hands on knees trying to catch her breath. She had not run since she caught Ray Ray with a Playboy five years earlier and chased him until she caught him.

Effie stood with her hands on her hips still struggling for air when she heard Danny calling out, taunting them, sounding as if he was closing the distance between them. She reached for Jaimey's hand again and started walking briskly toward the lake, moving forward with purpose as if she had a plan in mind.

On the edge of the lake closest to the cabin was a small boat house. Effie led Jaimey inside.

"Who is Danny; why is he after you?" Effie whispered through short shots of hard breathing.

"He is the man that kidnapped the little girl Madison that I told you about, the man I thought I killed. The man chasing us sexually abused the sweetest little seven-year-old girl you have ever seen for close to a year."

"Well, why is he chasin' us right now?" Effie asked confused.

"You heard him, revenge," Jaimey said through fearful tears. "I stole Madison and a bag full of money from him. I just can't believe he's alive."

"Well, he is and he's chasin' us right now," Effie said out of breath.

Jaimey shone the light from the flashlight along all the walls. Fishing rods and poles were lined up neatly along one wall. There were tackle boxes stacked just as neatly on a shelf. On the opposite wall she could see pictures of Cappy with fishing buddies and young boys standing in front of signs from the Make a Wish foundation.

Effie was busy preparing one of the three Jon boats that were in a line in front of them.

"Jaimey!" Effie called out quietly. "Help me!"

Effie was untying one of the Jon boats.

"Give me that lantern hangin' on the wall behind you."

Effie took the lantern, turned it on, and set it up on the front seat of the boat. She tied the trolling motor with rope, turning it slightly to the right. She turned the motor on its lowest speed and sent the boat on its way.

"It won't be long before he figures out we ain't in that boat, so we got to hurry."

Effie watched as the boat slowly made its way in the direction she hoped it would.

She took Jaimey's flashlight and taped it to the trolling motor of the second boat. With rope, she fixed the trolling motor so that it would run straight across the lake. She placed the motor on medium speed and sent it on its way.

"Where did you learn this, Effie"? Jaimey asked in amazement.

"Daniel Boone rerun, come on and get in," Effie said as she stepped in the third Jon boat.

"I see you," Danny said as he called out to the unmanned boats.

"It's workin," Effie said as she quietly paddled out of the boat house.

The other boats were slowly making their way in the direction she sent them, and now Effie and Jaimey were slipping quietly out of the boathouse and paddling across the lake.

"When we make it to the other side, we can hide out in one of Cappy's shootin' houses," Effie whispered, slowly sculling the paddle in her right hand.

"There he goes," Effie whispered tracking Danny as he

moved along the bank quietly toward the first boat that was slowly making its way in his direction.

"Dammit!" Danny screamed as he realized the boat was empty.

Jaimey and Effie had made it halfway across the lake when they heard Danny shout as he spotted the second boat. They saw him take the lantern out and throw it on the ground and get in the boat. Effie laid the paddle down and turned on the trolling motor. She placed it on the highest speed and in the direction of the bank. As she did, the rope broke on the second boat which sent the boat turning wildly in circles and lighting up the night in all directions. It wasn't long before the light shone on Effie and Jaimey, and Danny spotted them when it did.

"Oh God, he saw us!" Jaimey said.

Effie ran the boat up on the bank.

She and Jaimey both fell getting out. They could hear Danny taunting them from the middle of the lake. They moved quickly, ignoring the briars cutting into their skin, clawing at them and begging them to stay put, wrapping around them like kudzu enveloping the earth around it. They pulled and yanked their way free of the underbrush and pushed on until they came to a small game trail. Effie followed it, turning to the left and then leaving the game trail, she cut through a hardwood bottom. Their feet sunk in the mud, slowing their escape until the terrain increased in elevation. Effie stopped, sitting on a stump, catching her breath.

"Come on, we've got to keep moving!" Jaimey said.

"I ain't gonna make it, go on..."

Before Effie could get out another word, Jaimey grabbed her arm and helped her to her feet.

"Just walk as fast as you can."

Effie finally caught her breath and took the lead again. As the forest opened, the moon shone bright and the black night turned green in front of them.

The patch of ground covered in Rye grass left over from the previous deer season was longer than it was wide, and in its center was a large shooting house. Jaimey quickly climbed to the top of the stairs and impatiently stood waiting on Effie as she took another breather before she was able to trudge to the top.

Effie finally made it inside and plopped down on the small loveseat inside while Jaimey closed the door behind her. They both sat, trying to slow their breathing, and, in the distance, heard Danny call out again.

"Where are you?" he sang. His voice was coming and going but moving closer, and then it was silent. For several minutes the only sound was the slowing but labored breathing coming from Effie and then above them in a corner, unaccepting of their intrusion, a barn owl screeched. Jaimey grabbed at Effie, her heart thumping, feeling as if it would burst out of her chest.

"I just wet my pants," Jaimey whispered, crying.

"It scared me too; that's just an owl," Effie said reassuring her.

"That just gave me an idea. If he tries to come in here, as soon as he opens the door, I'm gon' take this broom and bump that owl out of here and maybe he'll fly right into his face and tear his ass up, and you be ready to shoot his ass at the same time. Okay?"

The shooting house was well-built. It was six feet by eight feet, just big enough to hold an old loveseat so Cappy could take a nap. In the front and on both sides, windows had been cut out and now covered by hinged plywood.

Effie slowly opened the front window sliding the hooks

on the end into the eye bolts to hold it open. She lowered the camo netting to cover their profiles.

They could hear Danny still talking and taunting them, but couldn't tell exactly where he was. Effie slowly and quietly took the shotgun from Jaimey and opened it. She placed two shells in it and slowly closed it. She moved the safety, hearing a slight click as she did.

The moon sat full and bright above them. It shone on the green grass below them giving the night a green glow. Effie and Jaimey kept their eyes peeled on the brightest spot hoping Danny would step into it so they at least would know where he was.

Effie handed the shotgun back to Jaimey.

"It's ready; just push the safety off and shoot," She whispered.

Jaimey nodded, too scared to say anything.

Effie saw the fear in Jaimey's eyes. She felt her hands trembling, and she held them, told Jaimey to close her eyes and she prayed.

As soon as Effie finished praying, she looked Jaimey directly in the eye.

"You're gonna have to get pissed off 'bout this shit. You can't let a man run you down like this child molester did and like your husband has," Effie looked at Jaimey for an indication she was heard and understood.

"I shot him; I thought he was dead," Jaimey whispered with a shaking voice.

"Well, good for you. This time you got to aim straighter and shoot more times that's all."

Effie placed her finger on her lips again with her eyes widening. Jaimey heard the same footsteps Effie did. They were slow and deliberate and then fast again. It sounded as if someone were kicking at the ground and scratching. Effie looked down at the ground and saw an armadillo scurrying and digging in the ground looking for acorns. They relaxed.

"I wish he would keep on talkin' cause that way we know where he is," Effie whispered to Jaimey.

Things had been too quiet for too long.

"Maybe he left," Jaimey said hopefully.

"That cracker didn't come all this way to stop now," Effie whispered. As soon as she said that, they both heard a creak on one of the lower steps. Effie grabbed the broom and looked up at the owl. She sat behind Jaimey facing the door.

Another step, another creak.

"Put your gun up. When he opens that door, squeeze the trigger," Effie said as she reached over and moved the safety.

A creak with every step and then a muffled cough that was gravely and loose. Jaimey remembered hearing that cough the day that Danny Crabs called her and later at his trailer. Her mind immediately focused on Madison and everything that she imagined that he had done to her and her fear turned into anger. She sat up a little straighter, now leaning against Effie, and firmly placed the butt of the gun on her shoulder. She kept telling herself to squeeze the trigger like her daddy had told her when they were dove hunting. "Let the shot surprise you," he would always say.

The door slowly opened into the moonlight. Only darkness dimly lit by the moon could be seen on the other side; and then slowly a foot emerged, and soon Danny Crabs filled the doorway of the shooting house holding his KA-BAR knife in his right hand. As soon as Effie saw him, she shone the flashlight in his eyes and hit the owl with her broom. The owl screeched and flew right into Danny's face, clawing at him. Jaimey pulled the trigger, but nothing happened. Danny Crabs fell back, flipping over the railing and falling the fifteen feet below him. Jaimey watched as the owl slowly flew off, screeching wildly as it headed to another perch somewhere in the far-off distance.

"Why didn't you shoot?" Effie said in a disgusted tone.

"I pulled the trigger, but it wouldn't go off!"

Effie looked at the safety. She had switched it on instead of off, moving the button too many times.

Taking the thirty-eight out of her bra, Effie moved quickly down the stairs. She stood over Danny Crabs, shining the light on his face, his eyes and mouth wide opened. She reached down to try to feel a pulse, and as her hand neared Danny's neck he grabbed her wrist, pulling her down on top of him at the same time. She took advantage of his weakened state and pulled away from him. She quickly got up and pointed the thirty-eight at him.

"No, let me!" Jaimey screamed taking the gun from Effie.

Jaimey looked Danny in the face. "This is for Madison, you sick piece of shit," she said as she unloaded the first round in his groin. Danny's scream echoed into the still night. A coyote answered from the hardwood bottom. Jaimey delayed the next shot letting him instead lie on the ground writhing in pain. A look of pained horror and unbelief showed on Danny's face.

"Shoot him again," Effie said, a sense of urgency placed on every word.

"Not yet; I'm letting him feel the pain," Jaimey said as she turned to Danny.

"That was for Madison."

"Shoot him in the heart," Effie said anxious to end the threat.

"He doesn't have a heart," Jaimey said as she looked back down at Danny.

Staring down at him, Danny's pained eyes were wide with shock. She could only see her uncle's face. She straddled Danny's waist standing over him. Every vile thing her uncle ever did to her streaked through her mind as quickly as lightning flashing in the sky.

"This one is for me," Jaimey said as she brought the pistol up from her side and shot.

The bullet entered just above Danny's nose. His once pained eyes turned still and unmoving. The body that, seconds before, was contorted in pain now relaxed. Jaimey fell into Effie's arms crying. They both stood, spent, unable to muster the strength to move a step, staring down at the lifeless body of Danny Williams.

"Oh God! What have I done?" Jaimey screamed.

She stood over his lifeless body and watched as blood flowed from his crotch. She stared at his fixed eyes swimming in blood, a feeling of remorse and fear covering her. The reality that she just shot and killed a man provided an overwhelming sense of regret and satisfaction at the same time.

"It was self-defense," she quietly moaned to herself almost as if she were asking herself a question.

The constant pain in the pit of her stomach that remained as she simply thought she had killed Danny before, will now never end, knowing she actually did this time.

"I feel sick to my stomach," Jaimey said to Effie.

"What now?" Jaimey asked Effie as if she had dealt with dead bodies for a living.

"We're going get him the hell out of here is what we're

going to do," Effie said, as she reached in Danny's pockets looking for his keys, but found nothing.

"He must have left them in the truck." Jaimey said.

"You stay here; I'll go get his truck," Effie said as she trudged up the small hill toward the house.

Effie returned driving Danny's truck and pulled up beside Jaimey still pointing the pistol at Danny's dead body.

"Let's get him in the back of the truck," Effie said.

"What are we going to do with him? Why don't we just call the police?" Jaimey asked.

Effie held up Danny's keys and showed Jaimey the clump of keys that included a key to the Lewiston Inn.

"We're gonna take this cracker back to his hotel room, put him in the bed and leave his ass."

"That's the plan?" Jaimey asked.

"Do you want to explain to the police why he's here? This ain't random way out here."

Effie and Jaimey each grabbed a leg, propped it up on the tailgate of the pickup and then both got into the truck bed trying their hardest to stay away from the head and blood. After several minutes, they finally dragged him into the bed of the truck and shut the tailgate. They drove back to the house, and Effie went in through the basement door and closed it behind her, wiping down the door and handle as she did. She reversed their exit from the house and made sure she left things just as they were. Walking back through the bookcase, she bent down and picked up the books and photos, replacing those as she closed the door. She swept the broken vase and poured the contents in the garbage can. She looked around the house, and decided it looked good. She made her way to the kitchen sink as Jaimey pulled the truck beside the garage and washed her hands and cleaned up as much as she could, then joined Jaimey in the truck.

"I'll drive, and we'll go the back way to the motel, once we get in town," Effie said out of breath.

As Jaimey moved, she realized there was no place to put her feet. The floorboard on the passenger side was full of bags.

"Turn on the cab light," Jaimey said with a sense of urgency in her voice. Jaimey looked down and recognized the green duffle with WILLIAMS painted in white letters on the side. She quickly looked inside; it was full of money. She was confused and couldn't understand how he had it. How had he found it? He obviously discovered where she lived; what led him to Effie to follow her out here? Questions racked her brain.

Jaimey pulled the bag onto the seat with her and opened it, showing it to Effie.

"Sweet Jesus, look at that!" Effie said.

"We'll split this. Thank you for helping me tonight and keeping me alive."

"What else he got down there?" Effie asked pointing toward the floorboard.

Jaimey picked up another bag and unzipped it, revealing a bag full of porn, mainly kiddie porn.

"This is so disgusting," Jaimey said, closing the bag back up.

"You mean that piece of shit likes babies? I'm glad we shot his ass now."

Jaimey continued the story of the day she had met Danny Crabs and Madison and what she could only imagine he had done to her. She recounted that she shot Danny that day and thought she had killed him. She told her again about reuniting Madison with her mom and dad, and then leaving Biloxi and coming back home to Lewiston, every detail she replayed, every smell she had smelled, every feeling she had felt. That day played over and over in her mind since it had happened. More than anything, she hated Danny for what he did to Madison.

The story ended as Effie pulled into the parking lot of the Lewiston Inn searching for number eighteen. The Lewiston Inn was a one story, thirty-two room motel. All of the odd numbers were on the front along the street while the even numbers were in the back facing a small field that separated two parts of town. Right on the edge of the wrong side of the tracks. The side the police wouldn't investigate too much when they found the dead body of a pedophile in a motel room full of kiddie porn.

Effie was familiar with the Lewiston Inn. In her younger days, she would extend the party that began at the Diamond Club and end there.

She pulled around the back of the Inn and found the number eighteen room. Luckily, the area was dark and there was only one other car in the parking lot.

Effie backed up to the door and gave Jaimey rubber gloves while she slipped hers on. She took the motel key, opened the door, turned the light on and looked around the room. Food wrappers and beer cans littered the room.

They cleared the bed and pulled the bedspread off, spreading it from the door to just under the tailgate. Each of them grabbed a hand and pulled Danny's body out of the truck, letting it plop down on the bedspread. They pulled the bedspread along with Danny's body back up on the bed and propped him up as if he were sitting up when he was shot. They took the bag with all of the kiddie porn in it, spread it all over the room and put a tape in the VCR. Jaimey placed his KA-BAR beside him on the bed and rubbed some of his own blood on it for good measure. Effie took the .38 and pulled Danny forward and saw where the blood was forming on the pillow. She held the .38 to the pillow and shot, and then laid him back against the pillow. They both grabbed a towel, quickly wiped down the entire room and stood in the doorway making sure everything looked as normal as possible.

Finished, Effie drove back to Cappy's house, got in her Cadillac and followed Jaimey to a carwash to wash the blood out of the back of the truck and then back to the Lewiston Inn. Jaimey parked the truck in front of the room, grabbed the bag of money, wiped down the inside of the truck and looked to be sure there was no blood, opened the door, threw the keys on the dresser, and she and Effie left. It was over.

"Let's go, I still got time to get to the clubhouse, I got cookin' to do for tomorrow."

"Can I go? I don't want to be alone right now," Jaimey said as she sat closer to Effie and placed her head on her shoulder.

"You just need to ask forgiveness, baby, I already have."

CHAPTER FORTY

The sun bore down on the inside of the open convertible. The white interior brightened an already clear day creating a need for the driver's Wayfarers. Cars slowed as they approached the 1968 red convertible Cadillac. The steer horns stretched from headlight to headlight was the first thing to catch their attention. The original candy apple red paint played well against the chrome of the bumpers and door handles.

The tag on the rear was from Arkansas. Pig Thrasher sat in the driver's seat patiently waiting for the line of traffic to move on so he could pull into the entrance of the country club. He crossed the highway and slowed as his front tires hit gravel. A county supervisor, mindful of votes, had his water truck there earlier that morning spraying the private road under the cover of darkness. It kept the dust down, but Pig still eased onto the gravel and slowly made his way toward the clubhouse.

The interior of the Cadillac was full. The four-man team from Arkansas, each with a woman on their laps, filled the interior of the land yacht. *Pig Sooey* sounded as Pig blew his horn announcing their arrival. The crowd converged around the car. They had been awaiting their arrival. Pig exited the driver's seat and held out his hand to his date and popped an unlit cigar into his mouth. He shook hands as he waded through the mass of people. The foursome was dressed as they were every year. Loud plaid knickers with knee-length socks and polo shirts. Red driver's caps with an Arkansas Razorback logo square in the center adorned their heads.

Pig and his crew arrived at the tournament every year in a similar fashion.

They all made their way to the score board and found their tee times for the next day. The players worked their way through the crowds.

"Hey, I got y'all on the calendar for the deer camp in December," Stan Peters hollered at Pig.

"We're ready, can't wait."

For three days, these men and their women, some wives, some not, converged on the little town of Lewiston to play golf and drink and gamble. The trophy wives rode the course with their husbands, held their beers while they made their laboriously contemplated shots and watched them when the young girls on the beer carts came too close and smelled too good and smiled too broadly wearing little in the way of clothes, fighting the summer swelter. These boys played in a smalltown tournament somewhere most weekends in the summer, always arriving in a similar fashion.

As in most golf tournaments, the schedule was usually the same from year to year. Thursday was the practice round. Friday was the qualifying round. Saturday was moving day, and Sunday decided the winner. Fridays were always the most anticipated because that was the night of the Calcutta and crawfish boil.

The Calcutta is pretty simple and straightforward. Individuals or teams are bought in an auction prior to the event starting. The highest bidder becomes the owner of the individual or team of players. In most tournaments, the individual or team can purchase half or all of their team known as a buyback. Depending on that, a sum total of the pot is determined. Payout is distributed to the top two or three teams once the rounds are complete. The bidder can purchase one or as many teams as he wishes. The more teams that are bid on, the more action the bidder has. Similar to stocks and bonds, spreading your money across multiple teams gives the bidder a more diverse opportunity. Once all the teams are bid on and the auction is finished, the total pot is determined by the tournament director. The cash is what is competed for in the event. It is an eighteen-hole stroke play event that is meant for nothing more than fun, but taken very seriously.

Russ and Cappy arrived at the Calcutta at 6:00 p.m. sharp. As soon as they exited Cappy's Ford Bronco, the smell of boiled shrimp and crawfish hit their noses like a freight train hitting a stray dog. People were everywhere; the club had the feel of a college fraternity party. Spanky and Fatboy joined Cappy and Russ and headed toward the crawfish table. Fatboy pushed his way through the boys and started to nudge Cappy, but Cappy turned him around and made him go to the back of the line.

They all finally got a place at the table and began the slaughter. Sucking and slurping sounds and shells cracking open soon filled the air replacing the murmur of old friends meeting for the first time since last year. The boys had a pile of shells in front of them that would make a horse choke.

Fatboy's face glistened as he rarely took time to wipe between bites. Oil, bits of crawfish shell and corn were hanging onto Fatboy's face like a climber hanging from his fingertips on the side of a mountain. There was a wet line from the bottom of his chin to the bottom of his untucked shirt.

Russ finished eating and cleaned his face. He walked away from the crowd for a moment, looking out over the lush green of the course. The moon loomed large and sat low in the sky and a humid fog hung over the green. The sounds of Cicadas and Katydids spilled from a sprawling live oak tree in front of him lulling the woods to sleep. The surface of the lake was smooth and quiet. The end of day when the water was still and looked like glass. The time of day fishermen call the bewitching hour. Frogs splashed the edges chasing insects. In the far-off distance a piece of equipment was cutting the last green in preparation for the morning's play. The combination of fertilizer, wet fresh cut grass and moisture permeated his nostrils. The golf course, any golf course, was like home to him, he was comfortable, the way most men are comfortable in their favorite recliner.

Cappy interrupted Russ's solitude.

"Hey, the Calcutta is about to start; come help me just a minute."

Cappy and Russ disappeared to the back of Cappy's Bronco and retrieved the two lawn chairs in the backseat. They made their way toward the stage. Suzie and her husband had done a great job of picking the location of the Calcutta. They situated the stage and area for seating under a live oak that created a beautiful canopy. From the clubhouse and over the stage and to the back of the crowd, lights hung brilliantly. On each corner, small trees resembling palms framed the spot. The night was clear and the band's song was interrupted by an announcement drawing everyone toward the stage.

The auctioneer and four spotters huddled on the stage in discussion. The band turned off their microphones and placed their guitars in the stands and the sticks on their drums. Two of the spotters fanned out into the crowd.

"All right, folks," the auctioneer began. "If we got any children or women with tender ears in the audience, you better close them or just leave cause it's about to get raunchy!" A swelter of laughter and yells came from the mostly male crowd while the women looked at each other for clues as to whether they should stay or go.

"All right, first team, Rogers and Neely. Now these boys came all the way from Arkansas to play with us this year. Take a look at these boys. Alright, who's gonna gimmee fifty? There's fifty, now sixty, sixty let me hear sixty. There it is, now what about seventy-five?"

"Ho," came a shout from a tobacco-filled mouth while pointing to a man with $65 in his pocket.

"Come on, y'all, now these boys traveled all the way from Arkansas to be with us here this weekend."

"Ho, seventy!" shouted the tobacco-filled mouth again. Come on now let me hear seventy-five. Everybody, get up off that wallet."

A raised hand gave the auctioneer what he was looking for, but he wouldn't be satisfied.

"Let's look at the numbers from last year; these boys shot pretty good if I remember right."

"Won their flight!" an auctioneer's assistant shouted followed by a long steady skinny stream of brown spit that hung in the thick air finally making its way into the garbage can at the bottom of the makeshift stage.

"Won their flight? Hell, that's worth a hundred-dollar

bill right there! Somebody's got to give me a hundred-dollar bill for these sumbitches, who's it gonna be?" the auctioneer sang.

"Ho!" Shouted the tobacco-filled mouth of the spotter, and $100 was in the bag.

"One hundred dollars going once, one hundred going twice, sold! Sold to Sam Macey... thank you, Sam!"

The night continued, human flesh and its ability to hit a golf ball were auctioned with wit and brashness. The auctioneer owned the night. He moved people to spend money they didn't have and on people they didn't know. The kegs of beer didn't hinder his performance, keeping the audience well-lubricated, the money flowing.

Russ and Cappy sat quietly, listening. It was the first auction of any kind that Russ had ever seen.

Fatboy and Curtis moved their carts by Cappy and Russ. Fatboy was eating a new plate of shrimp, using his shirt tail to wipe his mouth.

"Shit," Fatboy said without thinking and immediately looked toward Cappy to see if he had heard it. He hadn't, and he began wiping the huge blob of cocktail sauce from his shirt with his finger and then transferred the remains onto a shrimp that he quickly slapped in his mouth.

"You ready to play tomorrow, Russ?" Fatboy asked while chewing his food, rocking, keeping rhythm with each chew.

"I guess," Russ said meekly.

Fatboy grabbed two shrimp at once and drowned them both in cocktail sauce then rammed them into his mouth.

"So, what'll you think we'll shoot tomorrow?' Fatboy asked around the remains of the two large shrimp.

"Do you ever talk without food in your mouth?" Russ asked, finally tired of looking at dissected shreds of shrimp.

"Sorry," Fatboy muttered as he bit down on a corncob and sucked the remaining juice from it.

Their conversation, mutilated as it was, was quickly interrupted by the auctioneer as they both heard their last names called for auction.

"Now, folks, from what I've heard about Russ Crawford, this is a boy y'all will want to watch play. Heard he shot a 68 at Waving Pines earlier this week," the auctioneer said, looking toward Cappy for confirmation. The bobble of heads in the crowd turned toward Cappy and Russ, and Russ became increasingly uncomfortable with the attention.

The loud boom of auctioneer lingo rang out in the air as Russ and Fatboy's names were put on the board.

"All right! Who's gonna give me a hundred?" Cappy quickly raised his hand, an attempt to make the bids flow more quickly and increase the bids.

"Two hundred," a slurred voice said from a golf cart.

"Go ahead there, son! Two-hundred, who'll give me three?"

A coolly raised finger and the new price was three hundred.

"Five hundred dollars!" a female voice shouted

"Five-Fifty!" a voice from the back of the crowd sang.

Cappy looked at Russ and smiled. The look on Russ and Fatboy's faces were blank, unbelieving.

The price kept rising, and Fatboy couldn't believe his ears. He had never remembered a price so high before, and his name was on the card. In his mind, Fatboy's face had just appeared on a Wheaties cereal box.

Curtis looked at Fatboy and Russ and mouthed "Damn!"

The price was now at $1250, and interest was still

looming in the alcohol-soaked air. The auctioneer took a huge gulp, finishing his beer, and reached under his podium and retrieved another from his private stash.

Cappy continued to smile and sat quietly in his lawn chair motionless and cool. Fifteen hundred and the bidding ceased, a new record in the Calcutta for The Clubhouse Classic.

"Shit!" Fatboy shouted spewing whatever thick syrupy soft drink he had in his mouth. "Fifteen hundred, damn!" Fatboy now had a new reason to live.

Immediately, his entire future ran through his mind. He would have to lose weight and get more serious about golf if he would play on tour one day. His large, round face was red with excitement. He was a mediocre player at best. The bidding was mainly for Russ. Russ was the contender, not Fatboy. He was just getting a free ride.

The rest of the gang was gathered, high fiving as Fatboy disappeared toward the clubhouse. As he walked into the backdoor of the kitchen, he excitedly uttered his favorite word, "Shit!" and as quickly as it spewed from his mouth, a wet dish towel chased it right back in. Effie was there, and in his excitement Fatboy forgot. His mouth burned, and he felt a whelp begin to rise on his lip. He was doubled over in pain and dazed at the interruption of his gleeful activity.

"You know you don't curse in front of me, boy!" Effie said before he could come up with a good excuse.

Fatboy looked up at her with tears welling up in his eyes. She stood there like a statue, straight and reverent, her hands placed on her ample hips commanding respect. The rag dangled from her right hand, and Fatboy was amazed at her quickness. He still had one foot out of the door when she popped him. He barely got the word out of his mouth and boom!

"What you so excited 'bout anyway?" Effie asked not really caring.

"Me and Russ were just auctioned off in the Calcutta for fifteen hundred bucks!" Fatboy said quickly finding his exuberance again.

"Do you really think that impress me? All y'all white people doin' is gambling out there; y'all just playin' in Lucifer's playground, drunk too; just look at the mayor out there, fat, fallin' down drunk! An all those fools spendin' money they ain't even got, women half-dressed! It's the same every year," Effie's voice trailed off in a short-lived rant. Images of crimes she committed earlier flash into her mind. She had to keep reminding herself that she asked forgiveness. It weighed on her.

"Who's Lucifer?"

"Go read your Bible; go on now! I ain't got time for you, Fatboy."

Fatboy remembered he had to go to the bathroom and left Effie alone with her cooking. He finally made his way back from the bathroom. He peeked in the kitchen to see if there was any food he could steal, and if Effie was still in there. He peered through the door and saw Effie crying quietly while she was cutting onions and humming "Forget Me Not." Her whole body swaying in a slow, sweet rhythm all its own. He wasn't sure if it was the song, or the onions she was cutting that made her cry, and now he felt bad for cussing.

Just as he made it through the kitchen door, Effie's large round hand caught the back of his shirt, and she pulled him to her.

"Come here, baby, give Effie a hug."

She cried, still holding the onion in one hand and a large butcher knife in the other. She held him there longer than she usually did, and it became strange to Fatboy; it was as if something else made her hug him, like she needed him instead of the other way around.

"Push up my glasses for me, baby."

Fatboy pulled her glasses off wiped her eyes, cleaned them and returned them, propping them on her nose. They quietly stared at each other, and he turned and walked toward the door.

"They's some chocolate chip cookies in that bag yonder," Effie said giving Fatboy chocolate as a peace offering.

He quickly forgot about his diet and the Wheaties cereal box debut and grabbed a handful, and then reached again and got one more for good measure.

CHAPTER FORTY-ONE

Randy pulled into the parking lot of the casino. The amount of cash he had would allow him to play for the entire weekend. He meandered through the myriad of parked cars toward the back of the casino.

He sat for a minute. He reached into his shirt pocket and pulled out a bottle and shook three white pills into his hand. He popped them in his mouth and chased it with a beer. His head pounded from the night before.

It was Saturday. People were crawling the parking lots like ants after their bed was kicked. He watched as two couples slowly exited their cars. Canes and walkers extracted from the backseat. They laughed while they adjusted their clothes and prepared for the slow arduous walk toward the casino. He watched them disappear through the large doors as he finished his beer.

"I'll take five thousand to start," he said to himself, careful not to attract the wrong kind of attention as he had in the past.

He reached over the seat into the back, feeling for the bag. He floated his hand around the back, unable to feel anything. He stretched his body, pressing his feet into the floorboard, pushing himself farther toward the backseat. He frowned in confusion. His heart started racing. He began to panic.

He raised up on his knees and turned around. He moved clothes and trash, he still didn't see it. He got out of the truck looked under the seat. He bent the seat forward pushing his body halfway into the back. Frantically, he searched, trying to remember if he took it inside the house or if he maybe put it in the garage last night.

Rage slowly built in Randy. He milled around the outside of the truck pacing back and forth thinking. Trying to clear his muddled mind. He didn't remember taking it out of the truck. He noticed people staring. A man standing by the backdoor wearing a sport coat with credentials hanging from his neck looked his way. He sat back in the cab of his truck. He beat on the steering wheel and grabbed it with both hands and shook it. He was trying as best he could to tear it off, but he was too weak, he started hyperventilating.

He turned on his knees one more time and looked in the backseat. Amongst the clutter, he saw the bottom of a one-hundred-dollar bill sticking out of a folded piece of paper. He grabbed at it.

The note read:

Your whore wife stole my money; I got it back. Have fun with the cash; hope you win big.

"Son-of-a-bitch!" Randy screamed as loud as he could, his whole body shaking. He quickly began scouring the parking lot through the tears streaming from his face.

How in the hell did anyone know I had this money? Where

in the hell did Jaimey get this money from? Randy's mind reeled with confusion.

He looked at the note again and read the part about getting revenge on Jaimey. He reached into his pocket and found cash left over from the previous day. He had two hundred dollars. He needed a drink.

Randy sat at a slot machine transfixed as if he were a piece of stone, feeling nothing just staring straight, his hand resting on the pull stick when he was jarred awake. A hostess asking him if he wanted another beer, and he did. He slowed down on his play because he didn't want to run out of money or playing time for beer. He stuck another quarter in the slot machine and pulled it. Five dollars' worth of quarters began clinking in the tray at the bottom of the slot. The waitress returned with a beer, and he tipped her.

He took a large gulp and stared at the poker table. He watched as the crowd surrounding the table suddenly erupted, standing hugging each other.

He felt his numbness again. His mind started from the beginning as it usually did. Replaying college, marrying the beauty queen, living in a five-thousand-square-foot home then becoming homeless, owning the business, his ungrateful son. It went on and on, always the same. The same broken record. The same thoughts over and over until he became too drunk to think and passed out.

In his sober moments he knew he had blamed Russ for too many of his failures; he was just a kid, too young to be blamed for much. It made him feel better to place blame. The drunker he became, the able to blame everyone but himself. His self-loathing was interrupted again by the waitress delivering another beer, and he reached down and handed her a couple of dollars' worth of quarters.

As he sat and drank, Randy's mind continued to race. Thoughts of old friends, business deals, and his former lifestyle physically hurt to think about. It created an actual physical pain. It was almost unreal to him that this had all happened. He came from a good family, hell, a great family. His father and all of his uncles had been wildly successful in a variety of business opportunities. It was like a bad off-Broadway play and he was the star, a mean opera played out before the people of Mississippi to watch and laugh at... to laugh at him. The houses, the cars, the clothes, the Rolex his father gave him that had long since been sold to maintain some senseless materialistic lifestyle- it all laid heavy on him.

"The true measure of a man is not how he handles success, but how graceful he is when he has failed," his father's words rang in his ears.

He passed that threshold long ago. He had abused his wife; he had physically abused his only son. He had said things to him that couldn't be taken back. He mended fences and then broke promises. His favorite name to call him was Bastard...he was the only bastard.

"There is no way they will ever forgive me, and I'm not sure I deserve it," Randy said quietly to himself.

He quickly put every quarter he had in the machine and began pulling. With every pull, the little he had left dwindled. Every quarter was gone. That was all he had. He literally had nothing left. Nothing.

CHAPTER FORTY-TWO

C appy stood at the back of his golf cart in front of two coolers. This was the first year that he and Bill Turner had not played in The Clubhouse Classic in the fourteen years since Bill had moved back to Mississippi. The two coolers replaced their golf clubs- one for ice, the other for the condiments and the vodka.

Bill sat with his legs hanging out of the side of the golf cart watching through binoculars as Russ and Fatboy played. They followed them around the course quietly cheering them on getting a little too loud when Russ made a good shot.

Ice quietly clinked in the two highball glasses as Cappy added the V-8 Juice, followed by vodka, a dollop of Worcestershire sauce, Tabasco, a little salt and lot of black pepper. He squeezed in lime and added a celery stalk and a pickled okra, and they both settled in to watch.

"He is just as smooth as a good bourbon, Cap," Bill said as he watched Russ.

"I've got Russ at 70 right now. If he hovers right around there and Fatboy stays consistent, they have a chance of winning; and Russ has a real good chance of becoming the club champ," Cappy said as proud for Fatboy as he was for Russ.

Russ birdied the number thirteen hole while Fatboy pared it. Cappy and Bill crossed over ahead of them near the number fourteen tee box and parked under a weeping willow tree sipping on their drinks. Cappy read the instructions and prize categories for the hole. *The number fourteen hole was a par three with two prizes attached to it, closest to the pin and a first hole-in-one. The closest to the pin carried a new set of Ping clubs complete with bag, several sleeves of balls and the coveted Beau Chene umbrella, while the hole-in-one was a cash prize of a thousand dollars. If a player made a hole-in-one, the money and clubs went to the first player on the first day of regulation play to make it. Whoever the player was that was closest to the hole, they were just out of luck if a hole-in-one were made.*

"You know, there has only been one hole-in-one ever recorded on this hole since the classic started," Cappy said as he handed the instructions to Bill.

Fatboy and Russ arrived with the two golfers they were paired with, two older men that had been playing the tournament for the last fifteen years. They stood on the tee box leaning on their clubs waiting for the team in front of them to complete their putts.

There were usually two types of players who attended The Clubhouse Classic- the real serious wannabe PGA pros and the guys who just have fun, know they won't win anything and aren't worth a shit. The latter was the group in front of Russ and Fatboy. Two salesmen, a local dentist and the head of the Lewiston electric department. They all knew each other well; all graduated high school together, and all four were putting their way to possibly losing worse than they ever had before. Their goal was to lose and lose badly. Last place came with the coveted Beau Chene umbrella, and they all wanted one. They had done such a masterful job of creating a last place trophy that the anticipation of finding out who lost was almost as much fun as finding out who the club champ was every year.

In order to solidify the loss, they needed to come into the day with a bad hangover and a case of beer in the cooler.

As the dentist finally sank his putt on the par three, he was six over on the hole and just as happy as if he had just made a hole-in-one.

Although Russ and Fatboy were up, they gave first opportunity to their teammates. Each one teed up and struck the ball, both landing on the edge of the green. Next was Fatboy. His placement was great, but his loft was too high. Instead of placing his ball on the back of the green and allowing it roll toward the hole, it stuck in the soft-watered edge.

Russ's plan was to place the ball right where Fatboy did. The nine iron was too much, put the ball too far back. He walked back to his bag and replaced his nine iron with a pitching wedge.

Cappy and Bill sat up a little straighter as Russ walked back to his bag and traded clubs.

"What is he doing?" Bill whispered.

Russ approached the tee box and threw down a ball not bothering with a tee. After rolling it around with the face of his club, he lined up and swung softly letting the club do most of the work for him. He hit a quick fade and placed it center right in the green a tad above right of the flag. The ball turned in the air and hit the green and began a slow tumble toward the flag.

Bill and Cappy moved more toward the edge of their seats, and as the ball rolled closer to the flag, Cappy stood and walked toward the other side of the cart, staying just under the weeping willow tree.

The ball started slowing as it neared the hole.

"He's got closest to the pin," Cappy said excitedly, thrusting his hands up as if he were officiating a touchdown in a football game.

The ball stopped on the edge of the hole as if it ran into a brick wall. Russ crouched down and rested his head on the handle of his golf club, he jerked his head up when shouting erupted. The ball fell into the hole, a hole-in-one.

Russ stared, unbelieving. His ball was gone. He stood and jumped all in one motion. Bill and Cappy came running from their hiding place. The officials that were recording closest to the pin also stood and began celebrating spilling the contents of their lap. They all danced around Russ in unison in one big gyrating group hug. The whole place erupted, and they soon realized they were disturbing other golfers around them and stopped the celebration.

With one stroke, Russ won a new set of clubs and more money than he had seen his family have in years, and he had just shaved two points off of his score.

After the commotion ended and the witnesses signed the validation of the hole-in-one, the rest of the team approached the green. Russ walked toward the hole and retrieved his ball and stuck it up in the air. Cappy and Bill resumed their celebration.

The two older men putted, one making par, the other a bogey. Fatboy marked his ball, cleaned it and repaired his divot. He replaced the ball in front of his marker and did the ceremonial walk around the green as if he had never played it before. He lined up his put, remembered what he attempted to do on his drive and rolled the ball starting it slowly at first picking up speed as it started downhill. It rolled just as he had imagined it would and after jumping around the edge of the hole it sank. Fatboy birdied the hole. There was more clapping, and slaps on the back and thumbs up from Bill and Cappy.

CHAPTER FORTY-THREE

The highway was quiet and still as the last portion of the sun squeezed itself into the tight line of pine trees like the slow deposit of a coin into a piggy bank. The red hills of Neshoba County grew darker as the last of the sun finally rested in its evening place in the galaxy.

The truck survived on the remaining fumes in the gas tank. Randy, barely coherent, was unfazed by the needle dipping further into the red. As he passed the county line, the day grew darker and yet the scenery remained the same. Cars swerved as Randy came toward them floating into their lane. One dipped into the ditch kicking up red clay and dust, but managed to correct and return to the highway, fishtailing as it found pavement again.

The stretch of highway between Lewiston and the casino was heavily patrolled. Randy spotted the familiar form of a patrol car and managed to stay in his lane as he passed. The sight of the patrol car sobered him, and, for the next six miles, he kept the car in his lane as he entered the city limits of Lewiston.

With only a quarter mile left to get home, the truck began to sputter, vibrating as it's life finally faded. He eased over onto the shoulder contemplating whether he should try to walk home. Driving under the influence or public drunk, it didn't really matter to him.

Randy looked down both sides of the highway, and slowly slid out of the truck, and felt the ground with his feet. Everything around him was spinning. He shut the door and began walking, mindful of walking straight. His eyes darting up and down the highway, watching, searching for the city police or a highway patrolman. Prepared to jump into the ditch if he spotted one.

The last bit of light was consumed by the dark, and he felt more confident in the cloak of darkness. He pulled his last beer from his back pocket and downed it in a couple of gulps then threw the can into the ditch. Paranoia crept into his psyche and he increased his speed. The women he saw on television speed walking popped in his mind, and he considered how stupid he must look and stopped. As he slowed his gait, his feet became tangled together, and he slipped on the loose gravel, falling. His right pant leg tore at the knee, and he began to bleed from the minor scrape.

The pain didn't register with him, so he stood and continued walking toward home. As he approached the country club, he noticed a steady stream of cars and trucks turning into the long, dusty, tree-lined road leading them to the clubhouse.

He stopped walking when he heard music, and he turned and followed the traffic toward the sound of the band.

"Life's been good" by Joe Walsh was coming from the stage. The volume filtered in and out of Randy's ears, and he attempted to sing along:

I go to parties sometimes until four
It's hard to leave when you can't find the door
It's tough to handle this fortune and fame
Everybody's so different I haven't changed

After butchering most of the song, he jumped back up toward the beginning of the song and sang his favorite lines...

My Maserati does 185
I lost my license now I don't drive
I have a limo, ride in the back
I lock the doors in case I'm attacked...

His singing was quickly drowned out by a car full of teenaged boys who sped by him covering him in red dust, taking the time to moon him and flip him off.

"Old drunk!" they shouted as they went by.

"Bastard punks!" Randy screamed back as he raised his middle finger toward the boys.

Red dust clouded his face and he ingested a large plume of it. Nausea weakened him and he leaned over and rested his hands on his knees. His body heaved up and down violently, unable to produce anything.

The clubhouse sat at the end of the road to the right, and he could see the party as he got closer. On his right side was a pasture with grazing cows that were all settling down for the night.

Randy set out across the pasture toward the back of the clubhouse toward the sounds of people happy, talking over each other. The cows that were once bedded down for the night now stood staring at the dark form trying to lift his leg over a barbed wire fence.

Unable to lift his leg high enough to get over the top of the fence, Randy decided to simply slip under the bottom. His belt loop caught on the barbed wire, and he remained stuck until he finally mustered enough force to rip it. Once on the other side, he made a beeline through the pasture toward the sound of the band and the small light that shone by the side door that led to the clubhouse kitchen.

He stood against another section of fence considering the best way to reach the other side. He was able to squeeze the two top runs together and push down, giving him enough space to throw a leg over. He straddled the fence, hopping on one leg. He lost his balance and fell, ripping his pant leg.

A line of pine trees stood along the road separating the cows from the clubhouse. He hid behind them and watched as a group of young girls moved toward the dark corner of the pool and heard the familiar pop of a beer can.

"A Pirate Looks at Forty" started from the band when the back door to the kitchen opened. A large man bound down the two steps, went straight to a cooler and grabbed two beers from it. Once he disappeared inside, Randy noticed a row of coolers lined against the wall beside the kitchen door.

The coolers were barely noticeable in the dark of night. A red one with a Colonel Reb sticker on it sat directly under the light that hung just to the side of the door.

Randy stumbled to the line of coolers, grabbed the handle on the red one and drug it back to the tree line. He hid himself behind the largest pine in the row and quickly opened the cooler and grabbed a bottle.

"Dammit... wine coolers," Randy said out loud as he grabbed a Bartles and Jaymes. He turned to the metal fence post behind him, placed the edge of the cap on the post, and popped the top. He quickly began to drink it but just as quickly spit it out. It was too fruity for his taste.

He dragged the cooler back up to the line, opened the one next to it and retrieved three beers, filling his pockets, and disappeared back into the line of trees. He popped the top, emptied the contents, and quickly opened the next one. He sat in the night camouflaged behind the large pine tree drinking a new beer as two of the cooler owners appeared, extracted drinks and disappeared back inside.

Randy ran back toward the coolers and got three more beers and ran back to his hiding place in the wood line and continued drinking. He sat in the midst of a growing litter of empty cans and finally vomited, rinsed his mouth with a beer and then drank the rest.

Cars continued arriving, dust following them to their final resting place. Randy watched the group of young girls move from the pool and convene around a small sports car and light cigarettes. Out of the corner of his eye he saw movement around the coolers. He heard the slosh of ice as the dark form opened a cooler and dug around; looking confused, he grabbed a beer and closed the lid. He stood for a moment looking around scanning the area around him.

"Damn kids," the dark form growled as he went back into the clubhouse with his cooler.

CHAPTER FORTY-FOUR

Cappy stopped introducing Russ and walked toward Jaimey and Effie as he watched Effie's large Cadillac pull up to the clubhouse and into her parking space in front of the sign bearing her name. Effie was the main attraction of the classic every year, dancing long into the night. He hugged them both and complimented their dresses.

Effie and Jaimey spent the earlier part of the day shopping for the new dresses. They also both got manicures, and since Jaimey bought some new open-toed shoes, she got a pedicure. Jaimey was dressed in a sundress perfect for a country club summer lawn party.

Effie, on the other hand, was a little more practical and bought a dress that she could wear to church as well. She was full into her taffeta phase and was partial to dresses that sparkled. She bought the same dress in purple with silver sequins that she already owned in gold. She also bought the matching hat and as she exited her car, it was clear how proud she was of her new outfit and knew how good she looked in it.

The weight of what they had done the previous day pressed on them both. They stole fast, unspoken looks at each other. The voice continued filling Jaimey's mind. It kept reminding her it was self-defense. He molested Madison. The voice kept reminding her that she pulled the trigger. She let him suffer. She covered it up. She moved a body, staged the scene...she committed a crime.

Russ ran to Jaimey hugging her.

"Mom, I won a new set of clubs and a thousand dollars today!"

"What!? How?"

"I made a hole-in-one!" Russ said almost shouting.

"That's wonderful! I'm so proud of you," Jaimey said while hugging Russ. One after the other were coming up to the two of them, congratulating Russ.

"Your boy has had one hell of a day," Cappy said as he gave her a sideways hug.

Bill Turner joined the group and immediately hugged Effie.

"Don't wrinkle me, and stop flirtin'!" Effie said to Bill as he kissed her on the cheek. "I'm gon' have to fix my rouge, now," she said, loving every minute of the attention.

Bill Turner turned his attention to Jaimey.

"Your son has a hell of a future in golf."

"Thank you for saying so; I know how he loves it," Jaimey said as Bill led her to the bar area.

The immediate fanfare, and seeing Russ so happy, made walking into the lion's den more bearable. She saw people speaking to her, but didn't hear them, she only heard the voice. The voice of regret kept chipping away. Regret filled her every emotion.

Jim spotted Jaimey across the room. He watched her,

wishing he was Bill Turner. Wishing she could be on his arm tonight. The rough exterior he saw at Cappy's house was slowly fading. The edges were softening. She was slowly evolving back into the sorority girl he knew in college.

She moved several strands of hair behind her ear and held them. Her eyes moving across the room as she lost interest in the conversation Bill Turner was having. She locked eyes with Jim for several seconds and they smiled at each other before her attention was called back to Bill as he laughed out loud.

She took a sip from her drink and watched the movement of people under the lights. The decorations absorbing the lights making the scene bright and festive. The live music hit on her nostalgic emotion, taking her back to the late seventies. Taking her back to Ole Miss. Taking her back to Randy.

Suzie and her husband Jeffery quickly made it to Jaimey's side introducing themselves, giddy with excitement.

"Ladies, excuse us please," Bill Turner said, always the consummate gentleman.

"Did he just say ladies, plural?' Jeffery asked Suzie with his hand resting lightly as if he were offended.

Jaimey snickered, "Did you just say ladies to that man and woman?"

"I'd been prewarned by Cappy to watch out for those two. He described them to a tee. You need to stay clear of them, bad eggs, love to gossip, especially the lady standing next to his wife," Bill Turner said with a wink as he made his way to the stage to request a song.

After giving the bass player and lead singer a twenty, the band slowly started "Wonderful Tonight," and Bill moved Jaimey out onto the dance floor and pulled her close.

"I love Eric Clapton," Jaimey said.

Bill Turner lead her slowly around the floor. His job for the evening was to protect a little girl who had been damaged. Protect Noel Mitchell's daughter and keep anything bad from happening to his little girl. To keep her away from the vultures. To keep her away from the women, and the man, who do the devil's bidding by trading gossip.

Song after song played. Jaimey spotted Effie dancing to "Brick House." She was bent over with her hands on her knees thrusting her rear out toward the middle of the dance floor. With every bump, the purple taffeta thrust up and out. The silver sequins reflecting the lights. She looked like a one-woman disco ball. She danced through the line of people waiting their turn with her.

Jaimey and Bill moved over to the food table and fixed a plate and sat down on the edge of the dance floor. Bill left to retrieve her a drink and Jaimey's mind again wandered to the previous night and the second time she shot Danny Crabs. Remorse continued to creep in. She kept reminding herself that he was a child molester, and he deserved to die. She reminded herself again that it was self-defense. Bill returned with her drink and a new story about Russ's exploits of the day.

In the middle of the story, Bill and Jaimey heard Russ's name announced. The announcer gathered everyone in the courtyard in front of the stage. Bill took Jaimey by the hand and led her toward the front of the crowd.

Randy was draining the last beer when he heard the music stop and an announcement.

"Russ Crawford, please come up to the stage," the announcer said.

He stood unsteady from his hiding place, through the tree-line and made his way over to the fence next to the pool. The voice announced the category of Calcutta winners for scores at the end of play on Saturday.

Randy watched and listened, unsure if he had heard Russ's name announced correctly or not. He began scanning the crowd and spotted a black woman in a purple dress. Standing next to her was Jaimey, and, behind her was a tall older man. Randy immediately began making his way around the clubhouse and toward the courtyard. As he did, he heard the announcer mention Russ's name again. Randy stumbled around the corner of the club house and made his way toward the crowd. As he approached, it looked as if Moses parted the Red Sea as Randy approached the center of the crowd. They moved, escaping the smell, shocked at his appearance. Men stood in front of their women who retreated from him with their hands over their mouths and hearts stunned at the sight before them.

The announcer's voice echoed through the night. He reported how well Russ had played that day and recounted his hole-in-one and the fact that he had finished the day with a 71. Russ accepted the golf clubs and cash amid clapping and whistles. As the accolades began to die down, one lone person continued clapping.

Randy stumbled toward the stage, his pants torn and stained with manure, gathering them in the front with his right hand.

"You lucky little bastard," Randy slurred. "You're one lucky little piece of shit."

Jaimey immediately ran toward Randy, Bill trying to grab her. When she was close enough, he spit on her and moved to backhand her all at once losing his balance. He fell at Russ's feet at the edge of the stage.

Gasps and moans tore through the crowd. Bill Turner immediately grabbed Jaimey and moved her out of the way. Bubba and Cappy picked Randy up and removed him from the area. As they drug him away, Randy's voice trailed off calling them both names and telling them he never wanted to see either of them again.

"I wish you were never born; I should have left you in the same place...." The broken sentence was the last thing Russ heard from Randy as Bubba dropped Randy and stood over him and punched him in the mouth. It knocked Randy out cold, and they drug him to Bubba's truck and loaded him in the back.

Russ was frozen; the only thing moving were quiet tears streaming down his face as he shared stares with the audience. Women stood with their hands over their mouths in silent shock. Men who came to love Russ in the short hours of one day of competition stood bristled and angry. Jaimey's face turned to stone as an old familiar anger boiled inside her.

Russ thoughtfully propped the golf clubs against the table near him and couldn't move. He was embarrassed, angry, and hurt. His whole body grew numb. As he wiped the tears from his face, Fatboy made his way to the stage and helped Russ down and guided him away from the crowd, his thick arm around Russ' shoulders.

CHAPTER FORTY-FIVE

Over the years, The Clubhouse Classic had seen its share of brawls, usually the culmination of loose women, loose lips and flowing drinks. Jealousy and the bravado of youth spawned several of them.

The last memory of a fight occurred when the freshly divorced ex-wife drove all the way to Lewiston from Memphis to see her freshly divorced ex-husband with his freshly engaged girlfriend and confront them in the bathroom. The fight spilled out of the bathroom, down the hall, through the kitchen doors, across the kitchen, through the back door that Effie promptly shut behind them.

There were the few times when wives caught husbands there with a girlfriend or one of the call girls that were normally around for tournament circuits.

Husbands had walked into dark backrooms and caught their wives with strange men, which erupted in the immediate throwing of hands. And then there was the time when a wife caught her husband and her best friend in the janitor's closet and stole their clothes and then called the entirety of the partygoers to come and stare at them naked.

She promptly waited them out and made them leave the closet without a stitch on, covering themselves as best they could with brooms and mops. But, no one had ever witnessed a father embarrass and humiliate a child, especially at that child's finest moment.

Russ went from being on top of the world to once again having his spirit and confidence tamped down, back to where it usually stayed. The place it was when Cappy first met him. What had taken Cappy weeks to heal had taken Randy only seconds to crush.

Fatboy helped Russ into a golf cart and drove him away from the crowd. A low murmur continued throughout the crowd as they moved away from them. The deep echo of frogs replaced the hushed whispers as the boys neared the lake. Soon the slow roar of the band started again as if a turntable starting up again after being turned off mid song.

"He's done this to me my whole life. I hate that son-of-a-bitch!" Russ said through tears that were now flowing down an expressionless, hardened face. He had never said that out loud to himself, much less to anyone else.

The words and anger coming out of Russ were foreign to Fatboy. He was scared. He was scared of what he had just witnessed, but more so, he was scared of what he was seeing in Russ at that moment. Fatboy didn't understand fully what had just unfolded. He lived a "Leave It to Beaver" life. A home where his father told him he loved him every day before he left for work, and his mother fed him constantly. A family that went to church every Sunday morning, Sunday night and to prayer meeting on Wednesdays. Both sets of his grandparents were still alive and lived in Lewiston. They ate Sunday lunch together every Sunday. Their names were in good standing in the community. His life was happy and easy, and he assumed everyone was growing up the way he was.

Russ's mood suddenly turned- like a switch was flipped- from hurt to darkness. He was tired of being tired, tired of being mad, tired of the nervous feeling in the pit of his stomach, tired of looking over his shoulder and wondering when his dad would show up and embarrass him or worse, beat him or his mom. Tired of the flip flop. Tired of the apologies. The day or so of getting along and then nights filled with terror. Tired of believing his dad when he said he was sorry. Tired of being gullible. Tired of wanting a father so badly that he believed him every time he apologized and said he was going to do better. Too many friends witnessed this same thing happen over and over again. Russ feared it would never stop.

Fatboy watched the transformation. Russ wiped the tears away slowly from his expressionless face. Fatboy searched for the right words, for the right thing to say at the right time in the right way.

"I need to be by myself for a little while," Russ said as Fatboy made his way back toward the clubhouse. Please go around by the pool and let me drop you off there so no one sees me, Okay?"

"Hey, you aren't going to try to hurt yourself or anything are you?" Fatboy asked, more scared than before.

"No, no, I'm not. Thanks for helping back there."

Russ made a big loop in the road when Bubba and Cappy drove back up.

"Where are you going, son?" Cappy asked, starting to get out of the truck.

"Cap, I just need to ride a little bit by myself."

"Okay, no problem. You come find me in a minute

though, OK? Hey, all this will work out, and it'll be OK," Cappy said.

"Hey, we just took your dad to the barn to sleep it off, we'll deal with him tomorrow," Bubba said.

"I don't like seeing that boy look like he does right now," Cappy said, wiping the frustration from his face with a bleeding hand.

Russ drove across four fairways and turned left and followed the road toward Bubba's barn through the long line of live oaks. The full moon shone a bright white glow that poked through the trees. Sparse clouds blocked the moon randomly floating across it with the wind. At the end of the road, he took another right and followed a beaten cart path that led to Bubba's barn.

He parked beside the side entrance and took out his driver and a five iron from the bag in the back of the cart. He opened the smaller door within the larger one and made his way inside. He walked around the backhoe. It was where he had left it when he and Bubba finished working on the new green two days earlier. He began searching in each horse stall on the left side of the barn when he heard a moan from the opposite side. He walked toward the sound, and saw Randy lying in a stall, on top of a fresh mound of hay, bleeding.

The smell of vomit and urine hit Russ's nose. Randy's left eye was swollen. His lips cut and bleeding. He had a cut above his right eye.

Randy opened his eye that wasn't swollen shut and murmured something that Russ couldn't understand.

Russ grabbed Randy by the ankles and pulled him out into the middle of the barn, shocked at how light he was. The events of the last twenty minutes aged Russ by ten years, and he moved as if he were ten feet tall.

"Must be nice having two grown men do your bidding for you. I don't imagine you could have done much damage to me anyway," Randy slurred as he wiped blood from his mouth.

Russ began to speak. He spoke softly and confidently. He was clear minded. He moved close to Randy's face, staring Randy directly in his eyes, his own eyes fixed unblinking.

"I made a hole in one today; I won a set of golf clubs and one thousand dollars. I'm leading the tournament right now and will more than likely win. Mom was there. She was having a good time. For once in a long time, we were happy, and then you showed up and ruined it all... *again.*"

Randy slid himself to the wall behind him and stood up. Russ stood over him, both fists clinched tight. He stood nose to nose with Randy staring him down as he spoke, confidence and rage building within him as each second passed. He could feel his adrenaline speeding through his body and his heart pounding. He took a deep breath and moved closer to Randy.

"Get the hell off of me," Randy said as he pushed Russ back.

As if his body was waiting for an excuse, Russ erupted and punched Randy in the face knocking him back down on the ground.

"You're done! You're done hurting mom, and you're done hurting me! We are not worthless! You're done with the abuse and the name calling and the remarks, that all stops now!" Russ said with a newfound clarity and a brevity.

"You think you're something because you're leading a little rink-dink small town golf tournament? Your Grandfather won this same stupid tournament years ago. That's nothing. You're nothing. You're just a little piece of shit."

"What did you say?" Russ said as he gripped his five iron tightly in his right hand.

"I said you're a piece of shit!" Randy spit at Russ after he repeated himself.

Russ backed away from Randy to give himself room and swung the five iron and landed it into his ribs.

Randy's body coiled with the pain as he balled himself into the fetal position, rolling over on his side trying to regain the air that had just been knocked from him, his body convulsing.

Russ focused on his target that was now Randy's full back, and he swung the five-iron again. It landed square in Randy's upper back. This had the same effect as before, and he writhed on the ground searching for air.

"For most of my life, this is all I've known, Dad. You, drunk, lying in your own vomit. Do you know how many times I've picked you up from the yard and brought you into the house? I wasn't even sure how you got home. Do you know how many times mom and I had to go bail you out of jail, being sure we covered our bruises and fresh cuts and busted lips so you wouldn't get in more trouble? I couldn't play football because I was always too scared of someone seeing my bruises in the locker room and you getting arrested. I always thought something would happen and you would stop this, and I could be your little buddy again. You remember when you called me your little buddy? I don't remember you ever telling me you loved me. What happened to you?"

"You happened to me. I wish you were never born," Randy said between deep sucking breaths.

Russ stumbled back once again, stung, hurt at what

Randy had just said. All the beatings he watched Randy give his mother and all of the ones he took trying to keep him off of her. The words that just came out of Randy's seemingly on repeat, would never be spoken again.

Russ slowly walked over to the wall where he rested his driver and took it in his hand, replacing the five iron. He walked back over to Randy and straddled him, standing above his waist. He extended the driver as if he were lining up a long drive.

"I wish you were never born," Randy said as he stared up at Russ with hatred in his eyes.

Russ scraped the hay from under his feet so that he stood on the ruff hewn floor of the barn and placed the driver beside Randy's head directly on his temple. Russ's backswing was smooth; and as he reached the top of his swing, he increased the clubhead speed as fast as he could hitting Randy directly on his left temple. The impact made a loud cracking thud, and Randy's eyes blankly stared up at Russ as his life left him.

Russ calmly walked back over to his five iron and picked it up. He made his way back out to the cart, wiped them both off, and returned them to his bag.

He walked back to Randy's side and stared down at him. A weakness came over him and he collapsed beside his father. Tears fell onto the floor mixing with Randy's blood. Fear paralyzed him. His hand shook as it hovered above Randy's body, unable to touch him. Tears continued to fall as Russ' quiet cries turned to hard, long sobs. Relief and regret mixed into one emotion.

He finally stood and walked around to the other end of the barn, opened the two large doors, climbed up on the backhoe, and cranked it. He drove to Randy and lowered the scoop on the ground in front of his father, jumped down and rolled Randy into the scoop.

Back in the cab, he raised the scoop, backed out of the barn, and headed to the new portion of the number ten green. Once there, he turned his seat and swung the hoe toward the center of the green and dug down as deep as he could. He took out two large scoops of dirt. Satisfied that he was deep enough, he turned his seat around and drove the scoop around to the freshly dug grave and dumped Randy's body in it. He jumped down and walked to the grave. He looked in the hole staring at his father for the last time. Tears flowing. He sucked in a breath as he sobbed uncontrollably.

"I just wish I knew what could have been," Russ said out loud.

He picked up a clod of dirt tight in his hand and threw it into the hole. It landed on Randy's face.

"Maybe we can be at peace now."

He returned to the backhoe and began filling the hole, replacing the dirt on top of him, smoothing it out. He ran over the area and packed the dirt, and then lowered the scoop on the surface and smoothed it a final time.

Russ jumped down off of the backhoe and walked over the freshly dug grave.

"I'm glad you're gone," Russ said smoothly.

As he walked over the grave, he felt light, like he could float. Like he was finally free.

EPILOGUE

In the expanse of time much can be forgotten and forgetting can also be the best medicine. A decade can wipe away memories, returning to a place can bring them flooding back.

The Volvo station wagon rolled to a stop at The Nineteenth Hole. It had been twelve years since Russ had driven up the long gravel road, and now he sat in front of a place that held so many memories. He parked and sat for a minute just staring at the club house. He saw Ray Ray walk out of the back door and to the tree line with a mop bucket and pour the contents onto the ground.

"Ray Ray," Russ called. Ray Ray looked up and immediately dropped his bucket, ran to Russ and hugged him. He had not seen Ray Ray since Effie's funeral and the memorial that was held at The Nineteenth Hole. Effie had died on Thursday and the funeral was on Saturday lasting most of the day. The service at the church lasted three hours after visitation, and then the memorial at The Nineteenth Hole lasted into the night with the stories flowing long into the next morning.

"How have you been, man?" Russ asked.

"Okay, just hard since momma died. Sometimes I don't know how to run this place. It ain't as busy as it used to be, but we're makin it."

Ray Ray saw Jim and Jaimey getting out of the car and raced to the other side. He shook Jim's hand, hugged Jaimey and reached in to get Will out of the back seat.

"Hey Little Man," Ray Ray said as Will laughed at him and held his arms out to him.

"Everybody's here; y'all come on in," Ray Ray held Will as he walked through the door, announcing Russ's arrival.

Before Russ could get in the door, Fatboy ran over to him and picked him up and bear hugged him.

"Shit! It's so good to see you!" Fatboy said.

"Hey, language mister!" Jaimey said as she pointed at Will.

Spanky, Curtis, Duckhead, and Junior, all made it over greeting them and meeting Will, some for the first time.

Russ' wife walked in the door with a diaper bag and was met with the same hugs and pecks on the cheek. Fatboy's third wife was introduced to the group and she and Russ's wife found a table by themselves. Many of them had not seen each other since the wedding when they were all last together.

"Oh, wow! This is new?" Russ asked as he stared at a painting of Effie that Fatboy had commissioned.

"Yeah, I couldn't decide if she needed to be wearing her Sunday hat or not. Ray Ray said she wore it more times than not, so I had the artist add it. Thought about adding glitter to it, but that would have been too much," Fatboy said, swigging a beer.

"Can I get anybody anything?" Spanky asked as he moved behind the bar.

Russ waved him off, the others grabbed a beer, and they all sat down to cheeseburgers and fries. When they finished, they all made their way to the front of the clubhouse where a line of carts waited. Just as they had done so many times, they headed down the fairway in a single line toward Ol' Red. It still stood, less a few lower limbs that deflected too many shots adding too many points to a game.

They all stopped in a row and sat still in silence. Spanky was the first to get out of his cart and walked off from the group for a minute. Standing with his hands on his hips Russ saw him take a deep breath, wipe his eyes and then rejoin the group.

Russ put Will down and he walked over to Spanky and held his arms up to him to be picked up, and they all stood together in a circle surrounding a granite marker, a memorial to Cappy.

William Capstick
"Cappy"
Ol' Red will forever be known from this day forward as
"Cappy's tree"
Dedicated by his boys

Each of the boys spoke about Cappy and told stories that took place in their later lives. Stories that many of the boys didn't know. Stories about Cappy helping some of them with school cost. Stories about Cappy simply listening to them as they unloaded the minutia of their lives. Duckhead talked about how Cappy took him in to live with him for a year after a messy divorce. Fatboy talked about how he immediately went to Cappy after each of his.

When the circle made its way to Russ the first thing he did was introduce Will.

"I know this is the first time some of you have met Will. As you know his full name is William Capstick Crawford. You all know what Cappy meant to me, and you know what he did for me and my family. We are all the better for knowing him. Cappy was a man of few words, so in honor of that, I will keep this very short. Cappy was loved by everyone in this circle; he loved us all so much. He wanted us all to be good men, so when we leave here today and we have dedicated this marker to him, let's all be good men; that's the only way we can truly honor him," Russ said, his voice cracking, full of love for a man that changed his life.

With promises to keep in touch, the boys headed back to The Nineteenth Hole. Russ opened the back of his car and loaded his clubs on his cart. He strapped them in tightly, loaded up Will and called Jaimey to go for a ride and to play a few holes.

Russ stood on number ten tee box and teed up his ball. He stood, taking several practice swings thinking about Bubba and Cappy and Randy. He lined up and struck the ball and sent it sailing down the left side of the fairway setting himself up for a great approach onto the elevated green. As he approached his ball, the greens keeper was just finishing the final cut, so he leaned on his club resting with one foot crossed over the other.

"You know, when your daddy was sixteen, he and your uncle Bubba built this part of the fairway and the green; he designed the whole thing," Jaimey whispered as Will licked the remnants of a sucker from his lips, nodding his head as if he had heard the story a thousand times.

Russ held his pitching wedge and took a few practice swings. He struck the ball and placed it just on the edge of the green near the second cutting, and it rolled toward the hole stopping a foot away.

He drove to the edge of the green and grabbed Will and gave him his plastic putter and ball. Will roamed all over the green chasing a butterfly and laughing. The gnarled branches of the oak tree extending over the green blocked most of the sun and cast a long shadow. Russ and Jaimey held hands as they walked up to the ball.

He handed the putter to Jaimey, "Here, you do it. I've got you set up perfectly to make a birdie."

"No, I've made my peace; Russ, you go ahead."

"Mom, are you sure you don't blame me?"

"The day you told me what happened, was the first day I had peace in my life for so long. We weren't living, Russ. He was not redeemable. You needed a chance at a good life, and now you have that. I have Jim in my life now and he's the best thing that's happened to me besides you. What you did saved us, saved our family."

Will had forgotten about the butterfly when he found a small turtle at the edge of the green, and he was crouched down chin resting on his knees poking the turtle with his plastic putter.

Russ stood over his ball and drew a line with his eye along the path of the putt. He stroked the ball, and the ball followed the imaginary line that Russ had drawn and made the familiar clunk as it hit the bottom of the cup.

"Birdie," Russ said quietly to himself.

"Too much time wipes away too many memories and we forgive things we don't feel as though we should forgive," Russ said wiping a tear.

THE END

Made in the USA
Monee, IL
12 September 2023

42567863R00154